also by Michael Hopping

—

Meet Me In Paradise

MacTiernan's Bottle
stories by Michael Hopping

Pisgah Press
Candler, North Carolina

Pisgah Press

Pisgah Press was established in 2011 to publish and promote works of quality offering original ideas and insight into the human condition and the world around us.

MACTIERNAN'S BOTTLE
Copyright © 2011 by Michael Hopping

Published by Pisgah Press, LLC
PO Box 1427, Candler, NC 28715-1427
www.pisgahpress.com

Book and cover design: the whiskey priest
Printed in the United States of America

This is a work of fiction. Characters, places, institutions and incidents are either products of the author's imagination or are used fictitiously. Any resemblance to actual persons, institutions or incidents is purely coincidental.

"Complications" previously appeared in *The Great Smokies Review.*
"Toasted" appeared in *fresh.*

Library of Congress Cataloguing-in-Publication Data
    Hopping, Michael
    [Short stories]
    MacTiernan's Bottle — 1st ed.
    ISBN-13   978-0615558387
    ISBN-10   0615558380
    Library of Congress Control Number: 2011941562

Acknowledgements

This book has been long in the making. Dozens of writers and readers have contributed to the shaping of these stories, as have multiple writers' groups. Thanks are due to all of them. I especially want to mention Stephen Griffith, Ray Russell, Elizabeth Lutyens, the Great Smokies Writing Program, the Wednesday Afternoon Writers' Group, and the Asheville Barnes & Noble store where the latter has met for years. Finally, these stories are a small contribution to the ongoing conversation. They wouldn't have been possible without the brilliant contributions of previous speakers. Some of their names and thoughts are scattered through this text.

for explorers of the boundless frontier

MacTiernan's Bottle

Table of Contents

MacTiernan's Bottle

*H*OMO ERECTUS FOOTPRINTS have been discovered in Kenya. Imagine it: hardened remnants of mud that oozed between your toes on some random day resurface after 1.5 million years. Your unbelievably remote descendents trace the gritty, size nine contours of your puppy-prints and wonder. Where were you going? What was on your mind? Regardless of how grossly they misinterpret their thoughts as yours, in some sense you're sharing a moment across time.

Art is like that too, only the wonder usually goes both ways. As a creative wannabe myself, nothing used to seem more straightforward than an artist's hunger for connection with his audience. It hadn't occurred to me that somebody might paint a masterwork and intentionally take a chance on it never being seen.

No one suspected that the Wolfe River Motel & Tavern, a backwoods joint in the North Carolina mountains, was home to a thirteen by eight foot fresco. Demolition of the corner closet in Room 310 revealed a tease of color that continued on behind an adjoining false wall, where sheetrock above the wainscoting replaced the motel's typical stucco. Moldings concealed the façade's retention fasteners. Proprietor Rusty Boone watched his hired help, Kaz

Thanguld and me, unscrew them. The three of us tipped the façade backwards onto the floor.

Before us, a bluewater seascape faded dreamily to atmospheric haze and white plaster. Waves painted in a rich complexity of form and translucence hove on the verge of swamping the room. Atop the nearest crest a bottle containing a slip of paper lurched on the brink of a sudden drop. Such was the illusion that I swear I tasted brine.

Distorted by lenses of saltwater, shadowy human figures materialized in the swells. Here a fisherman casts his line into what might be the Wolfe River. There a naked toddler crouches beside its sunbathing mother, examining strands of her hair. Further back a farmer tops tobacco. Barroom drinkers sit hunched in solitary contemplation. Stripped of clothing and context, lovers entwine in an arabesque of blue-green limbs swirling in the wave.

Thang, the long-bearded genius of jabberwocky, was first to recover his power of speech. "Thus saith the Prince of Lies," he spat. Without further explanation he fled, dodging remnants of the demolished closet.

Rusty followed, shouting for his wife. "Lauren, come here. We're in 310. Lauren!"

I stayed behind on guard duty, as if fate might somehow take back what it had divulged. The water looked wet in the rising stripe of afternoon window light. But the January sun slipped behind Craven Knob before the Boones arrived. Lauren flipped the light switch. Nothing. Thang had tripped the breaker to these rooms first thing in the morning. Rusty sent me to restore power.

The master panel was on the ground floor. As I passed through the tavern to get to it, Thang jockeyed a keg into service position. I'd been told the bar only opened on weekends during the off-season. "It's Wednesday," I said. "Private party tonight?"

"Ask Boone."

"What happened up there?"

"Mark of the devil," Thang said. "I'll have nothing to do with it."

Well, okay then.

I returned to 310 to find my employers transfixed, more like goggle-eyed kids at Disneyland than the Charlotte society expats they were. Lauren, a stained latex glove at her mouth, whispered, "Look. Oh, my god, look."

An hour later the four of us were in the tavern, holding the bar down with pints from the new keg. A locally brewed porter, Rusty told me, an uncommon treat. It was deep brown and thick with roasted flavors. Rusty asked Thang, apparently for the second time, about his bizarre response to the fresco.

Thang bristled. "I told you. Let the Prince of Darkness and his works stay away from me."

"The naked couple? Since when did you become a prude?"

"*Res ipsa loquitur.*"

Rusty noticed my incomprehension. "He means the Thang speaks for itself."

The jibe drew a wounded snort from its target.

"Did anybody see a signature?" Lauren asked. "I certainly didn't."

"Not me," I said.

Thang launched into a screed about civilization's crimes against Nature. In the three weeks I'd lived and carpentered at the motel alongside the psychotic electrician, I had grown used to his inability to stay on topic. Behind the foggy wire-rims and onion dome lurked a high performance mind with a fried guidance system. Thankfully his rants weren't repetitive.

My first day on the job, Rusty'd pulled me aside to clue me in about his childhood pal and roommate at the

University of Georgia. Kaz Thanguld had supposedly been an outstanding student until a protest demonstration got him suspended in junior year. He hitched out to San Francisco in '67 for the Summer of Love but couldn't take the crowds in the Haight. So he dropped out of that too and, as Thang, came home to create his own reality in the mountains. I should expect tangents, Rusty said. Thang believed they counteracted mass hypnosis.

Lauren excused herself to the kitchen. Rusty looked pleadingly to me, like I should interrupt the harangue.

"Nature is fractal," Thang continued. "The mark of the beast is oversimplification: 666. Technociety is rectilinear hubris." He gestured at chairs, tables, walls and windows; "Rectilinear says, 'I'm not from this planet. My rules are different. Deal with it.' Earth is about to kick rectilinear ass and good riddance." He hoisted his pint and drank. The gray ironing board on his chin bounced at each swallow like a spring gauge pointer.

"You calling me an asshole?" Rusty inquired.

Thang's beard wagged in mid-guzzle.

"Clayton, did that crazy Hungarian just call us assholes?"

"Maybe tangentially."

The accused wiped his moustache with the sleeve of a shirt that hung on him like a worn-out potato sack and belched a malty cloud. "Just young punks like you, Clayton," he said. "A man who serves barley products of this quality is all right. Another measure of nectar, barkeep." He pushed his empty glass toward Rusty.

"If you didn't pull wire off the books for a pittance minus beer tab, I'd set your raggedy butt on the curb."

"If you had a curb," Thang retorted. "Licensed electricians of my caliber are rare."

⌘

4

Wood butchers for hire are more plentiful than licensed electricians in southern Appalachia. Qualifications for carpentry typically consist of possessing a tool belt, circular saw and reliable means of transportation. I owed my employment at the motel to chance and a pay agreement involving room and board. Call it an unscheduled sabbatical. I had a Master of Fine Arts stamp of approval that legitimized me as a studio artist in wood. Some of my gimmicks had the potential to earn a decent living. All I had to do was crank out product but I couldn't bring myself to keep doing it.

It's too easy to blame the critic who unintentionally slammed the centerpiece of my MFA exhibition. For me, the late Japanese graphic and materials designer Shigeo Fukuda ranks with Escher as a visual trickster. The centerpiece of my show, Rest in Pieces Fukuda San, was an homage to him. I situated a computer monitor in the larger of two jumbles of planks and mirrored planes and installed them in front of a wall mirror. When viewed at a certain angle in that mirror, the assemblies resolved into a computer hutch and chair. Passersby were, of course, also visible in the big mirror. They appeared normal unless they sat in the "chair." Then, from the hutch viewing angle, they were reflected as mismatched body parts and could view their shattered selves on the "desktop" monitor.

Reviews of the exhibition failed to grapple with Rest in Pieces' attack on perceptual certainty. Critics instead praised the lines of my more conventional furniture, the joinery, how Rest in Pieces' use of tapered boards solved problems with perspective. A young champion of tradition dissed Rest in Pieces as "a facile apologia for deconstructivist mayhem." His mossbacked mentor wasn't sucking up to anyone. He judged the installation "a pile of crap."

I discounted them. But Claudia Hammond from the Virginia Museum of Fine Arts attended. Her opinion carried weight with me and I took pains to be available. She asked my intention for Rest in Pieces. I told her. Whereupon she smiled sweetly and said, "People may not get that but they'll enjoy your take on the relationship between surfaces. I think you'll find a market for furniture incorporating it."

Graduation to the real world brought with it the usual financial realities. Luckily, Claudia had been correct. While I piddled with new art projects, orders for desks and other pieces mimicking Rest in Pieces' unorthodox angularity paid the bills. I hated every trained monkey minute. So I rang in the New Year by leaving Virginia, with no fixed itinerary. At Newport, Tennessee, I got off the interstate and snaked eastward through bypassed burgs wasting away under blankets of wood smoke. In the company of a few commercial pickups, log haulers and old folks on milk runs I took my sweet time ascending into North Carolina.

I was tired and thirsty when a sign below a three-story building clinging to a boondocks mountainside caught my eye: WOLFE RIVER MOTEL—REST UP AND WET YOUR WHISTLE BEFORE HITTING THE RIVER—BEER & WINE SOLD HERE. The vintage stone and brick construction intrigued me. Whitewater rafters seemed a reasonable source of modern clientele. I couldn't guess what had attracted the original customers.

A senior citizen dressed like a working man met me in the beer store. I bought a six pack and asked the room rates. Rusty introduced himself with the polish of a gallery agent. He regretted that the motel was closed for remodeling. But if I had cash and didn't mind a poorly heated room he'd make an exception. "It's Friday, so the tavern opens at six. Our beer selection beats anything you'll find up the road in Altamont. We've got good food and live music tonight."

A fifty-dollar deposit bought me a room key and distraction from stewing about consumerism's upside down priorities: the dominance of How over What and the banishment of Why from serious conversation.

The why of the motel was free for the price of beer. Rusty's grandfather had built the place in 1923 as a pleasure club for gentlemen seeking relief from the daily grind. Its location was convenient to the Coxe County line but far enough into Bernard County for the high sheriff of Coxe to conduct his personal business in privacy. The club weathered the end of Prohibition and World War II, only to fall victim to the IRS. In the early '70s, Rusty's dad, an Altamont doctor, had Papaw Boone's whorehouse renovated as a tourist motel. The venture failed.

The building sat vacant again until Rusty hung up his banking spurs in Charlotte and returned to the mountains. He opened a beer bar and package store on the ground floor, supplying good old boys with mass market lager and Altamont's jaded palates with fancy ales. Motel accommodations for the Wolfe River rafting industry were phase two. Phase three, modernizing the rooms, was in progress. When he learned my trade and current status he complained that the remodel had fallen behind schedule. His electrician had no sense for wood. Perhaps we could make a deal. Why not, I thought.

Rusty was a meat-and-potatoes amateur plumber who enjoyed running downstairs to sell beer. Lauren painted rooms and cooked. Once an accomplished dancer, she'd given it up for a career on the arts beat at the *Charlotte Observer*. Her access to society intrigues had been a casualty of the move west. Country life bored her. She and I chattered like displaced refugees about artistic events and controversies, not caring if her husband glazed over.

Despite Thang's peculiarities he was a competent electrician. I liked him. In his loopy way he commiserated with my angst, telling me, "Newton was a bloodthirsty demon.

Reject him and never abandon hope. The higher physics always needs spies."

For a second, I almost understood him. Then I lost it and laughed.

Without missing a beat he forgave me; "Unsavory informants are the backbone of any good intelligence service."

On the night we found the seascape Thang downed his second pint and left for what Lauren called his hermitage overlooking the Coxe County dump. The Boones and I sweated through bowls of Jalapeño Hot Head chili and chugged sweet tea by the pitcher. Rusty supposed the painting must have been done during the renovation. Business school had kept him away from home during those years. Still, he couldn't imagine not hearing about something as outlandish as a fresco.

While he began a search of motel records, Lauren and I trooped upstairs for a closer inspection of the painting. The initial shock now past, different reactions surfaced. "It's remorseless," I said. "Rolling people under. In a minute they'll be as gone as if they never existed."

"Yes, but what about the note in the bottle? If everything's hopeless, who's it to?"

I hadn't a clue. Out of habit I scanned the back of the false wall for a signature—that's where a carpenter would put it—and noticed a yellowed sheet of paper caught between a stud and the wainscoting. "Maybe this is our answer," I said. It was an invoice made out in a foreign language. I gave it to Lauren.

"It's Italian," she said, "a Florentine art supply house. Some kind of lime. And there's a list of *pigmenti*, powdered pigments."

"Who shops in Florence? Did anybody sign for delivery?"

"At the bottom here. Nice penmanship. 'MacTiernan, 3 May, 1970.'"

"Who's he?"

"Name's familiar," she said, "but I can't place it. Could be a workman. Where's the signature on the painting?"

We searched wave by wave until I spotted a three-letter pictograph. The capital letters M and T were superimposed, with the stem of the T extending below the valley of the M. Over its twin peaks floated a moony O. Lauren fetched her camera and snapped the first of many pictures.

Rusty was in the package store office thumbing through a scrapbook when he heard our news.

"I think the artist's name is MacTiernan," Lauren proclaimed. "Scoot over, dear. Let's Google him."

Wikipedia provided a concise overview. Osbourne MacTiernan (1903-1979): Scottish-born fresco painter active in the United States during the post-WWII period. Churches and corporate headquarters. Last commission for Parke-Davis in 1968 depicted the history of clinical drug trials. Died in Santa Monica after years of declining health. Major influence on contemporary revival of American fresco. A black and white photo shows the artist on a scaffold, brush in hand, nose to nose with a Roman centurion. MacTiernan sports an ostentatious mop of hair. His features are sharp, intense.

"He's in here," Rusty said, flipping scrapbook pages. "This is him in front of the motel. Ozzie. The caretaker Dad put in charge. Dad said he was a stucco whiz and did most of the renovation work himself." In the fading Polaroid snapshot, Ozzie's face is shadowed by a fedora. The hair seems shorter. He's wearing an open-collared white shirt and pressed khaki trousers, leaning on a shovel as if it's 1935 and he's a poster boy for the WPA.

"Great job, kids," Rusty said, swiveling to slap Lauren a high-five. "Oh, hell, let's *really* celebrate. Where's that fifth of Macallan?"

"Tomorrow's a workday," she said.

"The man was a Scot, dear. He deserves a single malt salute."

"You get into that and you know how you'll be in the morning. I'm going to bed. Watch out, Clayton. He'll have you passed out drunk too. It's a cold night to sleep it off in the bar."

"Killjoy," Rusty groused.

The no-show for work was Thang. Rusty, though baggy-eyed from lack of sleep, had resisted the call of the highlands. While we waited for the electrician, Lauren joined us to re-photograph the fresco in daylight. She documented everything, including layout marks on the façade's framing studs. MacTiernan's carpentry skills earned points from me. His false wall was precisely executed and struck a good balance between sturdiness and weight. He'd thought of everything, including sly gaps below the base molding and above the crown for air circulation.

We covered the painting with a plastic sheet. After the Boones left I sawed the façade into sections—by hand to minimize flying dust—schlepped the pieces to the furniture storage room, vacuumed 310 and adjourned to the tavern for lunch.

Rusty paced behind the bar like a shooting gallery duck, yelling into his cell phone. "What do you mean, 'I can't do it'? Here I am stressing over you being dead in a ditch and all I get is a load of cockamamie? You heard me. What? I'll tell you what's getting fired around here. Your sorry ass is what. As of now. That make you happy?" He flipped the phone closed.

Lauren, who'd been standing in the kitchen doorway holding plates of sandwiches, set them on the bar. "What's the matter?"

"Damned if I know. He's off his nut again, babbling about devils and fires of hell. Told me I ought to burn the place down."

"Oh, my god."

"He's just yapping. Don't worry about it."

The boss steamed out with Lauren close behind. Over her shoulder as they turned onto the stairs toward their second floor apartment, she said, "Go ahead and eat, Clayton. We'll be right back."

I gave them five minutes, then five more. Then I ate, contemplating arson and mental illness. Thang didn't seem the type. But what was the type and how did I know? I nibbled a second bag of chips, stalling around.

Still nobody. To look busy, I decided to haul the demoed closet to the dumpster in the parking lot out back. Papaw Boone had had a shrewd sense of design. The building blocked any highway view of the back lot. Customers could park there unobserved and enter at the second floor stair landing where a large game room welcomed them to reach into their wallets. I propped open the parking lot door.

A construction dumpster sat in the sunny end of the lot. Unseasonable heat glared off the blacktop and steel. As the last load of debris clanged home, the sound of a car engine around front disrupted my plan to bring out a chaise lounge and catch some rays. I went in to find Rusty. He'd heard the car too and was clomping downstairs to the beer store.

We spent the remainder of the afternoon spit-shining 310. When we took out the window curtains and the fresco's protective dust cover, the room sparkled like a rustic museum space.

At supper Lauren told us that Winston Fasteau, a curator for the Mint Museum, had forwarded her pictures to an expert in New York City. Also she'd learned that a fresco artist named Syd Bennett lived in Altamont. She'd spoken to him by phone. Bennett sounded enthusiastic and said he'd drive out on Saturday. MacTiernan was his favorite non-Italian fresco master.

"What about the newspapers?" Rusty asked through a mouthful of garlic bread.

"Winston said we should be very cautious. We're not absolutely sure it's a MacTiernan and, if it is, it's extremely valuable. We have to think about security. I'll call the *Observer* and the *Altamont Bugle* but Winston says to wait."

Rusty leaned back in his chair. "This thing has marketing potential out the wazoo. I don't want to skip too far ahead but, whatever happens, we'll need to block the corridor there. If we convert the three rooms on the other side to a suite, we'll limit the unrentable space. What if we forget the river rats, Lauren? Go with a retreat center. We'd be profitable year-round."

"Clayton, is that possible, building-wise?"

"You should be able to lose the common walls between rooms without a problem. Why not tear out 310's sink and bathroom and use 308 as your point of entry? It'd cost you a third room but—"

"That's where we'll sell tickets!" Lauren said.

"What about electrical?" I asked.

Silverware jangled as Rusty's fist smacked the table. "I ought to wring the bastard's scrawny neck. He knows I need him, but he has to show up for work."

"Calm down," Lauren said, sopping up sloshed tea. "We came here to lower your blood pressure, not give you a stroke."

"It's a hell of a time for him to go mental."

⌘

Later, I sat eyelevel with the toddler and its drowsing mother. The center of the fresco glowed in the ceiling light. There was an illusion of swooping into the scene at high speed. MacTiernan's figures were oblivious to the rolling annihilation in store for them. The mother's hair spilled like lazy thoughts through the fingers of her child. I wondered when *I'd* ever felt so at peace with anything. My situation was closer to the bottle's, teetering slantways on the brink of a stomach-churning dip. MacTiernan must have shared the sense of unease. Why else conceal his valedictory to the world of art?

Remodeling operations shifted to the game room. With Thang still AWOL, Rusty and I disassembled the pool table and took it to a storehouse behind the rear lot. Compared to that job, moving the dry bar and coolers was a piece of cake. An architect friend of Rusty's arrived soon after. They went upstairs to discuss the fresco wing while I prepared the first of many buckets of soapy water.

The game room, originally Papaw Boone's casino, had started as a windowless firetrap. Someone, most likely MacTiernan, added an exit at the far end. But the piney gloom of floor and walls overmatched his lighting upgrades. I scrubbed decades of neglect, cigarette smoke and the sweat of eight ball losers off the wood. Underneath, preserved in the amber of MacTiernan's varnish, lay a dark caramel patina of all-night poker and debauchery. Rusty popped in to say he liked the knotty pine but didn't cherish the history. He wanted everything stripped to bare wood.

At six I claimed a barstool and ordered one of Lauren's Double Wolfe Burgers. Rusty treated me to another pint of porter. The thick brew tasted faintly of dark chocolate and coffee. Too many weekends here and I risked becoming a beer snob.

Thirsty souls drifted in by twos and threes. They reminded me of my parents, half a generation younger than Thang and the Boones, members of the cohort whose TV dreams of free love were screwed by Ronald Reagan and the threat of HIV. Instead of joining the capitalist horde, they and their friends had boarded counterculture evac helicopters, carrying little else with them into exile but bongs, cynicism and the consolation of classic rock. Their futures turned out to be more literally out-of-sight than they planned. Now, for them, the ideals were threadbare, the hair graying or gone. No more lighters raised in seas of solidarity with the music. But at obscure meetups like this the dream sputtered on. They unpacked acoustic instruments and circulated among the tables, supporting each other's schemes to pay bills through moral forms of self-expression. I was invisible to this new wave of Wolfe River ghosts and comfortable with that.

Rusty leaned across the bar. "Get out there and dance, Clayton. Tomorrow we may go into overdrive. You'll be too tired to party. Whatever you do, don't tell anybody anything."

The band's first round of soulful reminiscences topped my tank for other people's nostalgia. I headed to the restroom. A new manifesto above the urinal raised my spirits: "Free a Clydesdale. Anheuser-Busch donations accepted here." Right arm, dude. I just wished the long-suffering son of a revolution had chiseled it with a gouge.

Next morning, unaware that Syd Bennett, the fresco artist, had come and gone, I sanded myself into a dusty headphoned trance in the game room. Lauren *did* think to introduce me to the Mint Museum guy. Winston Fasteau shook—touched—my hand, remarking that he'd been told I was a furniture builder. I offered my card. He performed a fingertip deposit into a pocket of his camel hair coat. "It's unbelievable, I know," he cautioned me, "but the painting upstairs is very special. You must remember that. I can't emphasize too strongly how careful you must be. No vibrations, no dust, no machinery around it. Treat the work as a national treasure, okay?"

Rather than punch his fleshy condescending mouth, I said, "I hope you'll visit my website," pulled up my dust mask and resumed sanding. Winnie's effetery pissed me off so much that the wall stripping was far advanced when I knocked off that night. The tavern scene didn't interest me. I holed up in 310 and sketched the seascape, memorizing the complicated harmonies of MacTiernan's curves.

"Syd said our painting is a breakthrough," Lauren told us at breakfast. "Traditional fresco style uses bright color and hard edges to stand out in poor light. But MacTiernan allowed light *inside* the frame to dictate his edges. They're soft. So are his colors. The closer you look the more difficult it is to tell what's fisherman and what's not. MacTiernan was renowned for his shading technique but this is unheard of, according to Syd. The way the light refracts *through* the waves instead of bouncing off them is the fresco equivalent of Vermeer."

Rusty said, "I warned you, Clayton. Assholes and elbows from here—"

"The other thing, Syd and Winston agreed, is the puzzle of how he managed to do it. Remember the invoice? The plaster is so white because it's made from white marble. But the conversion from lime powder to plaster involves distilled water, an insulated pit and at least a year of aging before the plaster is creamy enough for the intonaco, the top layer that takes the paint. How is it possible that no one noticed a bathtub-sized hole in the ground full of plaster?"

"Nothing in the records about it," Rusty said.

"Then there's the painting phase. Fresco isn't like canvas. Ours took weeks and a small crew to complete. It's labor intensive."

"Like we're fixing to be."

Lauren cleared her throat. "No doubt, dear. But Clayton is interested in this." She continued, "They grind powdered earth pigments—remember *those* on the invoice?—together with water. The particles have to be teeny tiny to soak in and bond chemically before the intonaco hardens. If the painter is too slow, too bad. He has to chip off what he didn't get to and start over."

Rusty chased syrup around his plate with a bit of sausage.

"Water-based paint?" I asked.

"Yes, the oil comes later. So anyway they trowel on a new section of intonaco, prepare all the colors and apply them. Then everything has to dry. They might not be able to do an adjoining section for several days." Her hands flew up. "Oh, I forgot. First, the artist draws a full-sized cartoon of the painting on the rough plaster undercoat. There's a process for transferring the lines to the fresh intonaco."

"Sounds complicated."

"It is. Syd said a fresco artist without an experienced crew is in deep trouble. But MacTiernan was supposed to be retired. Where did he get his help?"

"There's no record of any of this." Rusty repeated. "Ozzie earned a caretaker's salary. I can't find where Dad paid for marble plaster or skilled craftsmen."

Lauren patted her husband's arm. "The impression I'm getting, dear, is that Ozzie was slumming. He didn't need anything from your dad but privacy and the right wall. Dad was busy with his medical practice."

"He trusted the man."

"As he should have. Oh, that reminds me. Clayton, the wet effect you mentioned? Water-based fresco paint gives

16

a matte finish but the near waves have glossy highlights. Syd said those were added later, in oil. They strengthen the three-dimensional effect."

Rusty stood. "The bottom line is that we're in over-drive. Thang's coming in this afternoon. Clayton, get me a list of wall outlets, fixtures, whatever we need for the game room. I'm going to pull the sink out of 310."

Thang didn't talk about his boycott and refused to set foot on the third floor but his intuition for the electrical diagram in the game room was uncanny. He ran new wire with remarkably little damage to the woodwork. By midweek I was ready to lay down a basecoat of polyurethane on the pale, denuded walls. He disapproved the choice of finish, worried about a fume explosion. The look on his face was one of genuine concern. I assured him that I'd keep the room ventilated with doorway fans.

Overdrive for the Boones consisted of looking after their business interests. Rusty fretted about the word from his insurance carrier. There'd be requirements for certified security and hazard mitigation systems. Equipment costs alone might run far into the thousands. Lauren traded her painter's rags for stylish suits. While she was in Charlotte picking up an official from the National Endowment for the Arts, Rusty hosted a photographic team from the Mint Museum. He pulled me off the game room job to reas-semble the false wall and answer questions about it. Apart from that, my place was in the trenches.

It only remained to be determined whether I was the remodel's asshole or elbow. At night, while the Boones discussed their next moves, I visited with the fresco. It occurred to me that the bottle's undecipherable message was from another punk who'd smugly observed the futility of Friday night in the tavern. Lauren had said MacTiernan was slumming here. No more so than me, or she and her husband. Blarney vessels all, bobbing over the waves with urgent petitions addressed to shores nowhere in evidence.

Casual students of art history may not recognize the name F. S. B. Jewett, but they're likely to recall his tome on the subject: *Ages of Art*. It's the classic text. An early edition of Jewett was probably what Picasso and Braque threw out the window when they invented cubism. My dog-eared copy was with my chisels and planes in Richmond. I had no idea Jewett was still living. To learn that he was Winston Fasteau's New York expert, boggled me.

Lauren understood the importance of the call from Jewett's office. Her shrieks knifed through my earbuds and the whine of the floor sander. Rusty huffed upstairs from the package store on the double. The three of us met at the landing. Lauren waved her copy of *Ages of Art* at us. "He's coming. He's coming here."

Evidently relieved at the lack of spurting blood, Rusty caught his breath before asking, "Who is?"

"Dr. Jewett. The author of this book, that's who." Lauren bounced up and down as though Santa himself had called. "I can't believe it."

"You almost gave me a heart attack," Rusty said.

Her voice changed, betraying a trace of concern. "There's one thing. Dr. Jewett uses a wheelchair. His secretary asked if we're accessible. I told him about the stairs. He said they can deal with that so long as the doorways are at least thirty-two inches wide. They are, aren't they?"

Rusty said, "The exteriors are. Not the room doors."

"That's got to be fixed by Wednesday morning."

Papaw Boone had grossly overbuilt his den of iniquity. Double jack studs framed doorways where singles would have sufficed. I widened 310's doorframe to accommodate a fire-rated door of the specified width. So much for ambience. I also built a temporary ramp on top of the stairway to the third floor. The ramp's lower end extended across the landing toward the rear entrance. It moderated the incline but imperiled foot traffic.

Rusty called me out of the game room after Jewett's van pulled into the back lot. Dave, Jewett's driver, conservation tech and personal assistant, wasn't much of a physical specimen. He offloaded the professor to a wheelchair but it was my job to get the old man up the ramp.

Not that Jewett was heavy. The connection between his bulbous head and oversized wingtip shoes consisted primarily of cloth: suit, wool scarf, topcoat, and lap blanket. Nested in the middle, leather driving gloves clutched the brim of a Homburg hat—circa Battle of Britain—and a walking cane that projected stiffly onward. As I tilted his chair onto its rear wheels for the backward ascent, he quipped in a thin, ancient voice, "Young man, few exits from this earth are more glorious than a chivalric demise. If you drop me, see to it that I enter the final joust rubber side down, at a gallop."

"Never fear, professor. I'll wait till we're at the top. Dave'll never know what hit him."

"Call me Stansfield. I like your spunk."

The banter persisted until I rolled the great man into 310, turned him to the fresco and joined the audience at his rear. Jewett was still for several moments. Then he said, "Clayton, perhaps you'll hold my cane. Dave, take me close."

Jewett's slightest gesture directed his chariot from side to side in front of the painting, with frequent stops to don reading glasses and peruse a detail. The Boones and I waited, interpreting his grunts. Dave positioned him for another overall view.

At last the chair swung around. "What do you think of it?" Jewett asked.

"It's a breakthrough," Lauren said. "How he used light. Syd Bennett told us it's like a Vermeer."

"Did he now? True enough. Before the advent of the electric light this would not have succeeded. What have you been told about the peculiarity of location and presentation? Typically in the West, serious fresco is a public art form commissioned to instruct or inspire a community. Here also, Osbourne flouts convention."

"It's a genuine MacTiernan, then?" Rusty blurted.

"Oh, indeed. And I venture to guess the appraisals will shock you. Unless you are in a position to independently establish an endowment, you should seek additional funding straight away."

"I'm hearing that."

Jewett said, "And what about you, Clayton? How does Osbourne speak to you?"

"If it wasn't so beautiful, it'd scare me to death."

"Go on."

I reviewed the evolution of my reactions.

"Spoken like a true son of the Enlightenment. You and Albert Camus would have gotten on famously. I never had the pleasure of meeting *him* but Osbourne and I occasionally crossed paths. Your observation that he deprives us of a shoreline is significant. Most unchristian of him. This painting is a sermon for a new age.

"But if an old man may quote the challenge of Fowles: '*Utram bibis? Aquam an undam?* Which are you drinking? The water or the wave?' I must tell you that from the confines of this damnable chair I read Osbourne's message as reassuring. Water abides."

The Boones and I were out of our league. We didn't say peep.

Jewett smoothed over the awkwardness. "You folks surely have more questions, as do I. Dine with us tonight. The food at my hotel is inedible but you will have a better suggestion. My treat. For now however, there is work to be done. Are draperies available for this room?"

"Yes," Rusty said.

"Dave will appreciate having them installed. He likes to control the light for his photographs."

To my disappointed surprise, Lauren had a problem with hired help "tagging along" to dinner, ignoring what I'd thought was our friendship and the fact that I'd clearly been invited. As if my presence would somehow cut into her face time with Jewett. I told Rusty I'd drive myself if necessary. Negotiations continued through the afternoon. She gave in when he appointed me designated driver and loaned me a jacket and necktie.

We ate at a swank Altamont café recessed in a downtown alley. Jewett regaled us with the history of North American fresco, concentrating on the twentieth century Mexican renaissance. "As an aspiring young artist," he said, "I sneaked into the RCA Building to watch Diego Rivera paint Man at the Crossroads. I treasure the fragment I salvaged when Nelson Rockefeller had it destroyed. Rivera had incomparable talent but I came to hate his guts. The unauthorized addition of Lenin's portrait to the piece was, in fact, the communist slap Rockefeller took it for. An act of irresponsible flamboyance.

"I much preferred Osbourne's methods. He evaded his ecclesiastical Rockefellers with subtlety, imbuing the features of biblical persons with common humanity and pushing angels into the fantastic. The eyes of his Pilate are doubtful. Those of Jesus often burn with a conviction that may be insane. Gabriel at the Annunciation is portrayed as the hallucination of a desperate girl."

Lauren, who'd scarcely touched her antipasto, assured our server that nothing was wrong with the food. As the pasta course was served, she asked Jewett about MacTiernan's personality.

"Charming, held his liquor, schoolboy sense of humor. At the social gatherings where we met, he impressed me as an actor on best behavior. He had a reputation as something of a rake but one must be cautious of rumor."

Rusty twirled his linguini, perfecting the fork and spoon technique.

Pretending not to notice, Jewett continued, "It was also rumored that Osbourne modeled his signature pictograph on a type of salacious carving popular in medieval churches. In Ireland, female examples are known as Sheela-na-Gigs. I forebear to describe the exhibitionistic hags in detail. However if one imagines the arrangement of his OMT as a stick figure—the O of the head positioned above the superimposed M and T—the sprawling legs of the M and lowered post of the T can be read as lewdly androgynous. As I say, his rebellions had the grace of subtlety."

Rusty's fork tripped in the middle of a linguini spin and fell onto his plate.

No sign of triumph ruffled the professor's demeanor. "If that interpretation is accurate, Osbourne had the sense not to admit it. But the story fits my assessment of his temperament."

"Subtle my ass," Lauren cackled, raising her wine goblet. "Here's to audacity."

Dave asked for details about the art supply invoice and whether Rusty's records might yet contain undiscovered evidence of MacTiernan. Jewett was interested in why the façade hadn't damaged the painting beneath. I told him.

Then he asked, "You have a studio in Virginia. What brings you here?"

What the hell. I told him that too. "Trying to decide whether to sell out and become the furniture builder people take me for. Why create art nobody gets?"

Jewett sniffed. "Only decorators and the blessèd mad are spared that miserable thorn. The question becomes: Are you a slave to your vision?"

I shrugged.

"Speak up."

"I don't know."

"If not you, then who?"

I frowned.

"For an artist in thrall to vision, asking 'Why bother?' is gratuitous self-flagellation. Answers are meaningless. Art will be served. But if you *do* have a choice?" Jewett scowled and shifted in his chair. "You recall Klimt, the symbolist painter? His women leap off the canvas. Their eroticism shimmers in geometric cascades. As a youth I dedicated myself to capturing that spark. But the figures in my painting remained contrived, mannequins. At the nadir of my existence I realized that borrowed inspiration is insufficient." Jewett's eyelids gapped pink.

Lauren disallowed his vulnerability. "No, Stansfield, no. That's not right. You *are* an inspiration—"

He quieted her with a raised finger. "Art has use for secondhand visions as well. I became an author of interpretive texts, perhaps a small belated comfort to a few misunderstood slaves. But vindication is a hit or miss proposition. If being understood is important to you, Clayton, say only what your audience expects to hear."

What remained of my festive spirit washed away in the blustery mix of rain and sleet that had moved into the mountains during our meal. Dave and I brought the vehicles around. Ice water trickled down my neck as I assisted him with the professor. My shoes filled and my pantlegs were soaked to the knees. The Boones scrambled into the backseat of their battlewagon SUV little the worse for the elements.

Lauren lionized Jewett with the enthusiasm of a groupie who'd scored. Had the professor not predated the horseless carriage and been disabled, Rusty might have taken offence rather than finding fifty ways of saying, "Yes, dear." I concentrated on driving. Fogbanks along the river reduced visibility to near zero.

North of town the murk lifted. Bracketed by spectral trees and cliff faces I cruised into a suspicion that Jewett had accused me of being a poser. Which was my pretense: artist or handyman?

The outside thermometer registered in the mid-twenties next morning. I topcoated the game room floor anyway and opened the doors. Rusty had me dismantle the wheelchair ramp, a task I performed with uncharitable gusto. At lunch I announced my plan to return to Richmond. The Boones were fine with that. They had to rethink their business plan.

"If you don't need me this afternoon," I said, "I'd appreciate directions to Thang's house. I want to drop by for a beer and *adios*."

With two six packs of ale stashed behind the seat of my truck I turned downstream on the Wolfe River highway and took a right at the sign for the landfill. Hemlock branches still heavy from the storm sparkled green where Ivy Branch diverged from the pavement and commenced a rutted climb. I might have been a salmon splashing upward from one icy puddle to the next, the gravel narrowing imperceptibly at each weathered gate and gaggle of mailboxes until nothing remained but parallel tracks through the woods. I stopped at a barrier of pipes and woven branches. A placard warned, CLOSE GATE OR GET LOST GOATS.

I closed the gate. The driveway meandered across a field of fenced garden areas. Thang's pickup protruded from an A-frame tucked below the ridgeline. Behind the building a grandiose washing machine agitator stirred the breeze like a pinwheeling bell tower. Solar panels and miniature yurt structures sprouted from a long mound of stone rubble. Atop it, a trio of goats raised questioning heads. Lauren had said Thang's hermitage was unique. I didn't realize how unique until I saw a plume of smoke. He didn't live in the A-frame. The goats were resting on his house. I saw reflections off windows embedded in the mini-yurts and rockpile but didn't detect an entrance. I tapped my horn beside the rocks and waited in the truck. Thang appeared up ahead, at the end of the mound, in a short-sleeved shirt and overalls. Under watchful goat eyes I pulled forward and lowered my window. "I came to say goodbye," I said. "Brought beer."

"Well then. It's bread day."

He led me around the corner to a door set in the stones. Inside, a conventional flagstone floor emphasized the irregular arch of the mudroom/airlock's whitewashed stucco. Portholes and a skylight flooded the short tunnel with light. Thang deposited the beer on the floor, saving two for immediate consumption. I hung my parka next to his on a wooden peg. "Nice place," I blathered. "Reminds me of southern California."

Thang's beard scythed the air as he shook his head and opened the inner door. "Come on."

We walked into a blast of yeasty heat. His great room had the feel of a summer patio. Sunlight caromed around curvy plaster undecorated except for the beaded curtains hanging in a pair of archways. The limbs of a peeled tree trunk in the center of the room supported a domed ceiling. Similarly earthed, a freeform table held bowls of bread dough. Vegetables flourished in containers scattered around the sitting area and windowsills on the south side. Opposite them a section of oil drum closed the mouth of a pizzeria-style oven. Together with a wood-burning stove it anchored the food prep area: a sink and countertop with cabinets below, shelved niches above. The inward curve of the wall kept the highest jars within reach. A neat trick. I'd stepped into an earthship dream and was envious as hell. "This is fabulous. You built it?"

Thang uncapped the beers and gave me one. "I had a house trailer but we didn't get along." He drank, then smacked his furry lips. "These'll clear your head." He tipped his bottle at the dough on the table. "You bake?"

"I watched my mom when I was a kid."

"Sourdough oatmeal. The first batch needs to come out of the oven and the next is ready to go in. Punch down that last run there. I don't want to be up all night or have nothing to trade."

While the new loaves baked, Thang coherently detailed the transformation of his house from single-wide trailer to otherworld living space. General contractors could have filled a notebook with his low-tech workarounds for issues assumed to require special equipment. Although Thang had been working steadily for more than thirty years he didn't consider the job finished. I'd read about Gaudi and other eccentric builders who never said quit, but actually meeting one fascinated me. Success on a project of this magnitude, crazy or not, required a bunch of practical skills. I repeatedly asked Thang how he'd acquired his.

I got nothing out of him but, "You pick up things." Including bakery arts. The aroma of bread intensified as he scooped the second batch of crusty loaves from the oven with a flattened garden spade and slipped my dough in.

He stoked the fire and we went outside. I met chickens and goats. The revolving contraption above their A-frame shelter was a wind turbine creaking as it spun in the stiff ridgetop wind. Thang planned to eliminate the noise by replacing the turbine's main bearings with a magnetic suspension system. We inspected his root cellar, surveyed garden plots and gazed across Ivy Branch at acres of landfill blight. We must have been out there an hour. My curiosity cooled with my body temperature.

I was hypothermic before he was ready to complete the inside tour. The beaded-curtain archway to the left past the kitchen area led to rooms for storage batteries, tools and a large bathroom equipped with a wringer washer. Behind curtain number two was Thang's bedroom. Turkey feathers, dangling from a dreamcatcher over his bed, fluttered as we entered. "See how it does?" he said. "Only been up a few days. Old one clogged."

The willow branch hoop was strung with a web of beard hair. "You make these also?"

"Tourist kinds are useless. You know that."

A cruel streak possessed me. "How long until they clog?"

"I usually get a couple of months. You?"

"Varies," I said. "Then you restring?"

"Hell no. Burn the thing. He'll come back on you if you don't."

The temptation was too much. I fastened my seatbelt for a trip to Captain Thang's Wackyland and asked, "Who will?"

His beard snapped to attention but he didn't speak. I'd gone too far. "May I?" I said, reaching for a hinged picture frame on his whiskey barrel nightstand. In one panel a young soldier in an Army portrait glowers at attention.

Thang snatched the frame from me and returned it to its place. "My boy Mabry. Lives in California. He's a cop."

I'd also glimpsed the other picture, a washed-out Polaroid of a hippie couple and baby. They stand before a building that would have been unrecognizable had I not recently seen a very similar photograph. In Rusty's version, MacTiernan leans on his shovel. The hippie man in *this* snapshot was Thang. His intuition for the motel wiring suddenly struck me as less miraculous and I felt like a steaming sack of shit. He must have been gutted by the image of MacTiernan's beatific madonna and child, rendered in greens and blues possibly ground by the woman's own hand. "Sorry," I said. "I didn't . . . Hey, I'd better be going. It's been a pleasure working with you. This place . . . You put any ambitions I have to shame."

"Don't run off," Thang said. "Won't be dark for a while yet. Have another beer. I told you they'd do you good. It's the hops." He clapped me on the shoulder. "I'll take care of that bread."

I brought fresh brew in from the airlock. As he removed loaves from the oven, I told him how the fresco had set the Boones on edge.

"It'll get worse."

My mouth outran my brain again. "The experts say MacTiernan couldn't have done it alone."

Thang darkened. "The Prince of Lies—for if I call a devil I'll call him by his name. Didn't take him long to find his fools. Papaw Boone and me, for two. In the beginning I did whatever the devil asked. Had me bury the Coca-Cola chest to hold his special blend of plaster. White as death. Shit fumed and boiled. Scalded me like a hog. 'Don't tell Old Man Boone,' he said. 'It's a surprise.'" Thang tapped the bread loaves with a wooden spoon. "I was a dumb damn idiot."

I flashed back to the missing lime pit and recalled that water boils on contact with quicklime. Gardeners have excellent reason to buy their lime already hydrated.

Thang repeated the thumping process as if to double-check for proper tuning. "Devil drew pictures and mailed them to hell in the trash. Always. They'd cause trouble here, he said. They did, too. That's how he lured Moon Girl. Said he'd teach her to paint the ancient way. He should know."

"Moon Girl?"

"Mabry's mother. You saw her. Liar tricked her and she went to live with him. He used us for toys, Clayton. Down there he signed his claim with that painting. Get away like you say you will. Don't let him trap you." Thang's voice vibrated with emotion.

I'd caused this. The least I could do was try to calm him. "He's dead, Thang. Osbourne MacTiernan died thirty years ago."

"Read that somewhere, did you?"

The snarl changed my course. "Did you tell Rusty?"

"Told him he'd best mail the devil's mark back to him in fire. Boone's been warned. It's all a man can do."

"Maybe if I—"

"Don't you screw me over for a good turn. Hightail it to your strong place and don't look back. Devil comes to you lots of ways, including paintings, experts and reporters with tape recorders. Let them keep away from me."

Whatever else may be true of Osbourne MacTiernan, he devoted himself to the Wolfe River fresco and cast it adrift with utter calculation. The wall he selected to carry it into the future is stoutly built, out of the path of real estate development. He also had to know that the remote location would force intentionality on eventual viewers. It's a subtler marketing ploy than beating us over the head with Lenin. Effective or not, the seascape's short-term survival prospects may be better than they were for Man at the Crossroads. Thang would rather avoid his devil than confront him again.

Earlier this evening, my last at the motel, the Boones and I shared a loaf of Thang's bread. I didn't enlighten them about his past. Moon Girl and MacTiernan have wounded him enough. It isn't chic to interpret his rockpile as a monumental secretion of scar tissue but I do. Perhaps Jewett influenced me. Art minus empathy is just another pretty sunset.

Now, with Rusty and Lauren downstairs dreaming their dreams, MacTiernan and I are going a final round in 310. The man is a tough reach for me. He purposely skipped out on the fresco's unveiling. Did he have it in him to regret Thang's misfortune? Was his act of concealment a ruthless method of thwarting such questions? His elaborate pains brought us what? A koan? An arcane joke with an Italian punch line?

Fear that it may be both and he might be right is a cause for shuddering. His waves roll inexorable, majestic with passions expressed and unexpressed. The quiet, the boisterous. Passion celebrated, deferred, wreaked, wrecked and never realized. But if control is an illusion and there is no because, each is equal and I'm a glint in the water cringing. A glint who loves wood but not sufficiently to lose himself in it. My passion is pedestrian, closer cousin to the Boones than to MacTiernan, or Thang's abject enslavement.

Tonight, two weeks and a day after we discovered it, the fresco's sensuality of form does not suffice. I search for the humanity behind the brush strokes. Maybe that's naïve. Ultimately it makes no difference. I only know that I need it to.

Snow Boots

B Y THE LIGHT OF THE FULL MOON Natalya Korolenko walked alone beside a snow-covered lake toward the town of Lubotin. It would soon be dawn and she was returning from the cottage of Irina Govor, having replenished the old woman's supply of firewood. Natalya had stoked the fire in the big clay oven and put kettles of fresh water on to boil.

The lake and its changing early winter environs remained exciting new territory for her. Scarcely two months earlier had Yelena Biletska, proprietress of the dry goods shop in Lubotin, sent to her brother in Kiev, Natalya's father, for an assistant. Natalya, the third living daughter born into a family with more mouths than bread and potatoes to feed them, was old enough to despair for her fate in the merciless precincts of the city. She secretly welcomed her father's decision to send her east. Here in Lubotin the work was no less hard but the country people took more thought for the welfare of their neighbors. This very morning her aunt, whom she addressed as Aunt Lena, had sent a bit of sausage as a treat for Irina's soup.

The ice was not yet of sufficient thickness to permit a shortcut across the lake. Natalya followed the meandering snow-packed lane through harvested fields and regiments of slender birch trunks shining silver in the moonlight. Although Irina had complained more than usual with her rheumatism and delayed Natalya's departure somewhat, the girl dawdled under the protection of the benevolent birches.

Across the lake the tall thatched roofs of Lubotin were hidden behind a ribbon of trees. Feathery plumes from the town's chimneys ascended into the lightening sky and hung in a thin cloud. One of the plumes issued from the apartment she shared with her aunt. Natalya would soon add another feather to Lubotin's cap by building a fire in Aunt Lena's prized iron stove to warm the dry goods shop for customers. For now however, she enjoyed the crisp rural air, so different from the stench of Kiev's close and besooted warrens. In the city the splendors of trees and open spaces were reserved to the gardens of nobility.

A muffled clopping of hooves and tinkle of bells behind her broke Natalya's reverie. She recognized these sounds without turning to look and stepped off the beaten track. Soft snow engulfed the worn pair of boots her aunt had purchased at the cost of a sack of millet. In hopes that the cariole of Olexandr Olexyovych Dudka might pass by without stopping, Natalya averted her gaze. Dudka, a landowner's son, was a gnomish man of ruddy complexion and unconstrained personality. He kept the accounts at Lubotin's rooming house, stable and tavern, an establishment of questionable reputation. On the single occasion when she had accompanied Aunt Lena there to deliver mended linens, Dudka looked up from his ledgers in the gloomy office behind the front desk and shouted merrily for the manager as the two women bearing white heaps of bedclothes entered the tiny front parlor. "Winter will be fast upon us. The drifts are already blowing in!"

Since then, whenever Dudka's sleigh overtook her on the return trip from Irina's cottage, he had invited Natalya to ride into town with him. Naturally she refused as respectfully as possible, fearing to provoke him, well aware that except to her and Aunt Lena, her life mattered naught to anyone. The sleigh, once again, slid to a stop. "You should take care for your feet," Dudka called in salutation. "Don't freeze the poor things. Will you join me?" His horse snorted steam and pranced with impatience.

"Thank you for your kindness, sir. I cannot," Natalya replied, still studying the snow lapping at the tops of her boots. "I am not of your class."

"Does Mme. Biletska instruct you so? I must speak to her about it. Look at me."

Dudka blanketed his legs with a wooly ox hide. He wore no gloves, a fact Natalya found incongruous. His hands were chapped and gnarled, more like those of a laborer than an educated man. Still, he used the aristocratic French form of address and was, by birth, a landowner. She forced herself to glance briefly at his face, then stared again at the snow. The horse continued its pawing and loud exhalations of steam.

"Yours is the class of silly girls," Dudka taunted. "Perhaps I frighten you?"

Natalya, cheeks scalding with embarrassment, forgot herself and glared at her tormenter. "Tell me, sir, have you not considered what your friends would think to see a peasant riding with you? Have you no care for your reputation?"

The shadows across his broad cheekbones softened. In the approaching sunrise, Dudka's fur hat glistened with frost. His brows knitted but he said nothing.

"You are a rich man," she insisted.

"Is that what you think? What can you know of this?"

Natalya shook with a sudden chill.

"You are shivering, Mlle. Korolenko. Enough. You will join me at once." He drew back the ox hide, indicating where she should sit. "Come now." It was a command. "Not another word. You will sit here."

With great reluctance Natalya stepped out of the snow and up into his sleigh. Dudka lifted the lap robe higher and in so doing exposed his legs to her. Wooden stumps hung below the hem of his greatcoat. "Sir," she exclaimed.

The hide descended so heavily across her lap that she felt she could not move under its weight. A pair of canes projected from a sort of quiver strapped behind the graceful curve of the dash.

With a flick of the reins the cariole lurched forward. After the horse settled into a trot, Dudka said, "I learned the danger of assumptions at university, Mlle. Korolenko. Tsar Alexander is a stern professor. You must do better than I and protect your feet. These pegs make poor snow boots." He turned and spoke to her directly. "Rich, you say? A prince of Russia, perhaps? Hah! It is true that I have the use of this sleigh. But I ask you, which of us is wealthy?"

With a series of great jounces, they emerged from the birches and skimmed across a patchwork of grain fields. Daybreak washed the snow's cold blue dimples with pink. Natalya imagined herself sailing amongst the clouds in a world turned upside down.

"Your aunt will tell you that I am a criminal," Dudka said. "But what difference can it make on such a glorious morning?"

Had he turned toward her then she would have leapt from the sleigh, but his attention was drawn to a mob of crows in raucous pursuit of a hawk. When at last he took note of her cowering he said, "You have no cause for concern. My crime was going to the people on the wharves of Odessa. I talked with stevedores. I worked beside them and gave them books. For this I lost my feet under the wheels of a runaway freight cart during a worker's strike and was sentenced to internal exile."

The admission frightened her all the more. "A revolutionary? The authorities!"

"The authorities," Dudka sneered. "Our illustrious officials find me amusing. What harm can I do them? Am I to kick their shins? But you are correct. I do not accept the wisdom of bureaucrats. I do not follow the church. Nor do I admire the stern dictates of my former associates, for whom nothing exists but the revolution. They also have banished me. Is this not ironic?"

"Sir, you cannot mean what you say. Will you stop? I wish to walk."

Dudka spoke with harsh condescension. "Your given name is Natalya, is it not? You are from Kiev?"

Natalya shrank inside her coat but could not evade the inquisition. "Yes, sir."

"The name of your father?"

"Nikolai."

"What work does your family do in Kiev, Natalya Nikolaevna?"

"We are weavers." The line of trees marking the main road into Lubotin was fast approaching. She resolved to flee at the earliest opportunity.

Dudka shook his head. "You guard the sanctity of the old beliefs and those who uphold them? Before the so-called emancipation your parents were serfs. If we believed as our fathers did, a family like mine would own you and your family, body and soul. Biletska would do my bidding. But what freedom does she have even now, taxed half to death? She must send for you because she cannot pay wages. Such is the price of belief."

The cariole's heavy oaken runners carved neat arcs onto the wider road. Flashes of orange through the naked tree branches announced the rising sun. A dog and rooster exchanged customary morning greetings somewhere behind a weathered cottage and a boy burdened with sticks trudged toward its door. He regarded the sleigh without expression and went inside. Natalya, forgetting her resolution, peeked at Dudka around the edge of her scarf and asked, "Surely, we must believe—"

"Yes, indeed. Indeed we must." He flung the words at the distant town, or it may have been the horse's rump. "We must believe. I believe many things. I believe a driverless cart can do the bidding of the police. The death of my wife and son in childbed confirmed me in the belief that malice is the engine of the universe. Tender emotions do but serve its ends. I believe that the Tsar is not half so harsh a master as belief itself. I believe that only without belief can we be free. I want to believe in the people but, simple and intellectual alike, most of them love chains. And yet I believe the people are wiser than your revered authorities."

The tirade seemed to have deflated him. She said softly, "I do not understand."

Dudka chuckled, his humor restored. "Nor do I. You see how it is with me. My greatest belief, since you insist, is that I must be mad, an opinion shared by many of my acquaintance. Our petty officials find my ravings no more intelligible than the barking of that dog. Consequently, I am as free as it is possible to be in Russia and as useless."

In his fatalism Natalya heard Kiev's groaning shadows, ignored by passersby, and the creaky axles of the dead wagon calling out for the day's stiff, half-naked harvest. On the morning she bid the city goodbye, none save her youngest brother had the strength for tears. From her father she received a letter for Aunt Lena, from her mother a half loaf of bread. She arrived in Lubotin destitute except for the fugitive embers of indignation and hope secreted in her heart. She could not prevent them flaming up now. "How can you say you are useless," she scolded. "You are educated. You keep accounts."

"You are a sentimentalist, Natalya Nikolaevna."

"Yes, a seamstress," she said, mishearing. "One day, with the grace of God and instruction from my aunt, I will be a tailor."

Dudka roared with laughter and whipped the horse to top speed. "A tailor," he bellowed as the irregularities of the road threatened to eject him from the cariole. "I have no doubt. You shall be a tailor. You are the future of Russia, Natalya Nikolaevna. You must succeed. I have a book explaining why. Perhaps you would like to borrow it?"

Natalya clutched the sideboard and lip of the dash. "Slow down, sir, I beg you."

"Right again," Dudka shouted, reining in the horse as the sleigh rounded a final bend and entered the outskirts of Lubotin. "Mother Russia depends on your safe arrival."

⌘

18 January, 1905
Petersburg

Dearest Katya, such was the first glimmer of the unlikely relation that grew between my mother and Olexandr Olexyovych Dudka, the man for whom she and my unwitting father named me. I recount the story as she confided it, without embellishment. I have thought of Dudka frequently since the criminal massacres at the Winter Palace, an outrage that shall be known throughout the world.

"You are the future," he told my mother. He did not say it of himself. Radicals are comrades of the present. We can afford no sentimentality for the future or the past. Therefore I entrust the story of Dudka to you. The success of a revolution depends on the single-minded will of those who fight for it, but no less on its bearers of hope and care. My mother carried seeds of hope with her always, sowing them where she might. This also is your role, Katya, and I love you for it. Remain in Vienna until the battle is won. Now is the moment for radicals and, if necessary, for blood. Do not despair. The day when your crop can flourish in Russia will be quick in coming.

I must tell you a bit more of Dudka. Following the assassination of Alexander II, the police arrested him because of his former connection with the Narodnik plotter, Zhelyabov. After languishing for three years Olexandr Olexyovych was released without charge. He returned to Lubotin in broken health, a pariah to all but Mother. His sallow complexion and the premature graying of his hair moved her to tears. To me, a young boy at the time, Dudka was at first a terrifying scarecrow come to life, but he soon won me over with riddles and self-deprecating jokes. I particularly recall the day Mother and I measured him for a new suit. He teased me with his canes, brandishing them as if they were sabers. I think it delighted him to watch me run.

Not more than a year later, he died. Mother's pleading and the promise of a new cassock induced the priest in Lubotin to bury him. Dudka's emaciation was so severe I had no difficulty assisting Mother with the body. We dressed him in the clothes she made. And this I remember, Katya; this is of the utmost importance. In the coffin, she tied a pair of riding boots over his stumps, as though he were a normal man. When I questioned her about it she said, "He did not believe in God, but God may be pleased to believe in him. Olexandr Olexyovych will want his feet in heaven."

This is the necessity of hope, my dearest. It is what you are to me. I am well and miss you terribly.

Olexandr Ivanovych Stadnikov

⌘

Translator's note: On "Bloody Sunday," January 9, 1905 (Julian calendar), thousands of Russian workers marched on the Winter Palace in St. Petersburg to present Tsar Nicholas II with a petition demanding labor and political concessions. They were attacked by police and Cossacks. More than three hundred protesters were wounded; a hundred others died. Ironically the Tsar was not in residence at the time. This event sparked the 1905 Revolution, remembered mainly in the West for the Potemkin affair. Nicholas II was eventually forced to sign the October Manifesto, a guarantee of civil rights and democratic reforms. These were effectively scuttled within a year.

Nothing further is known of Katya or Stadnikov. His (originally untitled) story and letter were discovered by a New York book dealer in 1993. The handwritten sheets had been secreted in a volume of Russian verse.

Every Curry Tells a Story

I DON'T KNOW HOW GIRLS ARE SUPPOSED TO FEEL about their dads; I've read all sorts of things. Mine isn't loveable—Mom is welcome to him—but hating Daddy on a consistent basis isn't easy either. Gene Stratis is a naturalized US citizen, Greek by way of Belgium. At sixty-one he has the fitness of guys half his age and speaks five languages including Arabic. He works for an international services company—that's all Lizzie, my younger sister, and I are supposed to know. The fact that he wore a full beard for years after 9/11 was, I'm sure, a complete coincidence. Lizzie and I never liked the mysteriousness or his constant postings overseas. We've grown up with him being home for a week or a month, maybe five or six times a year.

Now I'm on visitor status as well. I was "home" last weekend, although Fairfax isn't really home anymore. My home is in Charlottesville, two blocks from campus. I have a studious roommate, a full load of prelaw classes, a cat and an ex-boyfriend. Treks to my parents' house are not that common. But Camille, my best friend from high school, got an extra ticket for the Avett Brothers at the Patriot Center. I'd have hitchhiked the hundred miles across Virginia to see them. Camille couldn't even spoil it by trying to hook me up with her boyfriend's technogeek cousin, who droned on after the concert about the potential for using artificially intelligent internet bots as virtual secret agents.

Saturday morning and into the afternoon I studied for midterms. Daddy went for a run. Mom took Lizzie to the go-kart track—it has an underage driver program. When I'd had enough, I sat through a bunch of inane TV commercials, waiting for a Women's Open tennis match that turned out to be a rerun. A network channel promised to restore my sex appeal with a stomach toner. Or there was golf, World War II, some black and white movie about drunks and a scruffy dog at a cocktail party. I don't know. I heard the front door as I cussed yet another probiotic online-dating ad for yogurt with a whiter smile.

Daddy was leaving for Brussels in a few hours, followed by two months at an undisclosed location. It had Lizzie in a snit. That's why she made Mom take her to the track. I've been through that revulsion phase. Now I'm like, whatever; at least he didn't regrow the beard.

The thing I loved best when I was little was the sound of his car in the driveway and running out to greet him. He'd scoop me off my feet and toss me so high. Once I remember seeing across our roof into the backyard. That can't be true. The point is, I used to think our life was normal. Later, even when I hated him with the passion Lizzie does now, I couldn't entirely suppress the thrill when he walked through the door.

So I turned when I heard him come in. He'd probably still throw me into the air if I let him. Not that he's the bodybuilder type. He could almost be a corporate VP out for a jog. Daddy wiped the sweat off his face. "You look bored."

"School's a bitch; we're a dysfunctional family and TV sucks. How trite is that?"

His El Greco eyes turned toward heaven. "Forgive Shannon her education and full belly." This is a favorite low blow of his, totally unfair and unanswerable, praying to a nameless Congolese baby who died of malnutrition during a civil war fought over minerals used in DVD players. The classic starving children of Africa ploy. But he's been there and seen it and can describe it in grisly detail.

Instead of letting it go at that, he rubbed it in. "Let's fix something special for supper. There's daikon in the fridge. Does Asian appeal to you?"

This was an unusual suggestion. Daddy in the kitchen is usually Daddy alone. For him, food is an improvisational art form. He excels at it. Says he learned from restaurant jobs when he was young. His specialty is transforming odd combinations of ingredients into meals people would pay good money for. It's a different culinary league from Mom and me. We depend on recipes.

"Fine," I said through clenched teeth. Rather than go off on him for mocking my restlessness, I added, "If there's squash in it." He knows I detest winter squash. It comes in two consistencies: mushy or undercooked and hard. Either way it has a washed-out, cafeteria taste. The request was spiteful. I wanted him to fail.

He considered for half a second before accepting the challenge. "Your mother's got butternuts curing downstairs. Pick out a big one and peel it while I shower. See what else is in the garden. Be adventurous, but keep in mind that we aren't investment bankers. We eat what we create."

"Daddy's garden"—that's how Mom refers to her organic kitchen garden—is a point of pride with her, not a weed or pest in it. I've literally caught her in the back yard washing zucchini leaves for a photo. She's a professional photographer. When Daddy's not home she gives away the produce that can't be frozen whole or stored in the basement. Last summer I confessed to her on the phone that I'm embarrassed at how she sort of puts herself out there with the garden for his occasional pleasure.

43

She denied that's how it is. "Ever think how nice it might be to forget your expectations and simply observe what happens?"

"Like in your perfect garden?"

"Spare me the sarcasm, Shannon. I'm referring to your father."

"Then why's Lizzie in trouble for sneaking out to a sleepover?" She'd been grounded for pitching a defiance bitch after Daddy flew to London and missed her birthday.

"Because dependability is also important, especially between children and parents. You have a right to expect that from us, whether or not you approve of how we do it. But Daddy and I don't need so much reassurance from each other."

"Simple as that, huh."

"Of course not. Want to know what terror is? It's a little brown ring in the bottom of a home pregnancy test tube when you're fresh out of college, your lover is married and you can't reach him for a month."

The terror admission was new information, a hint of vulnerability behind the certainty that's as recognizably Mom as the flecks of copper in her green eyes. "Exactly," I said, "He left it all on you."

"How else could it have been, under the circumstances? Thank goodness Gene was too thrilled to see through the confidence I pretended to have. Remember that baby picture of you I like so much? Your wide open delight at learning to crawl? It didn't dawn on me until then that our family was *actually* succeeding and I didn't need to feel like a fake any more. Your joy was mine too."

Sure it was. Camille and I swore an oath in high school never to put up with absentee lovers. Now that she's hot and heavy with Steve, an Annapolis midshipman, her standards are more flexible. Not mine. I don't care that my parents aren't married or that Lizzie and I have Mom's last name: Gregory. Camille agrees; it's a cool statement when couples stay together because they want to. She doesn't know Daddy was already married and still is. The wife's name is Dina; she's a fashion designer in Antwerp. Thank goodness Lizzie and I don't have Belgian siblings to look down their noses at the spawn of the other woman. Daddy's wife is a fact of life in our house. All the same, the situation isn't anything to share with a blabby best friend.

Despite a minor heat wave the end of the growing season was fast approaching and the garden wasn't particularly photogenic. There were bare spots. Some vegetables and herbs remained though, and the new fall crops looked good. I picked Chinese eggplant, red bell pepper, sugar peas, a late cucumber, lettuce, cherry tomatoes and, because tomatoes and basil go together, a bunch of basil.

As I transferred the butternut peelings from the sink to the compost pot, Daddy joined me in the kitchen and inspected the vegetables in the drainer. "You up for a curry?"

"Sure."

"Then dice your squash. Save the seeds; we'll roast them for the salad."

1 large butternut squash, peeled and diced (6 cups)

I took the chef's knife off the magnetic rack, recalling the time I tried to halve an unpeeled butternut and pressed so hard that the blade turned and cut the crap out of my thumb. I needed stitches.

Daddy saw my hesitation. "Let me show you." Knives and knife work are important to him. He's like a kitchen samurai.

Relieved, I gave him the knife.

"First thing is not to hold it by the handle for a job like this." He grasped the thick part of the blade between fingers and thumb. Only his pinky and the heel of his palm were on the handle. He sliced into the junction between the squash neck and bulb, neatly separating the two by rocking down with his wrist. "Like that," he said. "Now you try."

The blade was totally under control. What a difference.

"Notice how a sharp knife speaks to you. Each vegetable, each section, each ripeness, feels a little different."

The squash had a slippery, not quite buttery, fine granular texture. I got into listening to my fingers and was disappointed to finish the job.

"Excellent," Daddy said. "Now for some pizzazz. Let's bring your mother's lime tree in for the winter."

Mom bought the kaffir lime for Daddy years ago but, like the garden, she's the one who tends it. From a thorny stick in a gallon container, it developed into a four-foot bush that summers on the patio. Daddy can lift the pot by himself but can't quite see where he's going with it. I carried the drip saucer, opened the door and guided him to a sunny corner of the living room. When jostled, the leaves fill the front of the house with a wonderful scent. Daddy uses them as if they were citrus-flavored bay leaves. I've also seen him grate rind from the warty limes.

The fruits themselves are too bitter to eat. I wonder if Mom was aware of that from the beginning. But if she ever feels bitter it doesn't show. Grandpa and Grandma Gordon apparently had a fit when they found out about Daddy being married. Mom says she won them over by believing in herself and in us, him included. People might not imagine a kept woman having self-esteem or much personal sense of responsibility. They'd be wrong. Besides being the go-to architectural photographer in the DC Metro Area, Mom is a firm disciplinarian. Lizzie and I can't really complain about how she's brought us up. Aside from Daddy, she's less demented than most parents her age.

Stew until soft, stirring occasionally (about 20 min.)
 5 cups diced squash
 8 kaffir lime leaves
 2 TBSP unsalted butter
 1 cup chicken stock
Remove lid, reduce and stir until squash is the consistency
 of jam
Discard lime leaves
Remove from heat

"Chicken or vegetarian?" Daddy asked as we washed up afterwards.

"Chicken."

He got a leftover chicken breast and pint of homemade stock out of the freezer. I microwaved the stock while he melted butter in a skillet, added lime leaves and most of the squash.

When the stock thawed he poured some into the pan and lidded it. "You look comfortable with that knife," he said, passing me a cold daikon from the fridge—except for the mild radish taste, daikon could be confused for a giant albino carrot. "Peel and dice half of this. Then slice the eggplant thin and chop the snow peas into bite-sized pieces. Separate piles. Remember your fingertips."

I expected the radish fibers to be ropy; they weren't. Eggplant skin reminded me of cutting an aluminum can. I didn't notice anything about the pea pods but a hesitation before the knife clicked through to the cutting board. Daddy brought a bunch of shallots up from the basement, rubbed the papery skin off four big ones and set them beside my board. "Coarse chop. Half that bell pepper too."

Microwave until cooked but still firm (4-5 minutes)
 1 cup daikon radish, diced

the reserved cup of diced squash

I was surprised the blade didn't register the shallot rings. The pepper cut like it sounded: crisp and juicy as a stiff, waterlogged sponge. Daddy nuked the daikon and the rest of the raw squash. Between starting a pot of rice, cleaning the squash seeds, oiling, salting and spreading them on a baking sheet, he stirred the squash on the stove. There was a fragrance of lime and chicken.

Sauté until it begins to brown
   1 small-medium eggplant, sliced thin (chop to bite-size if necessary)
   4 shallots, coarsely chopped
   ½ red bell pepper, coarsely chopped
   2 TBSP unsalted butter

In another skillet he sautéd the eggplant, shallots and pepper, flipping them in the pan without spilling a piece. Restaurant jobs may have taught him the moves of commercial kitchens but I doubt that's where he developed his creativity. Kitchen staff at the off-campus café where I wait tables is too busy painting by number with pre-prepped food, yelling and getting high. No, Daddy's cooking is a taste of his other life.

"Why do you have to go to Brussels?" I asked.

"Not Brussels. Antwerp. *Trouw Mariage-Antwerp* is an important weekend for Dina. Buyers from all over Europe come to order next year's fashions in formal wear." He adjusted the heat under the sauté and took the lid off the squash. "Tradeshows are work. She's happy when I'm able to assist. And some old friends are in town."

The happy family aromas of butter, vegetables, citrus and chicken faded. I ripped into the salad lettuce, not caring about the size of the pieces. "I don't know how you manage it."

"Must we—"

"Mom doesn't care if she loses out to tradeshows but you see what it does to Lizzie."

"Better that I abandon the three of you?" He set the oven to 275°.

We knew this fight by heart but his threat of abandonment was an unexpected twist. A cold jolt flashed through my chest. "Of course not."

"Provincial mores are weapons of mass destruction. One day you'll discover that. Lizzie too." Back on familiar ground.

"Mom's not enough for you?"

"Because I love your sister am I excluded from loving you? Can't I love both Fran and Dina? We've been through this. Trite was your word, wasn't it? This discussion is trite."

As if I wasn't aware of that and didn't hate the predictable stalemate at least as much as he did. But I couldn't let it go so easily; isn't silence a form of permission? "I'm just saying, most of the world doesn't agree."

"It can't be helped." Simultaneously acknowledging my abuse of the lettuce and ignoring its meaning, he added, "Since you started the salad, cut up the tomatoes and whatever else you want in it."

The sounds of chopping, a spoon scraping the bottom of a skillet and the sizzle of sautéing vegetables replaced conversation. Why argue about how they live their lives, I thought. Mine is elsewhere.

Blend until smooth
    stewed squash
    1 14 oz. can coconut milk
    Thin it to gravy consistency with:
    ¾ cup chicken stock (approx)

Daddy spooned the gloppy squash into the blender jar, added a can of coconut milk and calmly, as if nothing had happened between us, asked for the remaining stock. He drizzled some into the blender and pulsed the mixture to orange goo.

"Done with the salad," I said, determined not to be undone by his maddening cool. "What now?"

His cell phone rang. "The squash seeds can go in the oven."

It was Mom on the phone. Something good about Lizzie at the track. Daddy motioned me to refrigerate the perishable items. I was about to wash out the sauté skillet when he frantically gestured for me to stop. Under panto-mimed "Hurry-up" direction I deglazed the pan with stock, poured the juice into the creamed squash, refrigerated it, turned off the oven and the heat under the rice. Except for the lack of yelling, I might have been an emergency kitchen fill-in at the café.

Minutes later, with Daddy's travel bags in the trunk of my Corolla, I was driving him to Manassas. I'd dropped Lizzie off at the go-kart track there a few times since she took an interest in the sport. They don't do bumper cars. Even beginner karts race a twisty Grand Prix course. The speed seemed slow until I tried it myself and got lapped by my little sister. Since then she's graduated to the regular karts with bigger engines. Mom told Daddy that Lizzie had entered the official sprint heats—an afternoon of six-lap qualifier races with the best drivers moving on to a final—and was kicking butt. We should come and watch. He could leave for Dulles directly from there.

What a delight. Thanks to lead-foot Lizzie I'd inherited primary responsibility for a meal featuring a disgusting vegetable. He talked me through completing it but I had him write down the instructions on an old envelope from the glove box.

A race was in progress as we entered the converted warehouse. Exhaust fans, rumbling at the ends of the building, weren't keeping up with the mugginess, fumes or lawnmower yammering of low-slung karts skidding around the course. A couple of dozen friends and families of racers whooped it up in the spectator area beside the long straightaway and finish line. One guy in Elvis sideburns, cowboy boots and a NASCAR windbreaker was styling at the expense of comfort. A gaggle of fire-suited adolescents shouted catcalls and encouragement while, beside them, a grandmother restrained a howling toddler from climbing the wall separating them from the course.

Mom didn't have that degree of adult supervision. She was leaning over the waist-high wall, her camera arm extended down to track level for action shots of the racers. People don't think of photography as physically demanding but being limber is a plus. For a woman in her forties, Mom does well in that department. When we got to her she straightened up and pointed across the snaking lines of orange and white barrier wall to a far section of the course. "Just in time," she said. "Lizzie's number 6, the blue helmet coming at us out of the S-turn. She's up to third. Whoo hoo! Go Lizzie. Catch them!"

Two karts, dueling for the lead, motored past us into the first turn: a hairpin. Lizzie kept out of the fracas, well ahead of trailing drivers. A straggler trying to close the gap misjudged his speed, rammed the wall and caromed across the straightaway. I sympathized with him, having done that myself.

On the last lap the second place kart clipped the leader's rear, trying to pass where there wasn't room. Both spun out. Lizzie slipped between them and crossed the line first. We cheered. Mom told Daddy, "They ought to disqualify that Darren. He's the same kid who tried to wreck Lizzie earlier." She pointed at the scoreboard. "Look! They're doing it. He's out!"

"Why's number 3 carrying the checkered flag?" Daddy asked as the racers came around to park in pit lane.

"Oh, no. That's the girl who got hit. I guess they don't think Lizzie would have won otherwise. But it doesn't matter. She's ahead in points. Her first try at the sprint races and she's in the final."

The noise subsided as drivers killed their engines.

"Lizzie," Mom called. "Daddy and Shannon are here."

Lizzie separated from the milling group of racers on both sides of the pit wall and took off her helmet. Her sweaty cotton balaclava framed a scowl. "Mom, did you see what they did? I won fair and square."

"Check the board, honey. It's okay. They disqualified Darren."

"Well, they should. Hi, Shannon. Hi, Daddy."

The NASCAR windbreaker strutted by with his arm around the girl awarded the victory. She was probably younger than Lizzie, maybe fourteen, a cool cucumber in color-coordinated pink and white. "Good race," she said over her shoulder. "Your first finals. I'll be easy on you."

"We'll see," Lizzie snapped.

Daddy said, "Big mouth on that girl."

"She's been karting since first grade but I can take her. Her name's Joslyn."

Mom changed the subject. "Let's get Daddy a burger in the snack bar. He has to leave after your race."

"I have to go, Mom. The 6 kart is handling real well. I need to claim it."

"Don't be rude. You have time to speak to Shannon and your father."

Daddy patted Lizzie's back. "Go on, honey. Show us what you've got."

Mom rolled her eyes with an expression that said, It's up to him.

"Thanks, Daddy." Lizzie dropped the oversized Star Wars helmet onto her head again and waddled off in a baggy fire suit that had faded to charcoal gray. Like most drivers other than Joslyn, she wore track-provided safety equipment. First come, first served.

"You shouldn't let her get away with that, Gene," Mom said.

"I was the same at her age. It's great to see her focused."

"The people here say she's a natural. I thought they were just buttering up the mother but maybe not. Let's sit. I didn't expect to be here so long."

"Shannon," Daddy said as we walked into the snack bar, "order us a round of something not too sugary?" He pulled a ten from his wallet.

As sweetly as possible, I inquired, "And what to go with that, sir?"

"I'll eat at the terminal. Fran, anything for you?"

Mom, to her credit, had the sense to say, "She's not on duty, Gene. *We'll* eat when we get home. Didn't you say supper's on the stove?"

Racers cranked their engines as I returned with bottles of flavored water. My parents got up from their table and we moved to the spectator area. The umpire or referee—whatever he's called—told the drivers to line up on the straightaway two abreast. There were eight of them. Lizzie and her beloved 6 kart inside on the first row, Joslyn beside her.

A horn sounded and they were off. Lizzie clung to a slim lead through two laps. Then, on the far side of the course, she dropped to second but pulled ahead again in the S-curves with Joslyn on her left rear, fighting for inside position down the straightaway in front of us. Lizzie glanced back, held her line, refused to be intimidated. Joslyn had to brake. They slid around the hairpin with a lengthening cushion on the field.

Lizzie kept Joslyn's inside charges at bay by swiveling in her seat, one eye on the challenge behind and the other on where she was going. Too close to the inside wall and she'd wipe out in the hairpin. Too far outside opened the door for a pass. In the previous race that strategy had frustrated Darren into trying to muscle Joslyn aside. She was smarter. On the final lap she emerged onto the straight directly behind my sister, almost glued to her bumper. Lizzie glanced left, then quickly right and left again, twisting far around. Suddenly she tugged at her helmet and drifted wide. Joslyn dove inside for the pass. My sister finished the race in second.

We hurried to the pits. "What happened?" Mom asked.

"I couldn't see. I turned and couldn't see anything to my left but the inside of this stupid thing. It's too big. Where was she?"

"In your back pocket," I said.

"Damn."

NASCAR dad, Joslyn in tow, introduced himself to Daddy. "That your girl? She sure give us a race. For a minute there I thought she might take us."

"You've got a wily daughter."

Joslyn beamed, "Thank you, sir. Libby, is it? You made me think today."

Lizzie pulled off her balaclava, displaying matted spikes of short dark hair. She squared her shoulders. "It's Lizzie."

"Glad to meet you," Joslyn said.

Lizzie chilled a notch. "I didn't see you back there."

"You weren't supposed to."

Mom hugged Lizzie. "You did so good. Didn't she do

good, Gene?"

"Absolutely. If this is your thing, honey, go for it."

A PA announcement called the top finishers to a po-
dium beside the track office. Joslyn won a small trophy.
Lizzie and the boy in third waved runner-up waves. Mom
documented the moment for posterity. Daddy had left us. I
saw him chatting with a clerk at the equipment counter.

Engines putted to life again as the track shifted from
formal race mode to walk-in Arrive & Drive customers.
Lizzie, after the obligatory handshakes, removed her
horse-collar neck brace and was unzipping the fire suit
right there in front of everybody. Underneath she had on
a soppy t-shirt and gym shorts. If she had any breasts to
speak of, she'd have drawn a crowd.

"What's wrong with doing that in the locker room?"
Mom asked, disapproving.

"It's too hot to wait."

"Daddy has to move his bags to my car. Change clothes
in the locker room. Just be quick about it. We'll meet you
in the snack bar."

Lizzie partially rezipped, gathered her gear and stalked
off in saggy pants.

"Shannon, let me borrow your keys so Daddy and I
can transfer his luggage. I'll drive him to the airport. You
take your sister home. I'll be back in a minute."

Mountain Dew was the closest the snack bar came to
offering the energy drinks Lizzie lives on. I bought her a su-
persized cup, sat at a four-top and sipped until she plopped
down across the table, wearing jeans and a clean shirt. She
tossed her gym bag onto a chair. My reward for sisterly
consideration was a grunt and the spectacle of her hollow-
cheeked sucking on the straw. The mosquito impersonation
continued until Mom and Daddy's arrival.

"All set," he said. He mussed Lizzie's slightly combed
hair and she stiffly allowed it. "Make your old man proud

while I'm gone. And check with the boy at the sales counter. He has a solution to your helmet problem."

My personal compromise for greetings and goodbyes with Daddy is the European double cheek kiss. It's respectful, by the book. We did our thing. "Be nice to your mother," he told me. "A plate of food tells a story. Let her taste harmony tonight."

Mom handed me my keys. "I'll be home in an hour and a half."

Daddy said, "See you at Christmas."

"See you then," I replied.

Then they were gone.

"Couldn't you at least say goodbye?" I asked Lizzie.

Her answer was a dismissive shrug.

"Well then, let's get out of here."

"Daddy told me to see Brian first."

"So, do it."

She disappeared into the spectators. I mouthed an ice cube from her soda. Seconds later she returned at a run. "He bought me a helmet," she squealed. "Help me pick it out."

My heart sank. I envisioned my sister modeling every helmet in the place, not being able to decide and trying them all on again. I grabbed her gym bag before it was out of reach.

I needn't have worried. Daddy and Brian had already settled on a model designed to prevent the eye shield from fogging. Lizzie's choice was limited to color: black or white. How did I know she'd pick black?

In the car she couldn't quit fiddling with it, trying it on, adjusting straps. Between the new helmet smell, lingering go-kart fumes and the aroma of Lizzie sweat, I drove with my window down. At home, showers were the first order of business for us both.

We didn't expect Mom to be back when she said, and

she wasn't. I brought Daddy's curry instructions in from the car and set about picking up with supper where we'd left off. The squash seeds in the oven, luckily, were browned and crunchy, perfect in fact. The rice only needed warming in the microwave.

Combine well in stewpot over low heat
    squash-coconut cream
    3 TBSP Thai red curry paste (or to taste)
    ¼ cup chiffonade of fresh basil leaves
Add
    diced daikon and squash
    sautéd vegetables

Lizzie's curiosity got the better of her as I poured the orange-colored squash cream into Mom's stewpot—my sister seldom ventures farther into the kitchen than the refrigerator. She found the tub of curry paste for me, opened the lid and threw the container in the garbage, proclaiming, "Phew. That stuff stinks."

"Not so fast," I said. "Let me smell it." My ex-boyfriend, who used to cook at the café, occasionally attempted Asian dishes. Let's be honest; some Asian seasonings smell bad. Thai fish sauce is the juice of fermented anchovies, for cripes sake. Nothing cooked with it has any right to taste good, yet it often does. As I suspected, the curry paste had a faint but unmistakable odor of spoiled seafood. I spooned three dollops into the stew pot.

"Gross," Lizzie said, appalled. "I'm not eating that."

"Doesn't smell any worse than you did. Daddy said it'll be okay. I'll make you a deal; I'll eat your curry paste if you eat my squash. That's our featured ingredient tonight." I whisked the paste into it. "How about helping instead of standing around? There's a bag of basil in the fridge. Roll the leaves and slice them into spaghetti strips."

Lizzie sort of managed to do it, then escaped before I thought of additional jobs for her. The leaves went into the pot. I stirred and sampled. The stuff was spicy, tangy, chickeny, sweet with coconut. Otherworldly delicious and down-home as dirt. I added the cooked vegetables, stirred, tasted again. Incredible.

Mom walked in and took a deep whiff. "Smells divine. What is it?"

"A Daddy special. Kind of a Thai curry with squash."

"Yum. You going out tonight?"

"I don't think so. Camille and Steve are trying to set me up with some computer security spook. One in the family is enough for me."

"Then would you like a gin and tonic? I'm having one."

Mom mixes hers with good gin and a dash of sweetened lime juice to take the edge off the tonic. Who was I to decline such an offer? She's moderately cool about liquor at home. Though I won't be twenty-one for almost a year she often lets me have one drink on evenings I'm not going out. This is to supervise my education about alcohol. I allow her to believe she's my primary source of knowledge on the subject. She allows me to pretend that lie is selling.

After the curry is heated through add
  1 broiled chicken breast, sliced thin
  snow peapods, coarsely chopped
  correct the seasonings

While Mom changed clothes, slathered praise on Lizzie and shamed her into setting the table, I luxuriated in my gin and tonic. Daddy would have approved the pairing of flavors between drink and meal. Harmony he'd requested and Mom had, by accident, achieved it.

For her sake, I visited the garden again to pick a presentation garnish of whole basil leaves. Daddy's concoction might as well look as good as it tasted. Damn him. Curry paste *does* stink. Squash *is* inedible and pigs, by god, do not fly. Except when they do.

Serve over steamed rice
   Makes 4 main course servings

Grass

RAY

I'M FUELING THE LAWNMOWER. Yesterday the new grass and wild onions were welcome harbingers of spring. Today they're a foot tall. I suppose I should be proud. The previous owner of our partially wooded two acres was a mechanic who worked at home. What passed for a lawn then consisted of an oily mix of gravel, clay and automotive junk. I had to beg grass to grow.

Last fall I didn't completely drain the mower's gas tank and over the winter the half inch of leftover fuel absorbed water vapor. The engine will cough and smoke, once I get it running. So be it. I don't believe in dumping gas or running the tank dry if all I'm doing is chopping leaves. The world is polluted enough already. With luck the starter cord will hang together. At least today. I pull, pull again. Nothing.

Our grandson, Jake, a freshman at NC State, is younger than this old push mower. In human years it's closer to my age of seventy-four. They don't make parts for it anymore, something I found out after a wheel fell off. I jury-rigged a new axle. It wobbles a bit but so do I.

When I bought the mower it was top of the line. Five horse, guaranteed to start on the first or second try. It'll do that again after we get through this opening day ritual.

The rust stains on the handle are from sweat. The deck remains solid, sandwiched between an underneath plaster of vegetable matter and a greasy top coat of dust. I tell my wife Althea that the dust keeps the paint from peeling. I don't want to think how many miles I've walked behind this thing. I pull the starter cord a few more times.

Althea and I live on a Blue Ridge mountainside. Apart from trees the main thing we grow here is rocks. Now and then I hit one. Lost a chunk of blade housing that way. Fortunately the debris shot out the same direction as the clippings. To be on the safe side I mow in high-top boots. They also protect against snakes. Yellow jackets are another matter but those buggers usually keep to themselves until August.

Our lot slopes. Most of it isn't too steep, but two or three times a year, not today, I do battle with the bank between the driveway hedge and lower woodlot. I'd let the trees take over if the septic leach field didn't run close by. I pick a day when the ground is soft and my boots get better purchase because the bank has to be cut on the horizontal. It's always a thrill scrambling along with the mower pinned to the bank chest high. I have to grip the handle with one hand low near the back wheel and the other up on the dead-man. So far we haven't taken a tumble. It amazes me that the handle mount hasn't broken.

My wife tells me I ought to hire a yard service or buy a riding mower. You'd think she'd learn to ignore my complaints about cutting grass. But she can't help herself. "Trade it in," she said again today at lunch. "Home Depot has that yellow tractor you were looking at."

Like a $3000 rider wouldn't spin out any number of places or roll over on the bank regardless of what the saleslady says. "It's the grass, not the mower," I told Althea. I was on my second glass of iced tea, fortifying myself.

"Then why must you gripe?" she said. "I swear, it's always the same thing. 'The mower is falling apart.' You're too old for a push mower. It's asking for a heart attack. What am I supposed to do if you keel over in the yard?"

"9-1-1 is only three numbers. With your memory it shouldn't be a problem. Or scroll down to Emergency on the speed dial."

"You'd be stiff before the ambulance arrives."

My wife is a fine woman to put up with me. She's had her gall bladder out, cataracts, a hip replacement and skin cancer. The dermatologist left a divot in her scalp. Then he prescribed a cancer cream that took the hide off her ears and face. He called it FU. Sounds about right. She looked like somebody scrubbed her with a wire brush.

"If you think I should trade things in just because they're falling apart . . ." I let her fill in the blank. She didn't appreciate the humor. Once upon a time I had an affair. We said all there was to say about it long ago.

After the grass is cut I'll treat myself to a beer out here in the shop. It's a detached four-bay garage equipped with refrigerator, portable TV and woodstove. Plenty of room for tools and shelves of what Althea calls "whatnot." I put in a custom workbench and three swivel chairs, the classic low-backed pattern with sculpted arms. The chairs were my first post-retirement woodworking project. Over the course of my teaching career only two manual arts students lost fingers. I'm prouder of that record than the Board of Education's sayonara plaque on the wall beside the clamps. I'm happy with the swivel chairs too. They're quarter-sawn red oak. One for me; one for an older neighbor who drops by and one for a guest. The guest is usually our cat, Clementine. Clemmie's chair has the cushion. She and I spend a lot of time here. In the house I can't sit down to a ballgame without hearing what else I ought to be doing.

I give the starter another spin. No dice. I consider checking the spark plug to see if it's getting gas, but I'd almost rather not know. Carburetors are inscrutable devices. I don't smell gas. The engine isn't flooded. I pull the cord again. Now it smells like gas. I take off the air filter to let the fumes dissipate.

I could sharpen the blade. It must be dull as Masterpiece Theater. OMG. OMG is Jake-speak for wow. Last summer he stayed with us to earn money for college. He and his dad weren't getting along. Jake agrees with me about Masterpiece Theater. He hid out in the bedroom with his laptop. Said he was doing homework. Never mind that he wasn't in school at the time. Transparent BS doesn't bother today's kids any more than it does politicians.

But I was young once too. Youth requires space. Most of us survive it. I joined the Navy and served aboard a floating gas station, the USS Cacapon, during the Korean War. The razzing we endured about the name of that tub was the worst part of the tour. Jake's online cruising may be safer than the '34 Terraplane hotrod I bought after I got out. He's less likely to sober up and find himself married. I tried to interest him in woodworking and mechanical things. He helped remodel the powder room but grime turns him off. He was nowhere to be found for yard work. I don't know how he'll cope with temperamental lawnmowers. Probably by living in an apartment.

The blade I'm using has ten years of steel in it yet, if I'm careful about maintaining the side-to-side weight balance. That's critical. New blades are unavailable for this model. Sharpening isn't on today's agenda though. Take it from a guy who's turned over a mower with gas in the tank.

I inspect the air filter. It could use cleaning. Maybe later I'll soak it in gas. I didn't used to sit around staring at dirty filters. I'd sweep up or rearrange boxes of screws. But

I'm learning the pleasures of blanking out. Complete peace with no sense of boredom. Puttering is my cover story. If Althea asks what kept me in the shop, I'll say I couldn't reinstall the filter until it was dry. It's best not to leave an exposed carburetor untended. A bug might crawl in and clog a jet.

Speaking of which, I put a finger in the carburetor throat. The brass flapper there is the choke. When closed it blocks air intake; opening it lets the engine breathe. I work the joystick on the mower handle. The choke moves normally against my fingertip. The smell of gas is less. I reattach the filter, set the choke and pull. And again. A fleeting sputter. I unset the choke and wheel the mower out to the driveway.

It's warm this afternoon, shirtsleeve weather. Five miles down the cove the summit of Laurel Mountain stands brown and sharp against the Carolina blue. Atmospheric haze will soon reduce the peak to a vague outline. We won't see it clear again until winter.

Althea and I stumbled across this property by accident. The move from Wilmington had us stressed out. I'd been lucky to find a new teaching position anywhere at mid-semester but the homes listed in the classifieds were over-priced and rent was eating into our down payment money. We took a wrong turn that day—there are no straight roads here—and the kids were in the backseat whining. Ray Jr., Jake's dad, spotted the FOR SALE sign and I thought, Why not look? Althea told me to turn around when she saw the cannibalized cars. I didn't get the chance. The owner was at my door wiping the grease off his hands before I could shift into reverse. Long story short, he had a good price and agreed to haul away the junkers. Althea liked the layout of the house. I promised her a grass lawn. It might have been penance for uprooting her from Wilmington.

I yank the starter cord. The engine races, puffs an oily cloud, sputters and dies. On the next pull the sparkplug hits again. I baby the throttle until the engine settles into a ragged growl and we begin the first cut of the season.

ALTHEA

Ray's crack about trading me in on a new model made me want to grab him by the ears and say, "Will you listen to yourself, Raymond Keller? Where's the man I married?" But no use to push it. He'd say that's the pot calling the kettle black. Maybe so but it doesn't get us very far. So I didn't say anything to him, just gathered up the dishes and let him go on out.

He was different in college, fresh out of the Navy then and cruising Greenville in that maroon hotrod with the suicide doors. He liked to show off his flattop; the hair in front jutted like a jaw. To heck with James Dean and motorcycle shades. Ray had the hollow-cheeks, without the self-doubt. He got away with ogling girls up and down, smiling at our embarrassment. Nice girls were not seen going out with him, but they did. He had that kind of attraction. I made a show of ignoring him when we were in the same class. It puzzled me, as he meant it to, when he took to calling me Red—I was brunette. I thought he must have caught me blushing, sneaking peeks at him. Eventually he confessed to borrowing the name from a racy cartoon. I was his Red Hot Riding Hood. Should I be ashamed to admit loving the big bad wolf? I was twenty years old and gloried in it.

We got married when I found out I was pregnant with Janelle. That's what decent people did. If Ray had other ideas I couldn't tell it from his excitement over being a father or the way he treated me. He buckled down and worked construction to supplement his GI bill. Somehow he found time to build an old-fashioned cradle for the baby. Janelle's youngest has it now.

Ray's first teaching job was high school math and manual arts in Wilmington. We still use the dining table and master bedroom suite he built afterhours in the woodshop. Later, of course, his extracurricular activities included an affair with the assistant principal. That time, it felt like he really *was* trying to trade me in but didn't have the nerve to tell me until he got caught. My mad carried me as far as a lawyer. Three kids too young to understand about the big bad wolf pulled me back. I'd known how he was when I married him.

Besides, I had never worked for a living and didn't realize I had a marketable skill. Who'd have thought all those hours practicing my penmanship with different styles of "Mrs. Raymond T. Keller," would lead to money in calligraphy? Ray does custom frames for me. It gives him an excuse to spend time in his shop. He did a lovely job on that oval frame for the old Chinese poem. It was a commissioned piece. The lines stayed with me.

Here at the frontier, there are falling leaves.
Although my neighbors are all barbarians,
And you, you are a thousand miles away,
There are always two cups on my table.

Since the kids left home, mealtimes here are different. I miss the gravy on the tablecloth and Janelle kicking at the twins for making faces at her. Their arguments weren't about anything, but they had life in them. It's more than I can say for Ray these days. He painted his garage battleship gray but doesn't get his own joke. That ship will never sail. He's drydocked on the side of this mountain for the duration.

Our dirty dishes aren't worth a sinkful of water. I turn on the hot tap and rinse the crumbs off the plates, looking out the window at his hideout. I wish he'd left both garage doors on it. In warm weather he used to keep them open. I could stand here at the sink and watch over him. I'd know if he had an accident. But after the twins left home he took out a door and walled in the space. It's too dark to see inside now. He disappears in the shadows. Anything might happen and me none the wiser.

The loss of that stupid door upset me. I hadn't expected it to. Surprise. Of all the hurtful voices in the heart's choir, surprise gets my vote for most cruel. Whether it opens the show or slips up on me later, surprise adds its own torment to bad news. It strips away an innocence I didn't know I had. Nothing to do but weep and kiss it goodbye.

My children were returning from school when the assistant principal's husband telephoned. For all the cussing and yelling, I didn't recognize the voice, much less what he was ranting about. I hung up on him, twice. Later, Janelle and I were in the living room discussing her schoolwork. We heard tires squeal outside and looked up to see our Falcon lurch into the driveway and skid to a stop. Ray hadn't driven like that since he sold his hotrod. The car was still rocking when he jumped out and slammed the door. He was in a state, snatching at the knot of his necktie. As he passed by the picture window he slowed down, trying to control himself. I shoved Janelle's papers at her and told her to go out back and play. I met him at the door. All he could say was, "Later, later. The kids." I followed him to the bedroom thinking that a student must have had a terrible accident. He shut the door in my face. "Please, not yet; after the kids are asleep." My head was spinning so fast I forgot the crank calls and burned the green beans.

Ray didn't have an appetite at dinner. For no reason he lectured Ray Jr. and Bobby about not riding tricycles in the street. That evening I went into a cleaning frenzy. The twins never went to bed with better groomed nails or cleaner teeth. Then I did laundry. Anything to stay out of

Ray's way, including hanging the wash out to dry in the dark. He scared the bejeezus out of me, laying hands on my shoulders at the clothesline. He said he was sorry. I thought he meant for scaring me. He pulled a bed sheet out of the basket. We sorted it out and threw it over the line. I remember saying, "What's going on, Ray? A man called. He was rude; I wouldn't speak to him."

"There's been a problem."

"What kind of problem?"

"With the assistant principal. The custodian . . ." Ray rummaged through the laundry as if he was looking for something in particular.

Now I was frightened. "What about the custodian?"

"He saw," Ray hesitated. "She and I were alone in my office."

"Oh, no. The custodian didn't think . . . Surely not?"

Ray turned away and whispered, "No, he didn't *think*. He walked in on us."

"I don't understand."

"Damn it, Althea. We were having sex." He stepped back, clenching and unclenching his fists. Then he began to pace with his face in his hands.

I caught his sleeve and made him stop. "No," I said. "It wasn't like that. The custodian was mistaken. You're a respected teacher. She's the assistant principal, for god's sake."

He wouldn't look at me.

I shook him hard. "Tomorrow morning you'll march into the principal's office and straighten this out. You can't have people thinking . . . It would cost you your job. And what about us? We have a wonderful life. You can't allow a custodian or assistant principal to take it away."

Through his fingers he croaked, "It's too late, Althea. I'm sorry." He sank to his knees.

I left him there and staggered inside. I locked the doors, all of them, including our bedroom door. Only then did the sledgehammer truly hit. Surprise.

Until that moment I'd been as naïve as Ray apparently was. We were building our marriage, raising successful children. I was learning to cook better. We Kellers were going places, ever onward and upward. Talk about innocent clichés.

It's not that good things stopped happening for us. We have six beautiful grandchildren and one greatgrand. I've got my calligraphy and still get excited about learning new things. But that night in Wilmington something inside me tipped from gain to loss. To my knowledge, Ray never cheated again, but that once created an irreparable void. We reached a new agreement, mostly unspoken. It was a deal for less.

I've been bargaining down ever since. At some point, everyday life takes on a hospice atmosphere. Every person I lose, every layer that's stripped away, leaves what's left of me raw. I'm dwindling, being peeled like an onion. One day I'm afraid there won't be anything left but that fool with her laundry basket and mouthful of clothespins.

As I dry my hands and think of cracked Chinese cups, Ray pushes his rattletrap mower onto the driveway. He stops and scratches his head, gazing into the distance. At what? He stoops and pulls the cord. The mower coughs, belches smoke and dies. He tries again. My husband and the driveway fade inside a blue cloud.

Sphinx

IN THE BEGINNING WAS SUMMERTIME, softball and unsanctioned wilderness expeditions. The Des Moines River, too mighty for boys to cross without a ship, rimmed our subdivision south of town. The floodplain along its bank teemed with monsters and battle spears in the form of sunflower stalks. Lyle Donaldson had the stronger arm but I aimed better. We extended the reach of our weaponry with atlatls like those the cavemen in library books used to bring down wooly mammoths. Our spears veered unpredictably, posing some risk to the hunting party as well as the lurking Cyclops. Sometimes Lyle and I crawled through the culvert under the highway and caught ringneck snakes in the forbidden highlands of Indian Hill or dug there, in the top of an overgrown mound left by a lost civilization. We dared not hope to discover a secret temple but worked like badgers anyway, spraying soil behind us with a broken board.

Other kids watched television but that was out of the question at my house. Our TV didn't have an antenna. The set was for videotape movies on Sunday night before prayer meeting. When Lyle and I weren't exploring or watching Scooby Doo at his house, we invented things. Sandstone ground together with water and glueberries from the thorny and poisonous horse nettle plant created paint. Lyle and I tested it on his dog's house. Chester didn't mind that there wasn't enough to finish both sides but Mr. Donaldson did. He made us wash it off. Despite soap and elbow grease a tan stain persisted. *Yes!* I thought, envisioning a career in science.

Momma found out about the doghouse a few days later while my sisters and I were in the garden picking vegetables. The whipping I got was only a few belt licks, mostly warded off with forearms, but this was already my third of the day and my arms were sore. She sent me to my room where I read a comic book about *Mutiny on the Bounty.*

Room confinement beat garden work, a fact that didn't go unnoticed by my older sister Claire. I heard her yell, "Why does he get out of doing chores?"

"You want what he's getting?"

"But it's not fair."

The screen door slammed in the middle of Momma calling Claire the curse of her existence, an opinion of my sister that I often shared. Through my window I watched her get slapped across the face. When she fell down and cried Momma told her to shut up; the neighbors shouldn't be subjected to the spectacle of sniveling children. Then Momma grabbed a broken garden stake and hustled Claire inside for a serving of welts and solitary.

All the while my baby sister Molly remained paralyzed in the garden with her grocery bag and nobody to fill it. Momma finally noticed and told the lucky duck to go play. Later, Molly got to help Dad change oil in the car while the convicts picked beans.

Punishment in our family was an evolving black art. The day Lyle's mother caught him and me returning from Indian Hill, the news reached home before I did. Momma said something about getting run over on the highway but

I couldn't hear it in the clacking whirlwind of lashes from Dad's thin Sunday belt, the worst of the three he owned. On this occasion she held it by the middle and got in two licks for every swing. The buckle didn't hurt so much as the silver cap on the other end. Thank goodness she didn't have a cat-o-nine-tails and hadn't thought of Captain Bligh's method of tying a lad to a grate before having him flogged. With the cell door at last slammed behind me, I salved my wounds with woodcraft and backcountry lore in the pages of *Two Little Savages*.

The belt had put a small hole in the wall of my room. I showed it to Dad when he visited me after work. Instead of spanking me again—a frequent delayed consequence for major crime—he lectured on true repentance, took away my books and grounded me to the house until I copied out the entire Book of Genesis. Two days of printing and erasing brought me to the end of Chapter 9, where Noah celebrates the end of the flood by getting drunk and naked in his tent. I was amazed that God didn't punish him for those sins, but instead cursed Canaan who hadn't done anything. Dad couldn't explain it and commuted my sentence. Momma, the unmerciful, had other ideas. I wasn't allowed to play outside our yard for a month.

Next morning I settled into a front room recliner to read *An Illustrated Library of Exciting Mystery Stories*. The detective in "The Sign of the Four" was new to me. Sherlock Holmes had a green cape and hat, a magnifying glass and a pipe to smoke when he needed to think. He was a master of disguises with awesome powers of deduction. Holmes could handle a tracking dog and even hired kids to assist with murder cases. I dreamed of being a Baker Street Irregular.

As Momma fixed supper she listened to the radio. They had an interview with a famous college protester from twenty years ago who said there would be a commemoration of the Free Speech Movement that fall in California. Momma cussed him and said his kind should be deported to Chile where they knew how to handle rabble-rousers. At supper she told Dad that I had conducted a sit-in strike against her all day. "I'm not raising a spoiled brat to go around yelling how odious America is. President Reagan doesn't stand for it and I won't either."

"What is odorous?" Claire asked.

"Odious," Dad corrected. "It means disgusting."

"I never said anything is odious."

"You are," Claire said. "You're odious."

Though it wasn't my turn, Dad made me wash dishes, also the jars for canning pickles. Then he banished me to the backyard with Claire and Molly. Odious rang in my head. Odious the pickle jars. Odious our prison yard weighed down by trumpet vines. Most odiously odious, sharing that space with odious sisters.

They were having a pretend picnic beside the garden. I kept my distance and excavated for artifacts in the digging ground, a rectangle of dirt against the back of the house where grass didn't grow. The archeologist trowel I used was a flimsy thing, better for scraping than digging hard dirt. Progress was frustratingly slow. So far the only artifacts I'd recovered were clinkers, the foamy rock leftovers of burnt coal. The one I washed off and kept on my dresser was rainbow-colored like an oily puddle. Although Momma told me Indians and cavemen didn't burn coal, the clinkers must have belonged to them; our house had a gas furnace. I expected to uncover skeletons or arrowheads and prove my theory correct.

The digging ground also contained pieces of flat sandstone that Claire used to build dollhouses. I'd talked her out of doing it on top of my dig—the rules were that it had to be backfilled at the end of every day—but she still insisted on imprisoning my Army men in her Flintstone houses. Her dolls were too large to fit.

I lifted the roof off her latest creation to check for captives and was surprised to find a beetle with a body as big and wide as my thumb and mandibles like ice tongs. What havoc might those jaws inflict? I grabbed him by the sides so he couldn't bite me and took him to the garden. He clamped his prehistoric jaws around a green bean and wouldn't let go. I had to pick the bean to show him to Claire. For no good reason, Molly screeched. Momma shouted from the kitchen. My beetle still held the bean pinioned like a green log. I took him to the kitchen window and stretched tall so she could see. The smell of dill pickles was overpowering.

"What is it?" I asked. This wasn't a dumb question. Before we were born, Momma was an archaeology graduate student. She often told us that if Dad hadn't talked her out of going to the clinic she'd be excavating the Incas. He didn't excavate; he taught college.

"It's a beetle," she said. "Get rid of it."

I already knew it was a beetle. "Look what he's doing."

"You're lucky that's not your finger. Quit pestering your sisters and do as I said. Now."

"Can't I—"

"Don't make me come out there."

I took the beetle to the back fence by the burn barrel and flipped him, bean and all, into Mrs. Livengood's okra patch. Her yappy pooch Buster must have been in the house. Too bad. A fight between him and my beetle would have been something to see.

I rescued three Army men from Claire's stone prison and was about to take them inside when she came over—for a change not to complain. She wanted me to cut her some trumpet vine for fairy crowns. The fence between our house and the next door neighbors' was covered with the stuff. You couldn't kill it, Dad said. I could cut it, though. My pocketknife was sharp enough to shave hair. Besides the cutting blade it had a can opener and an awl for poking holes in lids.

To me, trumpet vine was mainly good for rope and attracting wildlife. During the day, hummingbirds visited the flowers and chased each other in squeaky dogfights almost too fast to see. Sphinx moths with pink rear wings replaced the hummers in the evening. They weren't small, flittery or dumb like other moths. Sphinxes buzzed and hovered, quicker in flight than the human hand. At rest they had sleek backswept wings like fighter jets without the wing-mounted missiles and machine guns. According to the encyclopedia, sphinx moths lived almost everywhere except Antarctica and could fly for miles over open water. One kind in Europe had a death's head on its back, an extra touch of coolness. The thing I couldn't figure out was the reason for the name. Sphinx moths looked nothing like the lion-bodied Sphinx in Egypt or the Greek version with wings. That one was a monster who surprised travelers with a riddle and killed those who gave the wrong answer.

The moths were totally harmless, the furthest thing from scary, unless you were Molly with a flower crown on your head. When a sphinx tried to sip from it she went crazy, running and screaming as if from a MiG on a strafing run. Claire tried to hush her. Too late. The voice of doom rolled from the kitchen. Time to go inside.

The term of my parole wore on. Lyle couldn't visit. Bored and restless one afternoon I spotted a pair of sphinx caterpillars munching Momma's four o'clocks. They were friendly green sausages, one bigger than the other, with a double row of pink circles on their sides and alert puppy tails. Momma let me keep them in the garage. I lined the bottom of a big plastic bucket with grass, added a water dish and stems of four o'clock for food and climbing.

The larger caterpillar was Sherlock Holmes. His half-pint sidekick: Dr. Watson. They never drank their water and were picky eaters. Wilted four o'clock leaves didn't interest them. I had to keep the stems fresh in a jar of water. The caterpillars also liked suckers from our tomato plants, but not trumpet vines or the leaves of weeds or elm. Every day I took my friends outside for sun and exercise. Watson grew steadily. Holmes already seemed full-grown. I deduced that he was waiting for Watson, so they could pupate at the same time and be moths together.

On a perfectly ordinary Sunday morning while Dad was driving us home from church, he announced, "We've decided that you can't keep those tomato worms."

Beside me in the back seat, Claire cringed. Only yesterday the caterpillars had been guests at her Alice in Wonderland tea party. 'Fraidy cat Molly had even allowed Watson to crawl on her arm. Now, on the other end of the back seat, her finger remained contentedly in her nose.

I leapt to Holmes and Watson's defense. "They're not worms; they're sphinx caterpillars. They turn into moths like those in the trumpet vine."

Momma said, "I'll not have pests around my house. We'll destroy them after dinner."

"What?" I yelped. "You can't do that to pets."

Claire elbowed me in the ribs and whispered to shut up.

"Shut up yourself, Claire. They can't do this. It's not right. It's not." I leaned forward, shouting, "You can't do it."

Momma looked straight ahead. "Just watch me, young man."

"Dad, you can't let her. They're my friends. They're not hurting anybody."

Claire tried to cover my mouth with her hand. I pushed it away. "Holmes and Watson are mine. You can't kill them."

Dad turned into the driveway and parked. All four doors flew open at once. Momma clamped a hand around the back of my neck and marched me inside. Dad was right behind. As he gave her his belt I wriggled free. Claire and Molly dashed past us to the shelter of their bedroom.

Dad grabbed my arms and pinned them above my head while pulling me toward my room. Until we got there, Momma hit the hallway walls as much as me. But then she really cut loose. I had to go limp to make Dad let me go and tell her to stop. After a few more licks, including one that felt like it tore off my ear, she did. But Captain Bligh told me there'd be more of the same after dinner. Until then I was confined to quarters. No bread or water. I lay on the bed blubbering, rubbing the lash marks within reach. The spot of blood I noticed on the pillow had come from a fingernail gouge on my neck, not my ear. Far away in the dining room a chair leg scraped across the wood floor.

The cruelty of my parents enjoying Sunday dinner in these circumstances was unbearable. Desertion, even at peril of swinging from a yardarm, became an irresistible urge. I unhooked my window screen and crawled out of the house feet first. My toes didn't reach the ground. The windowsill scraped welt by welt up my stomach and chest. I fell, landing on my back in the yard, the wind knocked out of me. Clutching my sides, I staggered upright and ran.

No destination, except elsewhere and forever, occurred to me until I was on the county road leading to Fanscher Reservoir. Tracts of woodland lined its shores. Corn and wheat could be had at nearby farms. I wished I'd thought to bring matches and had changed out of my church clothes. A snot-faced kid in a white shirt and clip-on tie would draw attention. The tie went into a ditch; I pocketed the pearl tie stud. It might be useful as a fish hook. I always found discarded fishing line at the lake, sometimes lures as well.

My shirt presented a more immediate problem. I took it off. Behind the young corn in the field I was passing, I spied the rounded, gray-green tops of cottonwood trees bordering the Des Moines and headed for them at the next fencerow. Water and plant juice mixed in a rusty fender on the riverbank produced a dye that, if not exactly Army green, was a major improvement over white. The wet cloth felt good on my back. I wore the shirt unbuttoned with tails flying and cautiously returned to the road. The few cars on it were evident at a distance. None spotted me lying doggo in a weedy fenceline.

The trip to Fanscher took ten or fifteen minutes by car. On foot it was another matter. Fields floated by in slow motion. Holmes and Watson pests? Nobody could be so mean. God would preserve them like Daniel in the lion's den. Between praying that he would soften my parents' hearts, ducking for cover and planning my first night as a castaway, the confusion of roads I traveled knew nothing of distance or the broiling progress of the sun.

I'd never noticed the farmhouse at the crossroad near the lake and certainly not the German shepherd that now rushed snarling off the porch. He skidded to a stop in the intersection, snapping fangs enough for three dogs, and dared me to try my luck.

Against his teeth I could muster only a pocketknife, a tie stud and handfuls of road gravel. Even if the beast didn't tear me to pieces, he faced me with the undeniable fact that my new life in the woods wasn't happening. I stood in the road for a long minute. Then my shoes turned and did what they had to. Wretched, woeful, not bothering about secrets, trudging, dirt-kicking, counting out the miles foot by desolate foot, I beseeched the Lord to spare Holmes and Watson. Cars passed. Crows cawed. Mourning doves on power lines stopped cooing and whistled away at my approach. Rabbits peered from fencerows. The air tasted of dust.

Supper dishes were being cleared from the table when I got home. Claire and Molly went goggle-eyed and scuttled out back. I waited in the front room, uncertain what to do.

Dad said, "Where have you been?"

"The lake."

"Looks like it."

The baking dish in Momma's hand contained remnants of macaroni and cheese. She was stiff with composure. "There are leftovers. You may have some."

"Are my caterpillars okay?" I asked Dad. Like King Darius, he'd surely seen his mistake.

Momma took the mac and cheese into the kitchen.

Please, Jesus.

Dad spoke like a teacher explaining an Unsatisfactory to a kid who didn't do homework. "You were told about that."

Momma returned, minus food. "They were sprayed and taken out with the other trash."

"Holmes and Watson?" I burst into tears.

"What did I just say?"

Dad's tone softened. "I spent half the afternoon looking for you. Your mother was about to try again."

"Quit bawling," she said. "Take a bath. Then go to your room until you're called. Leave again and you'll be out all night."

Naked in the tub, bawling was all I had left to me. The pile of clothes on the floor belonged to someone else. I cried to hear myself live and wished it were otherwise.

Momma pounded on the door, "Shut up in there or I'll give you something to blubber about."

I stifled the sobs with a washcloth and gradually became aware that there were no other sounds in the house. My sisters' room, on the other side of the bathroom wall, was silent. No talking or muffled movie voices drifted under the door. Thoughts blared in my head. I strove to quiet them, lest they be overheard. The tiniest splash of bathwater hurt my eardrums. I retreated to a place far away from the racket and for the first time understood the meaning of alone.

The window screen in my room had been replaced. I was surprised not to see bars on the window but still felt trapped as I dressed and lay on my bed to wait.

Dad had no belt or Bible when he appeared in the doorway and said, "We have something to say to you in the front room."

My sisters were not in evidence. Momma sat on the couch studying the Yellow Pages. He sat down beside her and told me to sit also. I chose the recliner across from them, the one I read in, next to the picture window. They had closed the curtains although it wasn't yet dark outside.

Momma looked up from the phone book. "If you don't want to live here we can make arrangements with the Lutheran Children's Home in Elk Horn." Flat as that.

The man who resembled my father had fleshy lips.

I noticed lumps in the recliner. It didn't fit my body. The fabric had coarsened to steel wool.

The fleshy lips moved. "What your mother means—"

The woman impatiently cut him off. "This is the thanks I get for sacrificing my life to you? A houseful of disobedient brats?" The venom in her voice curdled the air. Momma would have flamed up and jerked me from the chair. This woman only scooted forward on the sofa cushion and crouched there unblinking. "Insolence will not be tolerated. If you don't like it here I'll drive you to Elk Horn myself."

81

Orphanages were where English beggar children used to live. Mean wardens hit them when they asked for food. I wasn't aware that such places still existed, but then I didn't know much about Lutherans either.

"Your mother cooks, cleans up after you kids, takes you to swimming lessons. The least you owe her is obedience. As long as you live under this roof you'll keep the commandment to honor thy father and thy mother."

"Aren't we going to church?" I asked. We never missed church, even on Wednesday night, except for high fevers.

The man looked sad. "Not tonight."

The woman, still crouching, hissed, "I'm waiting for an answer."

I must have appeared as confused as I was.

She continued, "You will obey without question or be signed over to the orphanage. Which is it?"

The man studied me like a specimen.

Out of nowhere a thought intruded. Were orphans also hit on a daily basis? Maybe there were too many kids for that. Other appalling questions followed. Did orphans go to school? Could they have friends? What about when they grew up? "I can't think," I stammered.

"You have until morning," the woman snapped. "I expect an answer before your father leaves for work. Go to bed."

The walls of my room, if it was still mine, had darkened in the dusk from white to the gray of spoiled meat. A hot breeze fluttered the curtains until I closed the door. Gradually the ceiling receded into blackness. Across the hall, my sisters' door creaked. I heard footsteps, then movie voices. The house came to life again.

It was disorienting to realize how grossly I had misunderstood my situation. This was not a family like other families. The longer I thought about it the more frightened I became of the people who called themselves my parents, especially the woman. She'd killed Holmes and Watson and was prepared to dispose of me too. I set the desk chair so it would fall over if the door opened and, just in case, brought my softball bat to bed.

Gradually it occurred to me that the case of Holmes and Watson wasn't really a break from the past and the strangers on the couch were not the doubles I'd imagined. These were my actual parents, ready as any English warden to strike me from the rolls. Strange to say, the flash of understanding brought with it a sense of calm. It wasn't a question of whether to live in an orphanage, only which one, this or another. For the time being I chose familiarity. Three kids compared to fifty or a hundred. Decent food, well-understood danger zones and best of all, a fresh choice every morning. Stay or go? The wardens needn't be informed of that part of our arrangement.

An early morning knock on the door awakened me. Mother said, "Brush your teeth and get dressed. We're in the dining room." I put on long pants and a long-sleeved shirt, prepared for a whipping.

My father's satchel waited by the front door. He sat at the table drinking coffee, pretending not to be tense. Mother stood ramrod straight behind him with crossed arms. "Well, what'll it be, the Lutheran Home?"

"Stay here."

Their faces didn't change. She said, "You'll do as you're told with no backtalk?"

"Yes."

She came around the table to glare down at me. "That had better be the truth."

"I know."

Father got up from his chair. "Good. The grounding is over. Behave yourself. Why are you wearing winter clothes?"

"I don't know."

"Go change them. And wake your sisters."

Claire opened their door at my knock and signaled me to step in. "Are you going away?" she sniffled.

"Not now."

"Not now?" She clabbered up, about to bawl. "Dad wanted to call the police."

"Why didn't he?"

"Momma said if he called them he could raise us by himself. He told her God expects wives to be submissive and she said she'd never be that stupid again."

Molly peeked out from under her sheet, sucking her thumb. I didn't recall the last time I'd seen her do that. She expected me to say something. So did Claire. Maybe tell them they hadn't heard what they heard. That our wardens weren't wardens and didn't mean what they meant. My sisters were handing me the power to undo the truth for them. Or I could affirm it, shattering them along with the family lie.

"Momma and Dad were just mad," I said. "Divorce is a sin."

If the meaning of words can be abused, addressing the wardens as Momma and Dad felt to me like abuse. As the days rolled on, other false notes crept into my voice. They went unnoticed. Lyle and I stopped hunting snakes on Indian Hill and played more softball. Whippings continued but the atmosphere was more cautious all around. On the whole, my position improved.

Nevertheless, I had no intention of being caught a second time unprepared. I began stocking a shoebox of escape supplies in my closet and asked to join the Boy Scouts. Dad, for reasons no doubt different than mine, approved in principle but said I wasn't old enough. I'd have to settle for Cubs. The first meeting I went to was my last; the den mother didn't teach survival skills, only how to paint small plaster animals. Campouts in Lyle's backyard provided better training. I got Mr. Donaldson to show us knots and how to build a fire. I hoped he'd start it with a fire bow but he didn't know how. He used lighter fluid and matches.

A friend of Lyle's big brother bought a new book bag and swapped me his old one for a dog skull with teeth in it. I got a dented canteen for nothing from another kid. Epoxy stopped it from leaking. Equipment-wise, my greatest lack was a small saw or hatchet. None were available for trade and I couldn't afford the ones at the store.

I'd been known to borrow things without asking, but outright theft hadn't previously crossed my mind. Now the sin seemed no greater than graduating from fibs to the conscious lies I was learning to tell. I resolved to steal my father's camping saw. It had a camouflage sheath with handy slits for carrying on a belt, exactly what I needed. We never used it. While my sisters played out back and Mother ran the sweeper in the house, I snuck into the garage by the side door, climbed onto the workbench, lifted the saw off the hooks where it hung behind the hammers and left as I had entered, the saw under my shirt.

Until then I hadn't realized how easily Holmes and Watson could have been saved. Remembering the thoughtlessness of my flight sickened me. It had cost my friends their lives. I richly deserved eternal hell for deserting them. Jesus didn't hear the prayers of imbeciles like me—and shouldn't. It was all I could do to skulk to my room without puking.

The softball bat was powerless against oppressive guilt. I slept fitfully and didn't hear my morning get-up knock. Noticing the bat in bed with me, Mother said, "Maybe Claire will loan you her Raggedy Ann. It's softer." The choice between staying and making a run for it was extra difficult that day.

About a week before school started, I woke up on my own and came to the dining room for breakfast. Claire and my father were explaining kindergarten to Molly, who didn't want to go. Mother had a black eye. I asked what happened.

"I went in to cover you up. You hit me."

"I did?"

"You did."

"I don't remember. I'm sorry."

"From now on if you freeze it's your own business."

I refrained from commenting on the probability of freezing in August. It was awesome to learn that I could defend myself while asleep.

In the second week of school, the nurse called me out of class. As we walked down the hall she assured me that I wasn't in trouble. Mrs. Stockwell was as round and old as our grouchy librarian and also wore horn-rim glasses on a chain around her neck, but she smiled a lot and used bright red lipstick. I didn't know much else about her because I didn't get sick and my shots were up to date.

Her office smelled of bleach. "How do you like your new teacher?" she chirped when I was seated beside her desk.

I said Mr. Penrose was fine. She congratulated me for having good grades last year, then asked more questions. Her teeth had lipstick smudges on them. It became apparent that I was supposed to talk about trouble at home, though Mrs. Stockwell didn't suggest at first what trouble there might be. I played dumb. She kept smiling, saying I could tell her anything. She wanted to help.

Eventually she tired of waiting for my confession. "How do you and your mother get along?"

"Okay, I guess."

"She's worried about you."

"Why?"

"She said you ran away from home? Because of some tomato worms?"

I admitted it.

Mrs. Stockwell leaned toward me conspiratorially. "Why not just let them go?" she whispered.

"I didn't know I could." And that, I realized to my great relief, had been the truth. I took a deep breath and felt almost giddy.

She shook her head sympathetically, tut-tutted those too-red lips, wrote something down, then looked up and pressed for details. I couldn't think of any.

"Do you have difficulty sleeping?"

"No."

"I understand that you sleep with a baseball bat."

"A softball bat. I don't anymore."

"Some people might do that because they were afraid. Were you afraid?"

"I like to dream about hitting homers."

"Good for you. And the night you accidentally struck your mother?"

"Did I hit her with the bat?"

"She said it was your fist."

"She had a black eye." I struggled not to smile. "Can I go to class now?"

"Is there anything else you'd like to tell me?"

"Guess not."

"Okay then. But anytime you'd like to talk, just tell your teacher. Will you do that for me?"

It was embarrassing to walk into class in front of everybody. Mr. Penrose paused at the map he'd pulled down over the blackboard. I slipped into my seat. He nodded at me and resumed identifying the oceans of the world.

I didn't mention Mrs. Stockwell to Claire on our way home that afternoon. But naturally, the first thing out of

Mother's mouth when we arrived was, "Mrs. Stockwell called." It was an accusation, like I'd been caught doing something.

"I can talk to her again anytime I want to," I shot back.

"What did you tell her?"

The reply had been too quick. I detected concern. "Nothing," I said. "Not one thing."

That night I left my door wide open and leaned the bat beside my bed. So anybody could see it.

Toasted

T ANNER WAS ALONE in the house on the day Our Lady of Guadalupe emerged from the broiler, scorched into a piece of French bread slathered with Italian dressing. The saw marks left by his knife had been transformed into beams of light radiating from Our Lady in the loaf. She even stood on a crescent moon, same as in the images that decorated the walls of religious homes throughout the Southwest. Her uncanny detail caused him to forget about lunch. In his oven mitt he held a sacred artifact and once-in-a-lifetime story. But, minus a corroborating witness, nobody would believe it.

With his wife out of reach at a Colorado State teacher's conference, Tanner next thought of friend and fellow tradesman, Chris Ramirez. Tanner couldn't believe how stupid his telephone request for a visit sounded and wasn't surprised at Rambo's mocking reply. "What's this bullshit? Momma Mona is away and your ass is too lazy to come to my house for a beer? You want company? Just say so."

Determined to recoup his dignity, Tanner spent the hour it took Rambo to drive from Salida to the outskirts of Saguache primping Our Lady for viewing. He propped her on a wad of paper towels in the salad bowl and set it on the stove. The range, with its pitted porcelain and cockeyed oven door, looked as if it had spent a rat-infested decade in a leaky barn before jouncing the length of the San Luis Valley on a trailer. Which it had. The GE cleaned up well though, worth every penny of the nothing Tanner paid for it. Mona could make a ham slice squeal with a twist of a knob, a vast improvement over the wood-fired cookstove in the house when they bought it.

Our Lady between the burners reminded Tanner too much of ordinary bread in a basket. He cleared the junk off the dinner table and tried her there. Better. A paper towel veil, creased to account for the protrusion of Our Lady's head above the bowl rim, added a dash of artistic mystery. He uncapped a beer and considered the presentation from various angles. Good enough.

The sight of Our Lady nearly poleaxed Rambo. His body turned to address Tanner but his gaze was stuck on the iconic image. "How'd you do that? You ain't Latino. You ain't even Catholic. It ain't right. This shit happens in a Mexican town? The town is on its knees. For real. They call her *La Virgen Morena*, the dark virgin. My old *abuela* in Nogales, the one who took me in, she's sick with cancer. If *La Virgen Morena* appears to her? Boom. She's healed. Why *Nuestra Señora* shows herself to a gringo atheist who don't know nothing?"

"Ask her, dude. I was only fixing lunch."

"You got to call the Church."

"Since when did you get religion? Broken-down L.A. gangbanger is what I heard."

"But this is *Nuestra Señora de Guadalupe*. You got to take pictures, call somebody. What about that priest over at the monastery, the one we did the bathroom for, Father Pat?"

While Tanner was leaving messages for Mona and the priest, Rambo sent cell phone pictures of Our Lady to everyone he knew. Tanner didn't learn about that until a few beers later when they were sitting on the back porch watching the sun flame out behind Cochetopa Peak. To the south, across the sage and rabbitbrush flats of the San Luis, dusty rooster tails approached.

A sensible sedan and elderly pickup pulled into Tanner's driveway. Two Hispanic families in their Sunday best got out. Tanner had never seen them before. Rambo greeted them in Spanish and collected five bucks a head, another plan he'd forgotten to mention. "Fifty-fifty split," Rambo whispered, out of the visitors' hearing. "They expect to pay. You'll get yours." Cameras flashed. Prayers were offered, a hymn sung.

Before long, Tanner's front yard filled with vehicles. He stationed himself in the dining room to protect Our Lady from worshipful manhandling. Rambo directed the parking. Along with the stream of pilgrims, nightfall brought plummeting temperatures to the high desert. Rambo, in a Coyote's Bar & Grill cap and denim jacket, was underdressed for the occasion. He'd stepped inside for a warm-up when Tanner's cell phone chirped.

"Dude," Tanner told him, "this is Father Pat's number. I'm going outside where I can hear. Mind the store."

Thirty miles to the east, the snowcaps of the Sangre de Cristos still glowed with dregs of daylight under an ultramarine dome already filling with stars. Tanner inhaled a lungful of sagebrush-scented chill and flipped the phone open.

Father Pat listened in silence, no doubt also hearing the hubbub in the house and the sound of yet another car finding a parking spot. Tanner pointed the new arrivals to the front door and had to interrupt the conclusion of his story by verbally reassuring them that they'd found the right place.

The priest asked, "You're Catholic?"

"Lapsed Methodist."

"Then forgive my confusion. What makes you think Our Lady has appeared to you?"

"Her picture is everywhere, Father."

"And you're asking what, again?"

"I'm not sure. Authentication, I guess. To know she's real. Things like this just don't happen."

"You do have faith then?"

"What do you want me to say? I used to believe buildings were built on the square and studs were sixteen inches on center. Reality intrudes, Father."

The priest thought that was funny. "Then you understand our situation with the Holy Mother. She seldom appears where we expect. Garage doors, pieces of toast. She's quite a jokester. Keeps us humble. What are you going to do, put her up for sale?"

"My buddy says I'd be a fool not to go on eBay. He's here now, charging people to see her. To me, it's not right to cash in on a gift delivered to the wrong house. But maybe he has a point. It's a hunk of bread. Bread gets moldy. You guys are the experts. What should I do?"

"Tanner, when Our Lady appears she makes her wishes known. She'll tell you; just listen."

To Tanner's chagrin, Rambo had turned off the dining room light. A plate full of candles in tin cups burned before Our Lady's bowl. In the flickering dim she glowed extra golden. Tanner, assuming the sooty worst, cursed under his breath. But dousing the candles in the presence of the faithful would be rude, probably sacrilegious.

By the time the last pilgrim left, Our Lady had marinated for hours in smoke. Tanner snuffed the reverent ambience and turned on the room light. As Rambo unloaded the take from his pockets, Tanner moved Our Lady to the kitchen for an inspection under bright fluorescent light. To his relief she wasn't stained. The image had lost a few bits of toasted Italian herbage. It was nothing compared to his discovery that a corner of the loaf had been sliced away, narrowly missing Our Lady's crescent moon.

He confronted Rambo with the damage. "What's this? Somebody got hungry?"

Rambo looked up from tidying two stacks of rumpled currency. "It wasn't to eat. The guy's daughter was in a bad wreck. They airlifted her to Colorado Springs. He took it to help her recovery. And he paid extra. Forty bucks. I let him keep money for gas."

"You *sold* it to him? Hello. See this? It's priceless. As in: Can't be replaced. What were you thinking? Who's going to pay for whittled bread?"

"We got $255 already. You saw how happy they were. *Nuestra Señora* rocked the house. They'll tell their friends."

"Tell them what, that for a couple of twenties they can take home a chunk of the Virgin Mary? Maybe watch a house burn down from so many lighted candles?"

"Chill, man. You didn't see what I saw. For most of them it was about *Nuestra Señora* hearing their prayers in person. This guy though, it was flesh and blood. His daughter, man, she's paralyzed. He'd cut his heart out for her. You can't deny motivation like that. Sometimes when something has to happen, it has to happen." He scooped up half the cash and stood. "It's past midnight. I got to go."

"Ah, shit," Tanner said, laying Our Lady back into her bowl. "I'm just saying it's a crazy end to a strange day, that's all. Too late to drive home. Take the spare bed."

"Stranger than strange. It's a miracle. I seen a lot of weird sh . . . weird things. Never nothing like this." Rambo looked confused. "I don't believe it. I can't cuss in front of her."

"We'll see how long that lasts."

"No, seriously. Don't you feel it? Like she's in the house?"

"That reminds me. Mona never called back." Tanner tried her cell again, and again was shunted to voicemail. He noticed her charger on the end table by the sofa. "Ah, hell," he said.

"You got the name of her motel?"

"Since we went mobile, we've been lazy about stuff like that."

Tanner thought better of leaving Our Lady out overnight. "Let's not have the mice finish what Whittling Man started. I'm going to line a spare toolbox with newspaper and tuck her in. Then, I don't know about you, but I'm as toasted as she is."

Rambo yawned, "Yeah. I'm ready for a blanket and soft pillow. But the pillow shouldn't smell too good." He cocked an eye toward Our Lady and grinned his gap-toothed grin. "I'm on good behavior."

The most recent occupants of Tanner's guest bed had been Mona's parents and their cat. With luck, a leftover flea might keep Rambo company until morning.

Tanner woke from a dream about swimming in candlelight and greeted the dawn with a pee off the front porch. Tire tracks crisscrossed the sandy soil of his yard. The struggling green scrub was mashed flat. It would take years to grow back. He barefooted across the bruised and frosted ground to pick up a fast food bag and three half-empty drink cups. The gritty cold on his tender soles served him so right that he carried the trash over to the bin beside the house before going in.

Our Lady's toolbox on the dinner table seemed to pulsate with demands. Beside her chrome-plated reliquary lay his share of last night's cash. There were also several puddles of candle wax and, outrageously, a new scorched spot in the tabletop. Swearing that he'd been out of his freaking mind to get involved with this Catholic nonsense, he went into the kitchen and dumped out yesterday's coffee grounds. He jammed a new filter into the holder and loaded it with French roast, direct from the can.

Floorboards creaked in the hall. The noise stopped at the entryway behind him.

Tanner flipped the switch on the coffeemaker. "How'd you sleep?"

"Not so good," Rambo said. "If I was still a banger, man, me and *Nuestra Señora* are long gone by now. Is she safe? Did you check?"

"I can't face her without caffeine."

Rambo shuffled through to the dining room and unlatched the toolbox lid. Tanner heard the rattle of Our Lady leaving her newspaper nest. "She's good," Rambo reported. "See?" He brought her into the kitchen, cradled like a premature infant in his rough mason's fingers.

The design was intact. Yesterday's illusion, however, escaped Tanner. Try as he might, the magic had gone. It solidified his decision. "You were right. About selling this. I'm going to do it."

"Oh, man, I was afraid of that. Ignore what I said, okay?"

"What's the alternative? I don't like charging people poorer than me, and the money's not worth the hassle anyway. Wait till you see what they did to the yard. And somebody burnt . . . Never mind; it doesn't matter. That thing belongs in a church. But why should I give it away? The Catholics are loaded. Let them bid."

"She needs to be out where she can do her work. Not locked up in a glass case."

Tanner set a couple of mugs on the counter beside the coffeemaker. "Come on. If she was yours, she'd be for sale this afternoon. You know it."

"No. I was wrong. Miracles, things of the heart, are not to buy and sell. Keep all the money from last night. I don't want it."

"Now you're saying you don't care about the bucks? You're shitting me."

Rambo stared at him, resolute. "Swear to God. I got work next week."

"Well, I'll be."

Rambo lowered his eyes and crossed himself.

As Tanner poured the coffee, a crazy idea lifted the burden of Our Lady from him. He didn't need the pilgrims' money either. His bills were covered. "What kind of job did you say you have coming up?" he asked, offering Rambo a mug. "Sugar or milk?"

"Black is good. I'm laying the block for a basement off Ute Trail."

"When do you start?"

"Tuesday. Why? You got something?"

"Maybe. Nogales is what, twelve hours from here?"

"If an old woman is driving."

"And today's Sunday. Okay, here's what's happening. Our Lady is yours. Take her to your grandma. The mojo might do her good."

Rambo returned Our Lady to her wrappings in the toolbox. "Don't jack with me, man. All I got is the cash in my pocket."

"She's yours," Tanner insisted. "What you do with her is up to you, totally. But if you're making the run to Nogales and expect to be worth a damn Tuesday morning, best get a move on. Take the money on the table. You'll need it for gas."

"I told you. Don't jack with me."

Tanner stepped away from Our Lady and, hands raised as if to ward her off, said, "It's a done deal. My share of the cash though, leave it here unless you're headed south to your grandma."

Rambo's expression transformed from skepticism to ecstasy. "What can I say?" he stammered. "*Mi abuela* blesses your name." He pocketed all the cash on the table.

"Good. You got time for breakfast? Sausage and eggs?"

"I could eat."

Before leaving, Rambo wrote a cardboard sign in Spanish announcing Our Lady's departure from the premises. Tanner was tacking it to the mailbox post when his friend's cherry red '61 Impala V8 rumbled alongside. Rambo killed the stereo and leaned out the window. "I don't forget this. We're blood now, *mi hermano*. Catch you on the other side."

"On the other side."

Tanner squinted into the midmorning sun as the Impala descended across the sagebrush toward Highway 17. At the intersection the red speck hesitated, then turned north toward Salida. Nogales was the other way.

Saturday's mail in hand, Tanner saluted the vanishing dot and shook his head. There was wax to be scraped off the table before the Bronco game at eleven. And Mona hated coming home to dishes in the sink.

Complications

THINGS WILL COME TO YOU at the strangest times. My neighbor Leonard had called me after work to have a look at the washing machine in the basement of his rental house. His tenant, Rita, said the spin cycle was out. It was. The tub was full of soggy laundry. She took care of that, but we couldn't completely drain the water. So the washer was heavy. Leonard tipped it backwards while I wiggled underneath into a cold, cheesy-smelling puddle. Loose belt. The motor carrier assembly wasn't sliding to keep it in tension. While Leonard and Rita chatted about who knows what, he forgot what he was supposed to be doing and let the rim of the washer cabinet ease down on me, harder and a little harder. Maybe it was being pinched between a Maytag and a concrete floor that triggered the thought. Or it could have been the spidery dust bunnies that kept falling on my face. Whichever. It came to me like a breath of freedom in a big wide world: *I don't need this.*

I don't. I grew up in a family that moved to stay ahead of rent collectors and process servers. People came and went. Deal like that, you get run over if you don't learn to fend for yourself pretty quick. Naturally we kids scattered at the earliest opportunity. No rich relations to cause second thoughts. I do fine without family complications. My wife felt the same way until her biological clock started ticking this year.

And so there I was, lying in a puddle under a washing machine, and it came to me. *Bud Ogden, you don't need this. You could pack your shit and hit the road tomorrow.* I didn't say that. What I said was, "Leonard, how about tipping this thing up again. It's tight down here."

"Sorry, Bud." The weight lifted off my arms. Another slop of soapy water hit the floor behind my head. He said, "What are you guys doing for Thanksgiving? Hard to believe it's only a month away."

"Same as always, I guess. Feeding other people's dogs." Suellyn and I bought into the Ritz K-9 Spa, a kennel and grooming studio owned by Nik Garabedian, the old man everybody calls Pop. The handyman stuff I do for Leonard is more out of friendship. He'd rather pay me by the hour than call a repair service that charges him seventy-five bucks just to show up. I don't blame him.

Rita said, "Feeding other people's dogs? That's pitiful. It's a holiday; you should celebrate." She moved into Leonard's rent house last winter to attend graduate school at the university. Some kind of management. On the side she writes reports for an online information service. Rita is good-natured, pleasantly feisty. Sweet face, freckles and a ponytail. Mostly wears sweatshirts and jeans. Keeps herself clean. I couldn't see from where I was lying but I'd have bet anything her running shoes were still dry. She had misunderstood the conversation between Leonard and me. He was angling for an invitation to Thanksgiving dinner and I was letting him stew.

"That's why we're booked solid at the kennel," I said. "People celebrating with their loved ones. The dogs have to make do." I didn't mean it as harsh as it sounded. "We'll finish out there before dinnertime, though. Never fear, Leonard. You too, Rita, if you're around. I smoke a turkey.

Suellyn makes stuffing and homemade pecan pie. You're both invited."

"His turkey is the best," Leonard told Rita. The washing machine weighed down on me again.

I groaned. Leonard overcorrected. Water sloshed and spilled.

Rita said she'd think about it.

"You'll be welcome," I said. "If not for us your landlord would probably spend the day squirreled up at his place reading books and sipping scotch. Might treat himself to a pineapple ring on his fried baloney sandwich."

"Don't listen to him, Rita. He couldn't get enough of the salmon I made last time he and Suellyn were over." Leonard's in his early thirties, chubby. One of those guys cursed with a permanent five o'clock shadow. The nerdy black-rim glasses are his own idea. He teaches English at a private boarding school and drinks scotch because it makes a statement. The single malt he serves is actually a cheap blend transferred to a better bottle. He says nobody can tell the difference.

"Look out for him, is all I'm saying. Got a rag and some oil?" I was scraping gunk off the moving parts of the motor carrier with a screwdriver.

Rita said, "I've got bicycle chain oil. Will that work? It's right here."

"It might." I held out my hand.

She dropped a dish towel and squeeze bottle into it. "Why should I watch out for Leonard?"

"He's crazy."

"No he isn't."

Leonard is a clumsy flirt but it doesn't stop him from trying. "Bud doesn't understand those of us born to the artistic realm. Allen Ginsberg is my spiritual father, although he could never acknowledge me without ruining his reputation. We lost Mom several years before my birth. Virginia Woolf, you may have heard of her."

"How terrible. Wait—"

"It's okay. We're a large family. Kurt Vonnegut is my favorite uncle, also deceased but a brilliant conversationalist. Would you believe he's into Batman? This evening we're watching *The Dark Knight*. Drop by and say hello."

"Vonnegut?"

"Sure. I call him anytime. It's the curse of fame. His fans never let him rest in peace. That's why I refuse to produce anything of lasting importance. My phone number is reserved for friends."

"He *is* full of it, isn't he?"

"Could be worse. He owns rental property and just turned thirty. To know him is to love him."

She said, "Bud, are you trying to hook us up?"

Leonard, bless his egg head, just had to keep on. "Procurement while you wait," he said.

I heard a swat. The washer slammed down across my chest. A housing brace grazed my ear.

"Ow! That's not what I meant," Leonard croaked. "Holy crap. Where did you learn that?"

"Rita," I barked. "Let him alone and get this thing off me."

"Oh, my god. Leonard, get it off him."

The sheet metal jaw released my collarbones. "If you two can see your way clear to let me live another minute, I'm almost finished. Do you mind?" I checked myself for protruding bone fragments. Nothing felt broken. My armpits burned.

"I didn't mean for him to let go. It's totally my fault. Are you hurt?"

"She kicked me."

"She can kiss it later. Not now."

Miffed, or pretending she was, Rita said, "What's *with* you two today?"

The motor carrier's springs and hinges soon functioned as designed. I rolled out from under the Maytag. Spots of blood marked my t-shirt where the sheet metal edge had scraped me.

Rita gasped like my guts were hanging out. "I'm really really sorry. Are you okay?"

"I'll live."

"At least let me get some peroxide to clean that cut. And I'll wash your shirt."

Leonard couldn't help himself. "She agitates, Bud. But are you sure she'll spin?"

Rita flicked a kick that snapped him on the hip like a wet towel. Leonard flinched and grabbed his butt. The woman had dangerous feet. And her shoes *were* still dry.

I stood and pointed at the electrical outlet. "Plug her in and find out." Rita wheeled in my direction. A sidelong warning glance backed her down.

Leonard limped over to where I'd taped the power cord, fumbled it loose and plugged it in. He was standing in a pool of water.

I shrugged, looking at it. "Better luck next time, Rita."

She grabbed the back of his shirt and snatched him to dry concrete. "Leonard, be careful."

"Remember about Thanksgiving dinner," I said, gathering my tools. "We eat at five." Before the words left my mouth I wished I'd kept my trap shut. Who could say whether I'd be there? The thrill of freedom still cruised alongside me like a girlfriend I wished I'd never lost. She drove a shiny new convertible. The top was down and I heard her call my name.

⌘

Not that I don't love Suellyn. She's a lovable woman. Has been since we met in high school. She was the cheerleader willing to take a chance on a free safety who transferred in from out-of-state. We couldn't resist each other. After the years of blind lust passed we found ourselves comfortable together. I learned to put the toilet seat down. She kissed me goodnight and became our bookkeeper. We own most of Pop's kennel business but he still lives out there so we don't have to.

Marriage isn't so much about sex as it is about trust. And there's my trouble. For sixteen years we didn't give kids a second thought. Then last winter our old dog Peanut died and Suellyn started up about having a baby. I said we could get Arnie, our poodle mix, a new playmate if she wanted—people are always trying to give us dogs. Suellyn said. "It's not the same. We're older now. There's a baby-shaped hole in my life and you'd make a great dad. Can't you just see those big brown eyes loving you?" She must have read that part about the baby-shaped hole in a magazine. It wasn't like her to say such a thing.

I said, "Big brown kid eyes are fine with me so long as they go home with somebody else at night. We have a deal about babies."

Since then it hasn't been the same between us. She's all babies, babies, babies and I'm the bad guy for saying no. It's not her fault about my attitude on the subject. I never had an interest in parenthood. Overpopulation isn't confined to dogs and cats. Excess people wind up in cages too. We just don't euthanize most of them.

I only wish I'd foreseen this baby-craving in her. It crossed my mind to wonder whether she was taking her birth control pills. They disappeared out of the pack as they should, but what if she flushed them? It wasn't a question I could ask without hurting her feelings. Even then, how could I be sure she was telling the truth?

Complications

Once when Suellyn was ragging me about getting pregnant and I was saying "No" for the hundredth time, I asked if she wanted a divorce. She broke down and cried, "How could you say such a thing?" To me it either meant I was more important to her or she was scheming. To be on the safe side I timed her cycles. With pills or without, I'll say this: her friend is my friend and she's regular. My antsiness about the calendar caused our lovemaking to get awkward a few times.

Any pet owner knows there's a better solution. Dr. Mulvahill is a top-notch veterinarian. I offered him cash to fix me. He thought I was joking; "That's not our operation. We shell the boys out under general anesthesia." I tried to stop him right there but he was on a roll. "If the owner is vain, Poochie gets a prosthetic set. The hard plastic kind has a tendency to rattle after a while; drives some dogs berserk. Silicone costs more but it's worth it. Squeezably soft. I'm guessing you for X-Large. Great Dane, more or less?"

Mulvahill has a sick sense of humor. I said, "No, thank you. All I need is a regular snip job. I'll pay a hundred bucks. A local anesthetic and a few stitches. What are we talking about, ten minutes?"

He turned me down. So I called the urologist he recommended and put money aside on the sly. A thousand bucks. It killed my beer budget and doubled the handyman work. Four months to raise the cash without raising suspicion. Another month waiting for the doctor appointment. On the day I repaired Leonard's washer my number was almost up.

The prospect of going to the urologist in the morning squeezed the breath out of me worse than any Maytag. Vasectomy is a deeply disturbing idea. I dreaded it like a man dreads the first time a woman backs him into a corner about saying he loves her. It's the way a big dog feels as he's being dragged down a long hall in a pinch collar, choking and bug-eyed. A fear in the gut that something is about to change forever.

I told myself I'd be okay, that it wasn't a big deal. Then I called myself a damned liar. There was no baby-shaped hole in my life. But it embarrassed me to be such a wuss. A good husband would man up and do what needed doing. My n'er-do-well blood told me to run. That night I heard my own clock ticking. In a matter of hours I would make a choice: shave my balls or hop into the freedom car bound for elsewhere, knowing that sooner or later I'd probably face the same situation again.

Suellyn noticed I was tense. I told her it was from Leonard dropping the washing machine on me. Bruises were already cropping up on my chest. She massaged my shoulders and back. One thing led to another. Pretty soon she had her hand in my boxers. Johnson was delighted. I was not. The time of the month was all wrong.

She purred in my ear, "Do it like you used to in our first apartment. Make my knees so weak I can't walk." She began pulling down my pants.

I stopped her. "You can tell how much I want to, honey, but that washer did a number on me. Every move hurts like fire. It might be a cracked bone. Or a dislocation."

"You weren't complaining a minute ago."

"Everything is loosened up now. Sometimes you can't tell how bad an injury is when your muscles are tight."

She turned her back and sat with her legs off the other side of the bed. "You don't love me anymore. Is it Rita? That's where you were tonight. I'll kill her."

I threw an arm around Suellyn's waist. "Stop it. I'm injured, that's all. If it wasn't so late I'd go for an X-ray right now. Let's just get through tonight. I'll have it looked at in the morning."

I hated to do her that way but it solved a problem. Later on when we were both lying there not sleeping, I didn't feel so bad. Resentment set in. It wasn't me trying to rewrite our rules. My balls were on the line because I loved her. And she was trying to blame Rita. Goddamn complications. I dreamed of the freedom car. All I had to do was let it take me.

Suellyn wanted to drive me to the walk-in clinic. She said Pop could open up and do the early feedings. My chest and arm muscles were sore as hell. But I assured her over and over that I'd be okay. Eventually she remembered she was mad and left for the kennel. It came to me that I'd been thinking all wrong about this. Vasectomy wasn't the optional proposition. That I would do. The choice came after: whether to tell Suellyn.

Scraping the frost off the windshield of our mobile grooming van hurt more than driving. So did getting in and out of the cab, especially after the urologist's office. A kicked-in-the-nuts feeling matched the ache in my pecs and triceps. And that operating room image was stuck in my head too: knees sticking up out of those stirrups and oh, lordy, what's going on behind the sheet? I went directly to the pharmacy. Took a pain pill before leaving the store.

The drive to the kennel wasn't long enough for the medicine to do any good. I tottered into the office hunched over worse than Pop. One of our groomers was advising the owner of a stinky pug on odor control. Out in the run for dog-aggressive dogs, a border collie herded a ball under Suellyn's direction. Through the fence I told her the clinic diagnosis was abrasions and deep bruises. Nothing rest wouldn't cure.

She assumed that the strain of driving had caused the hitch in my get-along. "It serves you right for not letting me take you to the clinic. You can't work. There's chicken in the refrigerator. Do you feel up to grilling tonight?"

I thought I could manage that.

When I opened the door at home, Arnie jumped up and planted a paw at Ground Zero. I almost puked. He dashed into the kitchen hoping for a lunchtime treat. Too bad. Since he'd made it so I couldn't eat, he was out of luck too. All I wanted was a pack of frozen vegetables. The doctor had said it would prevent swelling. The doorbell rang as I searched the freezer. Arnie barked and ran to see who it was.

Rita was still having washer troubles. It made a terrible racket and jiggled across the floor on spin cycle. She'd had to pull the plug. Rita is a bright girl but not mechanically minded. I cursed myself for not leveling the machine the night before and for not being a hundred miles closer to a new life. There was nothing for it but to grab a few tools and walk the two doors down to her house. She saw right off that I wasn't well and felt bad about it. I told her it wasn't her fault. To change the subject I asked what she was doing that day.

She said somebody had ordered a term paper on women's rights in Victorian society. Her original essay on the topic was a big seller for the service that contracted her. Rita guessed she'd customized the paper a dozen times for special orders.

I asked if it bothered her to be in the business she was.

"Some requests are legitimate; I never know for sure. But this is what technical writers and ghostwriters do. How many celebrity authors actually write the books with their names on them? Almost none. If it's okay to run for political office on the basis of a bogus autobiography, why can't I charge fifty bucks for a unique term paper?"

We went behind her house and into the basement. The washer had been prevented from walking farther by the drain hose hooked in the standpipe. We shoved the machine back into position. I showed Rita how to read a level and, wrench in hand, painstakingly lowered my sorry carcass to the floor. Thankfully, very little height adjustment on the legs was necessary.

She offered to pay.

"No," I said. "I should have done this yesterday. No charge."

"Come on. You need money too. Babies cost boatloads of money."

My heart flipped.

Rita's eyes widened. She blurted, "Suellyn told me. You've been doing these extra jobs. I assumed—"

"She's pregnant?"

"Not that she said. But she told me you were trying. Wasn't I supposed to know?"

Sore balls encourage a man to think first, maybe two or three times, before packing his suitcase. I deflected Arnie's welcome home leap and headed for the medicine cabinet, forgetting for a minute that the bottle of pain pills was still in my pocket. I took a second tablet, washed it down with a handful of water at the bathroom sink and read the label on the bottle. Didn't recognize the unpronounceable name. Probably Latin for useless. Suellyn's birth control pills were in the cabinet. She'd at least continued to pop them out of the pack.

The second pain pill put me out. I was snoozing in the recliner with a soggy bag of frozen corn on my crotch when Suellyn breezed in and kissed me on the forehead. She draped the corn over my right collarbone. I wondered why she chose that one.

"Feeling any better?"

I toyed with telling her what I'd done and what Rita said but knew where that would lead. It could wait. I stretched and stood, surprised at the improvement in all physical departments. "Not bad," I said. "Pretty good, in fact. But I wet my pants."

Suellyn thought I didn't know how it happened. "The corn slipped down. I'll put it in the freezer for you."

I gave her the bag. "Thanks. I'll change and light the grill."

As I turned to go she reminded me of our evening plans. "Better call Leonard too. Wasn't tonight the DMB concert?"

Leonard is cheap, everywhere except his entertainment system. He's got a sixty-inch plasma TV that beats hell out of anything else in the neighborhood. I'm amazed he hasn't been robbed. Our block is two streets over from respectable, a mixture of college students, blue collar workers and people like Leonard that polite society worries about. We were supposed to watch the Dave Matthews Band live on cable. Hearing those guys is like watching Troy Polamalu play strong safety for the Steelers. When 43 is healthy you don't have to know anything to realize you're witnessing greatness. "Let's go," I said. "Dave Matthews and a beer would do me good." And give me more time to think.

The concert was killer. I had a good time despite myself. So did Suellyn. Leonard, though, had something on his mind. He slugged down scotch and couldn't sit still. At the end of the show he offered us shots of fake MacWhatzit to hear him out. I let him talk me into opening a third beer. That's my absolute limit. Nobody with a hangover walks into a dog kennel the second time. Barking shreds inflamed brain cells. And the stenches and messes are guaranteed to turn even the strongest stomach inside out.

Leonard said one of his students had been expelled that day. A folder of tests from previous years had been found in the dorm room he shared with a notorious cheat. Suellyn said she didn't see the problem with kicking the kids out.

"Not both," he sneered. "Not both. Only the one with no prior record of violations. *If* DeShawn was guilty; he denied it to the end. The honor code wasn't the cause of his dismissal."

"What then?"

Leonard paced like an irate lawyer. "Here's how it works. Junior is brought before the honor council on charges of serious monkey business. Out of an abundance of concern for the student's future the headmaster personally notifies the parents. Any Ivy League dreams they may have had are about to go down in flames. What to do?"

He stopped in front of Suellyn and looked down his nose at her. "I'll tell you what. A generous contribution to the endowment fund gets Junior off with a warning. He is our special goose and his misdeeds our golden eggs. He and his kind financed the new gymnasium.

"But," he spat, turning to wag a finger in my direction, "object lessons are also required. The boy I lost was on scholarship. His mother didn't have the wallet." Leonard hoisted his glass and slurred, "Integrity our cornerstone, righteous striving evermore . . ."

"What crooks," Suellyn said. "And you work for them?"

"Time-honored tradition, my dear, since pharaohs and slaves. I live to serve in silence." He downed the last gulp of scotch and slumped into his chair. "Never mind. Thanks for listening. I had to tell somebody."

"No problem." I creaked to my feet, aching again, and fetched our coats from the hall closet. "If I was that kid's father the headmaster could kiss his kneecaps goodbye. Great concert, though. Don't get up."

"Don't think I *can* get up. Hey, Suellyn, what about Thanksgiving? What can I bring?"

The flaw in my vasectomy plan revealed itself when we got home. I had no explanation for Johnson's baby-fresh baldness. Thank goodness we didn't sleep naked in cold weather.

Pajamas and bruises got me through the first week undetected. The mess on my chest and arms darkened like the marks of a giant rat trap. Suellyn treated me as if I might break in two. There was no pressure for sex, a free pass that could expire at any minute. The doc had said to count on six weeks or more before I shot blanks. I purged the sperm inventory at every opportunity to speed the process along. But it wouldn't matter without an explanation for my prickly stubble. Of course telling the truth would solve the problem. By pulling the pin on a marital hand grenade. Lately I hadn't been seeing so much of the freedom car.

During the second week the answer I was looking for appeared in the form of an oily-chested hunk on the cover of one of Suellyn's romance novels. I picked a slow afternoon in the grooming studio to thank her for bearing with me lately. It wasn't a lie as far as it went. I told her that to show my appreciation we were going out to dinner at her favorite high-class restaurant. I'd clean up and do the early evening feedings. No need for her to hang around till closing time. With her gone and Pop doing his grocery run for the week, I retired to the studio. Johnson wasn't itching anymore when I emerged, shaved clean as a bodybuilder.

Suellyn's clothes and jewelry did her proud. She loved the meal. The chocolate truffles and champagne later at home scored big too. Her amusement at my great unveiling wasn't exactly what I expected. I haven't put on *that* many pounds since high school. Fully exposed, the inky bruise stains probably did look funny. Suellyn got over it though.

She wanted weak knees and I gave them to her. Her period started the next day, right on schedule.

Thanksgiving week in the pet care business is madness. Every kennel is full. Every groomer booked solid, shampooing, styling, clipping nails and brushing teeth. There's no time to smoke a turkey. So we did ours the week before.

My smoker-grill stays at Pop's place, a two-story white clapboard farmhouse on the grounds of the Ritz K-9 Spa. This year was the ninth for him and me to tag team on the bird. We have our act down pat. I prepped the turkey at my house by cutting slits in either side of the breast and stuffing peeled, frozen brats into them. It makes the breast meat extra-juicy. Slices resemble fried eggs. When Suellyn and I arrived at the kennel, Pop had the smoker ready to go. In went the turkey. Every so often one of us took a break from work to baste and add wood to the firebox.

The fence of the exercise yard near the smoker was soon lined with dogs, tongues out and tails wagging. After the bird finished cooking, Pop and I grilled turkey burgers for our guests. He taught us years ago not to forget the dogs at a cookout. Their owners didn't have to know.

He's a character, Pop is. Little guy, bent over with arthritis. Wears a roadkill-looking toupee to keep away the skin cancer. Over the years his head has shrunk but his dentures haven't. They're as wide on him now as the grill of an old Ford Fairlane. Pop is glad to see you anytime and tells you so in a nasally squawk.

My frontal hair was at the prickly stage again. He caught me scratching. "Fleas?" he asked.

"Crabs. Suellyn wants them fat for her seafood stuffing."

That tickled him into a coughing fit. As always he'd be our guest of honor on Thanksgiving. I told him Leonard was invited too. And Rita. From what Suellyn said, they might be sniffing around each other.

Pop couldn't believe it. "That crazy spaceman? What, is she crazy too, or homely?" Pop said that Leonard had once claimed to be from a planet where they live on great ideas. Whenever he visited Earth he had to put on a space suit. There was also something about astronauts dealing poker on the moon. That's how Pop heard it anyway.

I said, "She's all right. Smart like Leonard. Reads a lot of books. She can kick his butt too. I watched her do it. Maybe that's the attraction."

"I knew guys like that," Pop said. "My wife tried getting rough on me once or twice; rest her soul. I didn't allow it. One of our granddaughters takes after her grandma though. What did you say this girl's name is?"

"Rita. Rita Hershey."

"No, my granddaughter is Madison."

On Thanksgiving Day, Pop and I handled the kennel chores. Sunshine replaced the usual winter overcast. The dogs appreciated it. None were sick. They enjoyed themselves, best as kenneled pets can, by tearing around the yards with Pop egging them on. Dogs adore that old man. Heaven help us when he's gone.

Suellyn stayed home to bake pies and prepare oyster stuffing. Leonard was in charge of potatoes. He said the spuds would be Spanish, whatever that meant. Rita volunteered rolls and a cranberry-apple mold from her mother's recipe.

We'd frozen the turkey after smoking it. Through the afternoon Pop reheated it with his oven on low. It was ready when the sun sank behind the treetops toward town. By then our guests were exercised and in their pens. We'd fed all but the late eaters. Pop and I and the bird piled into my car and came home.

Arnie greeted us, already jacked up on the aroma of oysters, herbs and bread. The turkey sent him bonkers. In the dining room Leonard handed silverware to Rita who tucked it into napkins folded like sleeping bags. The dry leaf and turban squash centerpiece had to be her idea. And the vine wreath hanging on the window blind. She'd replaced her usual baggy clothes with a high-waisted royal blue dress. Until then I hadn't realized how good she could look. I introduced her to Pop and carried the turkey into the kitchen. A whiff of beer gravy simmering on the stove sent me about as wild as Arnie. I left the meat on the counter, kissed Suellyn hello and went to change clothes.

When I finished, Pop and Rita were filling wine glasses at the table. His dentures nodded as she talked. She probably thought he approved of what she was saying. Maybe he did. The squash centerpiece had been joined by a pink cranberry mold decorated with curls of orange peel. Also a steaming crock of mashed potatoes. I could smell the garlic and cumin from across the room.

My method of carving turkey isn't suited for the table. With Arnie at my feet in the kitchen, his tail on overdrive, I filleted the breast. Suellyn dolloped stuffing onto the serving platter. Leonard stirred gravy and told us about a new cheating scandal.

Two boys in his American literature class had turned in identical papers about a short story they'd been assigned. "Instead of reporting them to the headmaster I called him into class to hear a pair of exceptional essays on 'Death in the Woods,'" Leonard said. "Both authors came to the front of the room to read. For a mediocre student presenting A+ material, the first one did fairly well. The class got to watch the other jerk freeze in panic, not yet understanding why."

"You're a cruel bastard, Leonard," I said, handing Suellyn turkey slices and parts, including a boned thigh for Pop.

She arranged them with the stuffing on the platter and asked if either boy was the roommate of the scholarship student.

"Sadly, no. The second kid refused to read so I did it for him. Those wonderfully wrought phrases reverberated again as if within the walls of a tomb. Death in Third Period." Leonard poured gravy into our gravy boat. "The headmaster shot me a withering look as he took the boys out. I might have been a wolf who'd ravaged the academy's geese." Leonard tipped his head back and howled at the ceiling fixture.

The performance didn't distract Arnie. His concentration remained fixed on the turkey and got him banished to the bedroom.

Suellyn called us to the table. Leonard wanted to recite William Burroughs' Thanksgiving prayer before the holiday toast. I didn't see anything wrong with that until the line about passenger pigeons being shit out through wholesome American guts. I cut Leonard off with a loud amen. Rita clamped her lips together, stifling laughter.

Pop seemed merely puzzled. He was first to be served when I carried the turkey platter around. He forked part of a thigh onto his plate and said, "This old dog's choppers won't gnaw a drumstick anymore. Never let them pull your teeth. Falsies is like having a mouth full of piano keys."

Rita lost it, helplessly out of control. She couldn't quit laughing. The bug was contagious. I had to set the platter down.

Some time later with order restored and plates filled, people were too busy eating to talk until Leonard leaned toward Rita. "I was telling Bud and Suellyn about the essays on the Anderson piece."

She looked at us and gushed, "Don't you just love Sherwood Anderson?"

I'd never heard of him. Neither had Suellyn or Pop but we let it pass.

Leonard said he knew that neither of his students had written the report because it focused on the story's use of obscure Greek mythology.

That impressed Rita. "You're right, it does," she said. "Once I wrote a paper discussing 'Death in the Woods' as an Americanization of Hecate."

A confused expression came over Leonard. Something more than the blankness the rest of us shared. "Did I show you those essays?"

"No, why?" she said.

"'An Americanization of Hecate' is the title they used."

Rita beamed, "They *both* bought my paper? Wow."

Leonard sagged like she'd kicked him in the heart. I thought he might cry but he didn't. Eventually he blinked and sucked in a huge trembling breath. His voice shook. "It's brilliant, Rita. Rigorous yet elegant. I can't believe I'm actually sitting beside its author in the flesh. I just wish ... Why couldn't ... Do you have more?"

"Essays? Sure. Dozens."

"Lovebirds," Pop rasped. "Who knows what they say." He fixed me with his toothy grin, "But girlie here, she tells me this too: You and Suellyn might finally start your own litter? That right?"

Suellyn turned cranberry salad pink and shook her head, desperate to shush Pop.

He didn't take notice. "I've been tempted to dig under the fence myself, don't you know."

Nobody thought it funny. Suellyn cringed.

"Well?" Pop insisted.

Out on the street a car blasting hip hop rumbled past. Thin bars of light flashed through the window blinds and vine wreath. *Families,* I thought. *Complications. Who needs it?* The faces around the table had the same look that greets me at the kennel every day. Some dogs are excited and up front with it. Others plead, hoping against hope. One way or another though, the eyes all say, "Feed me, friend."

Then I thought: *Life could be worse.* I didn't say that. What I said was, "Suellyn's been working on me. You never know. Maybe next year we'll spin the wheel. Find out what's meant to be."

My wife's squeak of joy skewered me. *Damn it all.* Trying my best to smile I cleared my throat before anyone could raise a glass and asked, "Who's ready for seconds on turkey?"

Thirty-Eigth Parallel

A RKIE ARKWRIGHT VAULTED INTO THE CAB of his
pickup and slammed the door. A wave of nausea hit
him as he stabbed the wrong key at the ignition. The keys
fell jangling. He fumbled for the door handle. It opened just
in time. No—Edd would never ha—have cooked— Steady
soldier. Vile abo— Spew damn you. Told Nate. Leave the
sonofa— in the field.—Where it belonged. Oh dear Lord.
Oh—

Nate Cummins, who'd followed Arkwright out of Cap
and Edd Rosser's house, stopped at a distance from the
truck. The driver's door shuddered with the older man's
heaves. In the cone of barnyard light Arkie's freshly waxed
vehicle took on a greenish tinge. A shock of cold wind blew
through Nate's shirt. Only hours earlier he and Arkie had
sweated under game vests heavy with pheasant. It was hard
to believe the forecast for snow across western Kansas. No
longer. He bounced in place, rubbing his arms, waiting.

He and Jesse, Arkie's son, had been childhood friends.
Nate knew Mr. Arkwright as a standup guy, rough, depend-
able, generous, a railroad man with the strength to raise
the wheel of a compact car off the ground barehanded.
The harsh, sweet land incarnate. Arkie had a temper; who
didn't? But the man kept his cool. When he'd disowned

119

Jesse it was by force of personality, not physical violence. Tonight's scene was totally out of character. Thank god those old codgers, the Rosser boys, hadn't been hit by flying dishes. They'd sat stunned, hardly more befuddled than Nate. So what if there was jackrabbit in the stew? Wild game didn't come any cleaner. Not a pellet in the meat. Nate was proud of his marksmanship, nothing but head at the apex of a leap. Why shouldn't he brag a little? Arkwright had no call to go ballistic. But he'd snatched their bowls, dumped everything into the stewpot and was out the kitchen door with it. There'd been a loud metallic bong as the pan bounced off something in the dark. Now Arkwright was puking so hard he might hemorrhage.

Arkie raised his head as the spasm receded and fixed Nate with the glare of a cornered beast. Nate heard himself apologizing, though he wasn't sure for what. "If I'd have known you didn't like rabbit I wouldn't have let them cook it. Come on in. It's freezing. I'll clean up the kitchen."

"Get away," Arkie panted. "To trick me into . . . He was my son, you sonofabitch. Some men might forget their best friend. But how the hell could you?"

The accusation annoyed Nate. "I haven't forgotten. I didn't go for what he turned into at college but it hurt me that he died. It hurt bad. You don't forget things like that. Come on. Let's go in. We can talk about it there." Nate, with two young children of his own, couldn't imagine the "what ifs" and "if onlys" that must attend a parent's grief after a son shoots himself. But Jesse had chosen that unnatural life. Nobody'd made him forsake his upbringing. At some point a man had to be accountable for his own actions. And the disowning had happened two years before his death, for chrissakes.

Arkie didn't move from the driver's seat.

Nate tried again. "Is there anything I can do for you? Please. Come on, man. You can't stay out here." He approached the truck and caught a whiff of beery vomit.

"To hell with you. If you want to go inside, do it. But come one step closer and I'll sling you as far as your pot of slop." Arkie's chin burned. He wiped the slime off and pulled the door shut. When he bent to locate his keys he busted his lip on the steering wheel. Infuriated by the sudden taste of blood he grabbed up the keyring and rolled down his window, slowly, to avoid tearing the crank out of the door. The kid stood dancing in the cold like a damned moron. Arkie spat a rope of bloody bile at him. It missed. He wiped his chin again and warned, "I said, I'll beat your ass."

Nate yelled toward the house for the Rossers.

"Leave them out of this. That's an order." Arkie held his keys to the light, selected the proper one and snicked it into the ignition. Without another word he started the truck, jerked the transmission into gear and sped away, aimless as a rat skittering around the bottom of a dry stock tank.

The section roads that carved the prairie into square mile plots were deserted. He switched on the radio and reached for the fifth of bourbon he'd stashed under the seat in anticipation of this annual hunt. The Rosser boys and the cycle of seasons on their land grounded him year by year, each visit a homecoming. He never dreamed the celebration whiskey might be pressed into service as first aid. The news on the radio worsened his mood. Speculation centered on the Unabomber after the discovery of a fizzled explosive on an American Airlines flight. The Carter administration announced a ban on the importation of oil from Sandistan. Arkie swore out loud. A real president of the United States would negotiate for the release of American hostages by nuking a goddamned city. The degradation was too much.

He found a music station. Charlie Daniels sawed out "The Devil Went Down to Georgia."

Arkie kept to the farm roads. In his headlights the rushing lines of pale posts and poles unzipped and spread wide. He slipped between them, traveling a good bit of Trego, Gove, Scott, and Lane counties before his temper eased. North of the Ogalla crossroads he parked on the Saline River Bridge and got out to kill the fifth. The gusting wind made him wish he'd brought a coat. He took shelter on the other side of the cab. On second thought he'd had enough booze. What little was left he threw into the blackness and listened for a splash he never heard. He leaned back against the truck. It swayed and nudged him, stirring the whiskey warmth. A clot of rage gave way. Sadness tried to muscle in and slapped him to momentary sobriety. His presence was required elsewhere.

The liquor crept up again as he drove two miles west, one south, another four miles west, then south again to the fence-wire gate at the corner of the Rosser boys' land. He shut off the engine but left the high beams on to light the gate. Unsteadily, he passed through on foot and reset the keeper loop over the fencepost. Drunk or sober a man always closed gates. It didn't matter that Martin, the only animal in the pasture, had died in August. The Rosser boys, out of respect or forgetfulness, hadn't called the rendering plant to take him. Arkie appreciated the chance to say goodbye, even three months late. Martin was Jesse's bull calf, his Future Farmers of America project.

Arkie and Nate had first visited that afternoon, coming by way of the creek and milo field. The pheasants ran in the Indian summer heat but were no match for experienced hunters. Arkie had his limit and Nate was only a bird shy when they came upon the remains hunkered in the sedge. A faint dank smell lingered in the air, not unpleasant. The hide had darkened and shrunk tight against the ribs. Arkie's finger traced the brand scar, one of the few marks of his son's existence remaining on Earth. Jesse had been squeamish about applying it, probably suffered more than the calf. In the end the Rossers got a good sire for their money. Cap didn't have the heart to sell him after Jessie died. No words from Arkie were necessary. Cap understood what Martin meant.

Nightfall had changed everything. The pasture appeared insubstantial in the headlights, nervous waves of silver scratches etched on the dark. Pulled along by his shadow he staggered through them, groping for balance. His hands burned with cold. Canadian air lashed his cheeks stiff, brought water to his eyes. Martin's dim bulk in the weeds stopped him. The stinging water spilled and froze in a week's worth of beard grizzle. Arkie wobbled to attention and saluted.

Others might complain about the weather conditions but Staff Sergeant Arkwright had survived the 2nd Infantry Division's godforsaken retreat from the thirty-eighth parallel in 1950, a wet, frigid hell of firefights and sleepless nights that stretched from Thanksgiving to New Year's. The Korean winter was nothing compared to the ignominious hand fate had dealt him and his buddies. Was it worse to be killed by some whistle-blowing gook or live to explain why the US Army had bugged out? That year they said Santa Claus drove the supply truck that plowed into General Walker's jeep, killing the incompetent sonofabitch. It took General Ridgeway's arrival in January to rally the troops and show the ChiComs what America was about.

Arkie maintained his salute. Martin had earned the honor guard. The bull lay where it fell after a life of service. Single-minded devotion to purpose was all God and country asked of any man. Arkie lived by that code. Sophia might not care for it any longer but soldiers understood that softness was the worm in the damned apple. Martin would have been ashamed that the kid who raised him had perverted from the natural order. Best that the bull had no way of knowing. In death Martin deserved the same as any soldier, an honorable interment safe from the defilement of scavengers. Surely one of the farmers around owned a backhoe. Arkie would borrow it in the morning. For now, duty demanded that he get his butt in motion.

Cap and Edd's barn light, cattycorner across the section, hung as a low shining dot in the starless sky. Arkie turned away from it and tottered toward the headlights on wooden feet, flexing his toes to restore blood circulation. At the gate he steadied himself by holding on to the fencepost. With effort he unhooked the keeper, swung his body through the opening and reset the wire loop. He lurched at the pickup and caught the door handle going by.

The truck refused to start. He cut the lights. The starter, almost inaudible in the buzz of whiskey static, ground lethargically and quit. Arkie crossed his arms on the steering wheel and rested his head there, trying to assemble a train of thought. Cars ran loose, careening this way and that in a switchyard nightmare. Why hadn't he gotten around to equipping the pickup for winter emergencies? Should've been in bed hours ago. Screw them. Let them worry. His cap and a pair of gloves were behind the seat. He needed to piss. Gloves were better than nothing.

As he stepped from the cab his feet missed the ground and he pitched forward into an ungainly shoulder roll. Shivering complicated the task of hauling himself vertical again. He reached behind the seat for his hat and gloves and put them on. Where was his coat? At the house. Dumbass. His Remington pump swam into view on the gun rack. It couldn't be left in plain sight. He'd take it. Out of habit he double-checked the weapon for empty. With the dying headlights switched on to see him through the gate, he secured the vehicle and set out for the farmhouse.

The Rosser's barnyard star guided his second crossing of Martin's pasture. Beyond headlight range Arkie poked at the night with the shotgun, probing for the milo field fence, wary of the creek somewhere to his right. The shivering worsened. His teeth wouldn't stop chattering regardless of how he clenched his jaw. He inched through the weeds until the gun barrel scraped barbed wire, then ducked between strands. A barb ripped his shirt.

Rows of unseen milo stubble alternated with strips of bare ground. The field's monotonous undulation proved easy going. Cut stalks slapped at the toes of his boots like waves on an arctic sea. He sailed them northwesterly into the wind, yawing erratically from the effects of the bourbon. Stubbornly distant, the light drew him forward.

He stepped into thin air and slammed down as if tossed by an exploding artillery shell. Dirt clods cascaded with him down a slope. He came to rest on his back, head below his feet, the Remington caught between his legs. Staff Sgt. Arkwright shivered and flailed until he had the weapon in his hands. The barrel was unobstructed. His own condition was less favorable. Pain seized the right side of his chest and made breathing difficult. There was something badly wrong with his right knee. Still, he had to set up a defensive position. Pronto.

There were no more explosions or shrilling ChiCom whistles. He groaned for medical assistance. Received no answer. Then he remembered the milo field and ravine that meandered across it to the creek. He'd observed tillable land slough into the gully's advancing tributaries for fifty years. He cursed his stupidity, rolled onto his stomach and raised up onto his elbows and good knee for the climb to the rim. Due to the proximity of the enemy he stayed in the ravine while orienting. A spattering sound, sleet, advanced toward him. His guiding light, dimmed by the sleet, appeared through a screen of weeds. It seemed larger than before. Another spasm of shivering racked him, mercilessly aggravating the rib pain. He bit his forearm, muffling the moans until the shivering subsided. Where was the god-damned medic?

Unexpected warmth in his pants told him he'd lost bladder control. A couple of privates in Korea had pissed themselves on a night like this. The dumb clucks didn't see it as a problem until the wool froze and sandpapered the skin off their thighs. Arkie railed at himself for yet another mistake. Such gross stupidity ought to cost him a stripe. What had happened to his soldier's pride? His determina-tion and presence of mind? His adherence to procedure? No soldier worth a crap entered a field of battle unprepared. Rules are rules for a reason. Cap Rosser had drilled it into him since the day Arkie learned his first farm chore. How old had he been then, five? Derelictions of this magnitude were inexcusable.

Why didn't the enemy show? Did he suspect the United States Army, for once, wasn't going to bug out? Arkie would go over the top, bum leg and all, like Cap and his men had done in the Argonne. America expected it of her sons at times of threat. And never had she been more imperiled than she was now by the climate of moral rot. The stench attracted hippies, commies, ragheads and lunatic bombers. Their foul buzzard beaks picked at the nation's pride. Where was General Ridgeway? Or Black Jack Pershing? Arkie wouldn't stoop to the desperation of a solo charge. He'd witnessed one of those, a desertion by assisted suicide, committed by a man too cowardly to pull his own trigger.

Even Jesse hadn't been that weak. Arkie's eyes wa-tered again. He and Sophia had been so proud of their only child, the first Arkwright to attend college. They should never have allowed him to go. The university was a den of iniquities. It changed him, deafened him to the warnings of his father and real friends like Nate. How could you reach a son who rejected his nature? You couldn't. Arkie'd been forced to disown him. There was no other course of action. Sophia cried herself to sleep for months. Above all, Arkie resented Jesse for what he'd done to his mother. In a horrible way his suicide had been an honorable act. It allowed his parents to bring him home.

Arkie wriggled into firing position on the weed-line, daring the bastards. The wind slacked off. Sleet turned to snow. He listened for telltale sounds of the enemy. Forgetting that the shotgun was empty, he jacked a nonexistent shell into the chamber. The slide seemed balky. Maybe it was only the combination of leather gloves and numb fingers affecting his grip. He'd go barehanded when the attack commenced. He'd not let Cap down.

Nate probably thought of Captain Walter Rosser as half of an old joke. These days Cap did resemble one, so thin and mentally out of it that he might lose himself in his coveralls. The years had brought a proud soldier low. Captain Rosser hadn't yet been Nate's age when he braved Boche gunners to rescue Arkie's eventual father from the mud of an Argonne no-man's land. Cap and Edd saved Pa again after he lost his farm. They gave him work and the use of the cabin where Arkie's sisters were born and died of the croup. Though misfortune turned Pa meaner than a snake, Cap had a way of appearing to prevent the worst family violence. It was a sixth sense. Had to be. But it failed him on the day the Shorthorn bull gored out Pa's life. Regular landlords would have sent the Arkwrights packing. Not the Rosser boys. They adopted Arkie as their own, even to the point of letting the boy sleep over with them on special occasions. Ma became their housekeeper and lived out her days in the old cabin.

The night sparkled with crystals. He'd never seen the like. They hid the barn light from him. Cap and Edd were out there though, stuffing wood into the stove. Arkie had brought them two cords, sufficient to heat their drafty house to body temperature, the way they liked it, for weeks. He pictured Nate sweating in the kitchen by the stove. Except for the beds there was no other place to sit. Mostly the house was a waist-high maze of girlie magazines. The boys had been collecting since year one, though until Ma passed, the porn was stored in the barn. Nate's eyes popped to see it for the first time. Yes sirree Bob, Nate was sweating now. He deserved every minute of roasting the boys could dish out. And he'd do it fully clothed. Last night the kid had tried going shirtless. It wasn't ten minutes before Edd sidled over to him, cue ball head and toothless grin, and latched onto Nate's titty like the Gerber baby. Poor Edd, so far gone he mistook Nate for his mama.

Arkie's mouth was parched. The shivering had finally stopped. Frozen clods raked his side and pulled the shirttail out of his pants as he struggled to roll onto his back. The shotgun clattered to the bottom of the ditch. He ordered himself to hang on; Ridgeway was a month away from turning this thing around. The US Army should be fighting, not running with its tail between its legs. Not lying half-naked. Not like this. Blessed flakes of snow settled on his lips and tongue.

Leadership. Where was it? There'd be no medic. The boys had never bothered to get telephone service. Nate wouldn't have any idea where to search and Cap couldn't tell him that a soldier guards what his nation holds dear. The dead and wounded of too many battles lay entombed within the span of Martin's ribs. Two hundred years of American sacrifice demanded that Arkie prevail.

The cancer of appeasement. FDR had flirted with it. Then Truman and Acheson. Now the world marveled at Carter's humiliation. Hostage to a bed-sheeted Persian? The desecration of America couldn't go on like this. Kids smoking dope, aborting the next generation, becoming outright homos. The heartland was dying. The tears in Sophia's eyes. Her pleading, "Surely he'll grow out of it." Jesse might still be alive if Arkie hadn't taken action. Sophia might still speak to him. But what else could a father do? The cruelty of this earth dismayed him.

There they are, he and Nate, vests full on a balmy afternoon, paying respects to Martin. Golden, weedy fingers pulling the bull to rest. Arkie drops a wrapper. Bends to retrieve it. Looks up as the jackrabbit springs from a hole in Martin's paunch. Nate's 16-gauge locks on. Arkie tries to shout, *Run you sonofabitch. Dodge. Git.* But it has defiled and he cannot speak. The boom still echoes in the shimmering crystals. The rabbit's head vaporizes, gone. Jesse crumples in a cheap motel room. Cap can't save him and Ridgeway is still a month away.

Avatars

ONCE, KAFKA TELLS US, a stressed out salesman could wake from unsettling dreams to find himself transformed into a capsized bug and do nothing about it but flail his pitiful bug legs. These days we outgrow such quaint terrors about the time we discover that game controllers work better with thumb out of mouth. Given ultimate futility and so forth, we delight in waking on planet Pandora to join the Na'vi resistance. Or becoming Neo in the Matrix, battling Agent Smith. Oh, give me a home where I can save a planet and break damsel hearts without breaking a sweat. Am I right?

Avatars R Us. I was prepared to wake as darn near anything except a figment of my own imagination. At first I thought even that was cool. I'm a field biologist who enjoys the smell of unfamiliar dirt and a game of hide and seek to discover what lives there. Whether or not this represents a closeted rejection of the digital age—and it might—it does mean that woo-woo is not my typical beat. But life is what it is. I discovered that I have a double and can't shake him.

Here's a taste of my problem. Tomorrow I'm due to testify against the Air Force in a North Carolina zoning duel. There's a proposal to expand a bombing/firing range on the coast. Air Force attorneys will attempt to shoot holes in my environmental assessment, corner me into testifying that blasting some of the few remaining wild Venus flytraps isn't a threat to the digestion of endangered red wolves and migrant manatees. I'll be told that information about the toxicity of depleted uranium is irrelevant to the case because the military hasn't disclosed which munitions will be used there—never mind that standard armor-piercing bullets are made of the stuff. I imagine pouring pints of sparkling uranium water for the lawyers. Drink up. They'll do it to spite me, probably be awarded Purple Hearts for the damage to their kidneys and polished brass gonads. All well and good. The problem is that I'm not the one tending bar in the Uranium Lounge. Can't be. The barkeep is visible in my frontal lobes. I watch him do his stuff.

For about ten seconds the distinction between him and me is clear; then I'm sucked into another scene as phony as the computer-generated illusions of *The Matrix*. There, my avatar seems realer than me. He has a history, a future, adventures I'll never have. I forget myself in the characters he assumes and have to ask who's who. Of course any answer I get comes from the guy who's not me. For clarity's sake I call him Luie. My name is Matt, Matthew Donnelly, born April 29, 1980. A body answering my description resides in the foothills above Denver when not on assignment for the Wild Heritage Conservancy.

This morning as I boarded a flight out of L.A., Luie lectured me on the triumph of concept over material reality. *Images devalue creation*, he argued. *Why not subpoena an actual manatee to court?* I considered his position ironic and told him so while storing a carry-on in the overhead bin. Debate continued as I navigated past a portly granddad in 19D to my window seat. The question became less pressing when a good-looking woman about my age slipped into 19E. Black hair and the palest aquamarine eyes. But for a pair of styling sunglasses cocked up in her hair, she wasn't dressed to impress: cargo jeans and a shapeless shirt. I surprised myself, or Luie, by not fumbling the hello.

"Nicole," she replied. Then she whispered, "It's a little tight in here," indicating the wheezing bulk on her left. "Mind if I raise the armrest between our seats?"

Not at all.

"Thanks," she said. "Much better."

She pulled a movie star's purported autobiography from her knapsack and scooted the bag under the seat with her foot. River sandals, silver ring on her pinky toe, no nail polish. Unthinkingly I dissed her book. "Another celebrity extolling the posterized life?"

Luie cursed.

Nicole frowned.

A screen flashed on my mental console.

GAME OVER
GAME OVER

Commentaries such as this make Luie an irritating skullmate. So much so that he's become my personal devil. Thus Lucifer. Not that he's satanic. An adversary of biblical proportions would be wasted on me. Luie is quite adequate; thank you very much. In his defense, the devil business is recent. He's been my tireless mental stand-in since childhood. We—at the time I thought it was only me—rehearsed wheedling things out of my parents. High dramas in the practice room frequently translated to actual results. Luie and I still waste ludicrous amounts of time searching for the perfectly nuanced performance. Luie's downside is that my bringer of light and understanding has also become a filter separating me from the world. Beating him to a sensation these days is as rare as it is unexpected.

For a moment the world is new again. Then he recovers and takes it away.

Our plane jerked as it began to pull back from the gate. Nicole said that the star of her book might turn out to be more than cardboard. "It says here she's been married for almost twenty years. Doesn't that indicate real character?"

Luie and I went on defensive alert, as men do in these circumstances. "Not necessarily," I hedged. I had demonstrated an ability to commit—*or mental commitability*, Luie snarked—by living with Roxie for several years. In retrospect, it's a good thing we never married. She developed a taste for cocaine and, given the choice between it and me, made up her mind about ten miles off the coast of Belize. We'd rented a Boston Whaler to dive on an obscure reef. Since it's crazy to leave a craft unattended in those waters we had to take turns on the bottom. Roxie volunteered to let me go first. I thought nothing of it until I surfaced half an hour later to find the boat missing. I bobbed unnoticed until sunset. A trawler full of drunken fishermen almost whizzed me to cuisinart. At least they spotted me. The gargantuan former defensive tackle who jerked me aboard asked if he could hang me upside down for a photo. His brokerage clients would get a kick out of it.

Nicole said, "You're probably right." The jets throttled up and shoved us into our seats. Her thumb stroked the sales slip marking her page.

Luie delivered a swift kick to my parietal cortex. *Take a shot*. In the gravitational uncertainty of leaving the runway, I did. "Last minute trip?"

She brushed the cover of her book as if liftoff had dirtied it. "The funeral for my great aunt Eula." Annieula, as she'd been known, was a retired Army nurse who dedicated herself to improving medical care for Gullah communities along the South Carolina coast. She'd had to overcome generations of distrust for outsiders, especially whites. The old lady's example had inspired Nicole to become a nurse.

"In Annieula's last letter, when she knew she was failing, she wrote about not needing hospice because a Gullah auntie, her favorite folk healer, was taking care of her." Nicole's voice quavered. "But my family, in its wisdom, is holding her service in Beaufort, at a white funeral home. It's so wrong. Her Gullah friends won't go. Annieula's spirit isn't too Christian to rise up and raise hell. I hope she does."

"Nobody knows how to screw you like family."

"Tell me about it," she sighed. "But my sister Vicky and her husband are meeting me in Atlanta. I do look forward to seeing them. She was fond of Annieula too. We'll cry together while John and the other guys watch baseball. Even the sorriest human being deserves to be cried over when they pass, and this is Annieula for heaven's sake."

So Matt, Luie said as a flight attendant butted in, hawking headphones for the in-flight movie, *you want I should leave youse alone?* Luie's mobster impression isn't bad. Absolutely, I told him. "Not that you will." *Yeah. You don't do so good in these type situations. No disrespect.*

"What's that?" Nicole asked.

I hadn't realized I'd spoken aloud. "How'd you happen to be so close with your aunt?"

She gave me an "Are you sure you want to hear this?" look.

I nodded.

"My mom died when Vicky and I were small. After that, Daddy raised us alone. I don't know how he managed to juggle two pre-schoolers and a job on the Baltimore docks but he did. Occasionally he'd bring home a girlfriend. He said I ran them off. When I was in eighth grade he developed a mortal fear of me going boy crazy and sent me to Annieula's for the summer."

"Quite a transition from Baltimore."

"It was great. I asked to go back the next year, and the third summer Vicky came too. Everything was fine until she told Daddy that we went with Annieula on house calls to black people. Oh, my god, I thought he'd have a stroke."

Luie stifled my crack about racism.

"What did Daddy think, that we sat around crocheting doilies? There'd come a knock on the door and a man, hat in hand, speaking that wonderful Creole you don't hear anywhere else." She sighed, recalling. "Because we belonged to Miss Annieula, we were okay too. Mr. Oree used to carry us across the sound on his homemade pontoon boat. It had lawn chairs screwed to the deck and a beach umbrella for shade. We traveled like queens."

One moonlit night, some kids had taken Nicole along to watch a loggerhead turtle lay eggs. She told me she'd felt sorry for the ungainly mother as it flopped sand over its clutch and humped laboriously across the beach to the surf. "The rollers tried to shove her away. But, all at once, the crashing stopped and she just slipped between the waves. I could almost hear the angels sing. I'd give anything for those summers to take me back in."

Compared to her aunt's home health practice, Nicole's work in a neuro-trauma unit was no doubt hectic. Her customers dined intravenously and were breathed by ventilators. Luie pictured them cradled like prize squashes in networks of tubes and wires. He prompted me to ask whether the high tech is worth the effort.

"Some recover, more or less. Relatives drop by with old patients to show us how good they're doing. It's funny; I remember families but not patients."

Flight attendants arrived at our row, selling sandwiches. Grandpa paused his nap and requested turkey. Reaching for his wallet, he elbowed Nicole into my lap.

"Sorry," she said, reclaiming her seat after the thrashing subsided. She bought a ham and cheese.

"You don't remember your patients?" I asked.

"Head trauma bloats faces. And they're in medically induced comas to keep them from fighting their breathing tubes. I get the willies when a patient comes up enough to follow me with his eyes. Patients have seizures; they code; they die; I can handle that. But not them watching."

Luie whispered, *Geez, cut a dude some slack.* He descends a high country dirt road on my mountain bike, the roar of wind and thrum of knobby tires in our ears. We race into a blind curve, laying the bike over to conserve speed. Suddenly, an SUV in the middle of the road. Lock brakes. Our rear wheel washes out in slo mo. Cartwheeling. Then . . . then a moving shape. It has black hair. I'm here, I try to say. *Matt, on second thought, don't go there.* No shit, genius. "Have you done this kind of work long?"

"Yes, but only since last fall in L.A. I move a lot. Places with good outdoor sports. You'd suppose an ICU nurse might know better than extreme kayaking and hang gliding, wouldn't you? What do you do?"

I told her about my recent bio-census of a parcel near Palm Springs. The developer hoped I wouldn't find a particular species of kangaroo rat on the site of his proposed "green" golf course and gated community. Tough luck. He had rats. "He fired me, shredded my report and hired a friendly hack to redo the study. My contract contained a confidentiality clause; I'll be sued if I blow the whistle on him."

While we talked, Luie and Nicole ran my favorite stretch of whitewater, a continuous Class III rapid in the San Juans. Above them on the mountainside, a steam train chuffs a black plume up-canyon toward Silverton.

I interrupted this interruption to listen to what I was saying to the actual woman. "I kayak and mountain bike.

And I have a peach of a motorcycle: a restored '65 Triumph. Ever strapped one of those on?"

Nicole presses against Luie's back, whooping as the Triumph speeds along a deserted ribbon of asphalt, westward before the morning sun.

I heard, "The Gauley is a hoot."

My cell phone got better reception than Luie was allowing me. *Oh, yeah?* he retorted. *Why not fantasize? It's all you get.* And that, in a nutshell, is the hell of Luie. I, or rather he, can be anywhere, do anything, with anybody, anytime. Mental masturbation has its satisfactions. One is that nobody gets hurt.

I took the muffuletta I'd fixed for this flight out of my carryon. Muffulettas withstand TSA inspectors and hours of elevated temps without going bad. The olive oil is sloppy but greases the skids when you're short on fluids.

Nicole unwrapped her ham and cheese. "Thanks for keeping me company."

"*De nada.*"

She tasted the sandwich and made a face. "Is there a dog on this flight?"

It was an unfiltered moment. All mine. Laughing. No Luie. Just laughing.

But, with that realization, he took my place. The bastard had the stones to console me with snake oil schemes for outmaneuvering him, though forethought precludes success and we both know it. See how Byzantine this gets?

Luie suggested that I accompany Nicole to baggage claim in Atlanta. In his scenario, Sis doesn't show up. Forget my puddle jumper flight to New Bern. We'll rent a car. I'll chauffeur her to Beaufort, then drive north up the coast. Blushing, she accepts. Soft focus. Cue mushy love song. *Thanks so much, Luie.* His sarcastic streak is wide as an eight-lane throughway.

The ham in Nicole's sandwich must have been rubber. When she was finally able to swallow a bite of it, I said, "If that doesn't digest any better than it chews, you're risking the pork equivalent of a fur ball. Care for a muffuletta?"

Luie cringed.

"Thanks, but no. A fur ball at the funeral might please Annieula no end."

Granddad lurched Nicole into me again and went back to sleep. Luie took the opportunity to counsel a change of topic.

"One gypsy to another, how's it going?" I said.

"How do you mean?"

"I've lived in five states and had assignments in fourteen others. Set up shop; write a report; move on. I enjoy watching places disappear in the rearview. I've lost a dozen suitcases but never a single obligation. Those keep piling up. Do you ever wonder if freedom is a fraud?"

She considered the possibility, far too seriously, before brightening. "A friend in Gainesville said I'm as attached to nonattachment as he is to his couch. He likes the couch better because he has a place to sit."

I scored a second flash of unfiltered joy. Luie made a snide remark about dharma bums.

"Annieula said I have happy feet, but they're beginning to crave a couch that knows them." Her eyes widened to madwoman proportion. "I dream of owning a washer and dryer."

"Oh, no," I recoiled.

"Oh, yes. When I leave L.A. I may be done traveling. For a while anyway."

"Where would you settle?"

She shrugged.

"Ever been to Colorado? It's got everything a gypsy heart desires except coconuts on the beach. Though with global warming, who knows? I'm speculating on a little parcel near the Spanish Peaks. The beachfront property of tomorrow."

"Have you bought your boat?"

"Not yet. Still waiting for the right deal. Next time you're in the neighborhood give me a ring. I'll show you around."

"Deal." A flight attendant walked by collecting trash. Nicole chucked the sandwich and raised her tray table. "Who am I kidding?" she said. "I can't settle down no matter how much my feet hurt."

After the Roxie debacle, Luie—though I was still ignorant of his separateness—masterminded my reentry into the dating pool. I was surprised at how women had matured in my absence. Sex wasn't fast food anymore; it was fine dining. But the mornings after were usually most memorable for dirty dishes. The exception was the day I also awakened to Luie and his role in the ongoing farce and put him on a short leash. Now he slipped off it. "What's the matter with us," he asked Nicole, "drifting around, living out of suitcases? I wonder if my Velcro has lost its stick."

Her eyes softened, leading him to believe he'd charmed her. "That's it, isn't it?" she said. "Peeling off. Not fitting, or not really wanting to. I feel so guilty. Annieula never peeled off. There was always a place where she kept you, regardless of where you went or what you did. She was the same with everyone, a perfect pearl who reflected us all."

"Excuse me?"

"I'm sorry. Obscure reference. I used to be fascinated by the idea of Indra's net."

I'd heard of Indra. Luie laid down a djembe beat and bawled like Kerouac, *Go, man*. I couldn't resist. "Lord Indra the Hindu god? It's not nice to dangle a god." I ignored the shadow darkening Nicole's face. "Tell me."

She frowned. "The net was above his palace. It stretched endless in all directions and forever in time." Her hands cast it above our seats. "Instead of knots where the cords crossed, Indra's net had pearls, each so shiny it reflected all the others. And those reflections contained reflections. The net always appeared whole, whether seen at a distance or in the reflections of reflections in a single pearl."

"Cool."

"It *was* a cute story." She reached into her knapsack for a Kleenex and dabbed her eyes. "This is a weird fricking day. I'll stop bothering you now."

"You aren't. Go on, please."

The wadded tissue covered her mouth. She blew her nose. "I haven't always been this way."

"What way?"

"Not this," she indicated the Kleenex. "I mean I was settled once, happily married. We traveled but it was different then. Gary was a professional bareback rider. It's a tough sport. The concussions crept up on him. He started having trouble controlling his emotions."

"They say it happens to a lot of pro athletes."

"I did what I could for him, played the good nurse. His parents lived close by. They begged him to get help. Nothing we did was right."

I nodded, having been in her position myself. Roxie agreed to check into rehab a dozen times but never followed through.

"He said he needed space. So I took a temp assignment out of town and rented an apartment there. Gary seemed to perk up. One night when I was home, I asked if he was ready for me to stay. He said no. That was devastating. I went to bed without him. In the morning he was lying beside me, dead. The autopsy report said aspirin. He overdosed on freaking aspirin." The Kleenex trembled in her fist. "What kind of wife sleeps through such a thing?"

"That's terrible."

She traded the sodden tissue for a new one and composed herself. "It was four years ago. Appearances to the contrary, I've made my peace."

Luie's interference reduced my response to an incoherent mumble.

She said, "No, really. Gullah people call it recollecting. When you pass near the graves of loved ones, you should stop and recollect them. Their spirits remind you of who you are." She blew her nose again. "You never know, is all. I thought Annieula was reflected in me but I had to face facts."

"Sorry. I don't understand."

"Shouldn't there be an age when we're old enough for the truth? We keep reassuring each other; 'It'll be all right.' Who's *that* for? When a family asks me how a patient is, I say, 'Fine. Carlos is better today.' What's left of his brain is a bloody bruise. He won't ever be the same but hey, he's got stable vitals and good gasses. He's doing well. Who am I to take away his family's hope? It's their teddy bear. But the truth is I don't want to deal with the reality of Carlos either. It's cowardly. I hate myself for it."

"Isn't that a bit harsh?" *Luie, this was your idea. We could use a little help here.*

She stared straight ahead. "Annieula didn't lie. When she attended a dying person she'd say it straight out. 'Look around you, darling. See your family here, all we you're leaving? And Jesus and the old souls on the other side? Take my hand. We'll cross over together.'"

Nicole turned to me. "She'd hold that hand and hum in a kind of moan. Before long somebody would start singing. It might be a packed trailer house, smelly from all the people, but you couldn't help clapping and moving. After a while though, you began to feel oppressed. The pressure didn't let up until the spirit passed. You felt its relief. Then

Annieula would come back to us and say, 'The old souls are singing now.'"

Luie and I nodded, clueless.

"She told me souls are like ships. They need a steadfast beacon in the storm. That sounds beautiful but what's it supposed to mean?" Nicole shoved the dirty ball of Kleenex into her bag. "When it came her time, I stayed away. I didn't want to fail her. Her niece isn't a beacon; she's a liar."

My voice came from nowhere. "People like Annieula put the rest of us to shame. We shouldn't hold it against them."

"What?"

"I'm just saying it's a brutal standard. I'm not steadfast, not even for myself. I sit in my head watching TV with the channels in shuffle mode and no remote. Steadfast is great but we're not all heroes. I only play one on TV. Escapism at its finest."

She rewarded me with an embarrassed smile. "Mine is old movies. My first summer with Annieula, she caught me playing Scarlet O'Hara, teasing a store clerk. She grabbed my arm so hard it left a bruise. 'Don't you be pretending with people, Little Miss. Life is too short.' I'm so sorry, Annieula. I'd rather be skydiving or drunk. Anywhere but at your funeral." She rummaged through the bag under her seat for a pack of tissues. The butt of a compact umbrella peeked out.

Bless him, Luie improvised. "Tell you what, this trip is going to end up sucking for me too. You're a skydiver?"

"I have my license, why?"

"Your umbrella reminds me of Mary Poppins. Let's order a bottle of wine, grab a picnic blanket and take the D. B. Cooper exit. What do you think?"

"I'm not sure a folding umbrella is up to the task."

"No worries. Did I mention that I fly? Learned in my sleep. It's like the jump program in *The Matrix*. Free your mind and good things happen."

"Is that so? Then tell me, Neo, does the offer include an upgrade from Mary Poppins?"

"You bet, Trinity," I said, referring to Neo's martial artist girlfriend. "Go on; suit up. I won't look." The view out the window was green and hazy. Cotton balls floated on a southern pine forest. Not a care in sight.

"How's this," she asked. "Am I presentable?"

"Your movies don't do you justice."

Behind the stage where Neo and Trinity flirted, something else happened. Nicole and I met in a state of mind that outclassed the everyday as much as life beggars the finest digital. We met, except there wasn't any her or me to do the meeting. We were jet rumble, cramped quarters, emotional baggage and the curve of the earth sparkling on a universal sea.

The moment was rudely broken by an announcement of initial descent into Atlanta. "Shit!" Trinity spat. "There's an agent on this plane."

Luie materialized as well. "It was inevitable," he said, with the cold menace of Agent Smith.

"Vicky and John are coming in from Pittsburgh. I hope they didn't have any trouble." Nicole consulted her wrist for a watch she wasn't wearing. "Are we on time?"

My watch said we were. We were on it, in it again and perilously close to out of it. Luie barraged me with syrupy stuff: lawnmowers, babies with aquamarine eyes. If only we'd met on a whitewater trip down a Western river. We'd have time to warm the nights with private campfires and send red-hot embers to join the starry legions. *Never mind the ashes*, Luie countered.

Did I mention he's a killjoy? But the point is valid. People in love do their best to ignore the accumulation of unromantic byproducts. Luie morphed into the host of a reality show. *Who takes this rap for better or worse? Will Matt and Nicole fight for the right to assume the blame or accuse each other? Find out tonight on "Been There, Done That."*

I wasn't in the mood and told Luie to pipe down. *Stop me then*, he crowed. *You'd rather make believe than scrape your knees. People get hurt no matter what. Quit whining.*

Atlanta rushed beneath us. Streams of vehicles flowed like corpuscles along highways zooming in size. We bumped down and the pilot reversed thrust. Cabin activity commenced despite the programmed objection of the voice on the PA.

"A dive would have been fun," Nicole said, repacking her bag.

"I should have thought of it sooner."

Time. I wanted more of it as we fidgeted in our seats and followed Gramps into the egress line. Time for what? There was nothing here. How much time does it take to say ba-bye? Ask any flight attendant.

I said nothing as we entered the sparsely populated gate area. My flight to New Bern was ninety minutes and two concourses away. It could wait. We dawdled in the direction of the escalators down to the train tunnel. Without warning she said, "Can we stop a minute?"

"Are you all right?"

"That gate's empty. Let's go to the window."

A Delta 757 taxied by outside. As we watched it, Nicole was superimposed on the scene. She looked at me in the glass. "You remember my escapist movies," she said, drawing herself up tall. "Can I tell you a corny story?"

Anything for more time.

"Just now I imagined my leading man and I had flown in on a DC-3. It was a murky night, grainy black and white. We were crossing the tarmac toward the terminal lights.

He wore a fedora. I had on heels and a floppy-brimmed hat. Fate was about to sweep me away from him and I was frightened. I snagged a heel in a crack. He caught me."

"Lucky—"

"No, wait. I was all innocence and eyelashes, and innocents aren't responsible, are they? Ingrid Bergman is *my* teddy bear. But you deserve the truth. I tripped on purpose. You were supposed to catch me and you did. Thank you."

If she could confess, I could too. "Glad to do it. Want to know *my* dirty little secret? I'd do it again. Trip you myself if necessary, as often as you'd let me. I like to feel needed, and I keep score of good deeds. But for a moment up there you had me seeing things differently."

The knapsack slipped from her hand. "You too?"

"Just a glimpse of who I'd rather be. Annieula must be proud of you right now."

We embraced, carefully, as if we might break. I kissed the angle of her jaw. She shuddered. "And now?" she said.

"And now."

What I recall of our train ride to the terminal is Luie throwing elbows. *Get her address. Send a sympathy card, at least.* I refused to listen to him. *What's the matter?* he fussed, raising his voice. *Wake up you damned head case. Shame about old Matt. I hear his balls fell off from disuse. Get with the program, sport. You'll regret this; I promise you.*

Some time later we found Nicole's baggage carousel. She scanned the waiting crowd. By the information kiosk, a woman with bleached hair waved. She and a lanky man in a leather jacket started toward us. Nicole squeezed my hand.

I said, "Next time let's jump. You'll know it's okay if I forget to ask about that kiss."

"God bless you, Matt." She walked away.

Luie and I doubled back toward the security lines. *Nice touch at the end*, he said. *There may yet be hope. You may rely on me, Matthew.*

Right, I thought. Right.

Snakebit

M ANNY KRUG USED TO JOKE that his permanent tan was a product of Newark smog. He once told me, "If I coulda bottled that crap for suntan oil I'd have got out five years sooner, either rich or in the pen for causing cancer." Patio furniture had been a mundane venture by comparison, but a home store chain paid top dollar for Krug Fabrications just the same. When I met him, three years ago, he was in his mid-fifties, retired, a sharp-dressed engine block of a man, trophy wife on one arm and faded dice and daggers inked into the other. "Damn graffiti. Whatcha gonna do?" he shrugged. "Kids like me got more balls than brains."

His wife Connie was fifteen years younger than he, a busty farmer's daughter type who toyed shamelessly with Manny's libido. The perky redhead he breakfasted with might be a raven-haired temptress by nightfall. She kept him on his toes that way. Her variety gratified him, as did the stares she drew. He considered them a fitting tribute to his success. Connie, less grandiose than her husband, winked at her own advertising.

She liked to say that their ongoing honeymoon began in a southbound Cadillac blaring Springsteen the week after Manny sold his company. They wintered in the Keys and drove north with spring, partied in South Beach, learned the finer points of she-crab soup in Charleston and golfed at Pinehurst. Then they fell in love with the Blue Ridge Mountains.

Manny bought Lytle Camp, a sprawling tract at the head of Lytle Cove, on the strength of a realtor's yarn about the seller's ex-husband. He'd supposedly failed to inform her of the property's existence, let alone include her in the weekend romps he organized there for business associates. Although the story was mostly false the Krugs told it for true and embroidered it with lurid details, adding another dimension to a place already brimming with appeal.

Their farmhouse sat on a rise overlooking a private lake and waterside party house. Ducks and geese were seasonal guests. Bears wandered through. In the woods, pileated woodpeckers yammered like jungle birds in a Tarzan movie. Turkeys were tame and frequent visitors. While Manny mowed and pruned, Connie reclaimed weedy flowerbeds. The wanton greenness was a delightful change from Newark and the Oklahoma ranch where she'd been raised.

One Saturday last spring Manny phoned me. I met him and Connie at their garage. He was on the verge of hyperventilation.

"It ate the Ashleys," Connie indignantly told me. "All twelve of them. Ashley Mae, Sarah Ashley, Ashley Judd, Aunt Ashley. . . . At first I thought they were slipping out through a hole."

"Who?" I'd been in the cove almost as long as the Krugs and hadn't met any Ashleys.

"The Ashleys. Remember the feed store special on quail chicks?" Connie said.

I had no idea what she was talking about.

"Bobwhites. In Oklahoma I used to call them with a slide whistle."

That wasn't the confusing part. "The Ashleys?"

"I've known lots of Ashleys."

Middleclass conventions are a world away from Lytle Cove. It had been the rural disdain for them that lured me out into the county after my wife and I split up. Before then I'd thought of myself as a townie. Jennifer and I supplemented my income from the university counseling center by renovating derelict houses. We lived in them, saving money for the nice home in a nice neighborhood. But we never got there. Sawdust and mold and seven-day workweeks wore her down. The marriage was fortunate to crash before the housing market did. My share of the property settlement swung a loan on five acres and a trashed-out rancher in Lytle Cove, across the road from the Camp. Repair projects were my therapy. What can I say? I'm a fixer, even when the fixable stuff isn't what's really broken. Delicate projects, such as finishing sheetrock, were sometimes a trial for divorce blasted nerves. But the woodlot out front had recently been clear cut and was overgrown with brambles. There I slashed with gusto.

During one of my early sessions in the thicket, Manny and Connie walked over to introduce themselves. He wondered why I didn't hire a bulldozer to flatten the mess; I could come back with grass and ornamental trees. He knew a guy. I said I'd rather restore the natural vegetation and showed him more than a dozen species of sapling I'd already identified. He was impressed but worried about poisonous snakes. "Alf Waldrup killed a copperhead in my drive. Says there's rattlers in that rock outcrop above your house. One of those bastards gets you, oh boy."

No self-respecting snake wanted a taste of anything as rank as my boots and I told Manny so. In retrospect, I shouldn't have mentioned hoop snakes, the mythical beasts with deadly stingers and an ability to roll like a wheel, tail in mouth, destroying everything in their path. I made matters worse by telling him about the Appalachian religious tradition of snake-handling. Believers consumed by the Holy Spirit literally take up vipers and dance in church. Flicking reptile tongues test the air for imperfections of faith. Worshippers are occasionally bitten; a few die. Manny's discomfort with the subject eventually tipped me to his snake phobia. It took a while to reassure him that hoop snakes exist only in folklore.

On the Saturday Manny called, he needed another talking down. He stood beside Connie, trying to be supportive, while nervously shifting from foot to foot.

Connie said. "My chicks were so cute, like squirmy popcorn balls."

"We couldn't figure out how the damn things were getting away. They weren't going through the wire," Manny said.

She leaned into him for comfort. "Only Rasta Ashley was left. But this morning she was gone too. There was a snake. In the coop."

Manny patted her shoulder. "We'll fix that bastard, sweetie," he said. "Go on inside."

He waited for her to go in the house before pulling a shovel from his rack of garden tools and giving me the pick of what remained. It seemed impolite to decline. I chose a rake and eased into the empowering patter that calms phobic clients, reminding him that he didn't hesitate to shoo bears away from his trashcans. Dealt confidently with hornets. His steam engine breathing calmed as we neared the old apple orchard and homemade coop under the trees. Step by step. More and more confident and in control. We stopped well short of the pen. Manny'd built it of two by fours and screen wire, sensibly roofed with an oversized piece of plywood. I walked up to the coop alone.

A four-foot black snake regarded me coldly through the screen. The species is non-venomous. They're excellent mousers and take baby birds as well. Unfortunately, the Ashleys had been available. One corner of the plywood had warped away from the cage beneath, allowing the perp to enter. By ballooning the snake's craw too big for escape, Rasta Ashley had exacted her revenge.

Manny stabbed the blade of his shovel into the grass behind me.

I pointed to the gap under the lid. "The weather turned your coop into a diner."

Rather than come closer, he bent down for a better look.

"Nobody's fault, really," I said. "In a way, you have to feel a little sorry for this guy. Imagine it. You're on the road. It's mealtime and your stomach's growling. The smell from this place tempts you in. The food is pig-out heaven. But all of a sudden you're staring up a cop's gun barrel. It's all you can do to keep from freaking out. 'Wait a minute,' you say. 'Whatever's going on, it's not my fault. I'm just here for lunch.'"

Manny stabbed the ground again, less forcefully.

"But today, thankfully, we're on the other end of judgment day. We're the cops and it's this guy begging for consideration."

He hemmed and hawed and fingered the shovel handle. "You want that thing? Is that what you're saying, Doc?"

"My place has room for him."

"Well, he'd better stay there. If I see him again, he's dead."

Nothing more was said about the incident until several days later. I was in the checkout line at the grocery store, buying a six-pack of remedy for frustration. My last client of the afternoon, a computer science major, had complained about having to read novels for his humanities class and hated the hocus pocus of literary interpretation. To quote, "If it ain't on the page, it ain't there." I was at sea with him, a concept he couldn't entertain on dry land. Blindness to metaphor is becoming common among my clients. For these computer age literalists, paradise will no doubt be habitable software. The flat-earthers of tomorrow may be souls clinging to the irrational flesh.

My cell phone buzzed. Manny again. "You've got a pistol, don't you? Bring it over. We'll kill the son of a bitch! Bit me in the goddamn neck! I'll shoot him deader than hell!"

I told him I'd be there in fifteen minutes.

Connie ushered me into their bedroom. Manny sat on the bed in a red-faced rage with a gauze pad pressed to his neck. An uncapped bottle of rubbing alcohol trembled in his other hand. She took the bottle before he could spill it. When he removed the gauze I saw the long scrape over his jugular vein, a vampire bite minus fangs.

He told me he'd come in at the back door, pivoted into the kitchen and Bang! was struck by a black snake dangling out of the top of the pocket door slot. "Did you bring your pistol?" he growled. "Let's tear into that fuggin door."

The story sounded farfetched but his wound was indisputable. I set a bag of shooting gear beside him on the bed and loaded the clip of my .22 semi-auto with rat shot I'd been totting around for a decade. Better to risk a misfire than have long rifle slugs punch holes in the walls. "Ready," I said, snapping the clip into place. I didn't hand Manny the weapon. He wasn't in any condition.

He armed himself with a long flashlight and a short sword of a screwdriver. We lifted the pocket door off its track and removed it. No snake. No snake in the kitchen cabinets or under the sink where assorted paint cans and cleaning supplies assured a splatterfest of a shootout. We went downstairs to the earthen basement, tapped the duct-work, illuminated dark corners. No snake. The water heater sat on cinder blocks; the spider webs in the holes hadn't been disturbed.

Humans are wired to fear snakes. Some of us are able to suppress it. Others tempt fate by literally or figuratively embracing the feared object. A young woman I treated for dating anxiety discovered her cure in a photo of an ancient Minoan figurine. The outstretched arms of the wild-eyed, bare-breasted priestess held serpents as if offering them to the world at large. In her day, snakes were considered masters of the dark mysteries of life and death. The image inspired my client to arrive for our next session with snakes tattooed around her forearms. The inquisitive heads, on her wrists, came into view when she turned palms up. She wouldn't have been Manny's type.

He and I inspected the attic. No snake. Out of places to check we nailed a strip of baseboard over the empty slot where the pocket door had been. Connie mixed a pitcher of daiquiris. It was twilight, the air unseasonably hot, hazy as ground glass. Despite the heat and a snake in the house she wanted to stay on the front porch rather than go down to the party house at lakeside. It seemed that snakebite hadn't been the day's only trauma.

The morning had begun on a good note. While Connie went to the lake to sunbathe, Manny did yard chores. Still basking in the afterglow of his mercy at the quail coop, he'd seen a garter snake and spared it. To celebrate this latest display of compassion he took a break from work and adjourned to the porch to enjoy his lordly view.

"The water's sparkling," he told me. "Connie's there on the deck, sunbathing. Not a stitch on."

"Manny!"

He shushed her. "I go in for the binoculars. When I come out she's running up the steps screaming."

"It scared me half to death," Connie said. "Willis Wal-drup was in the party house, peeping through a window."

I was incredulous. Willis was Lytle Cove's most recognizable character, a good-natured scarecrow in bib overalls who kept a mouth hole singed in his graying Fu Manchu with unfiltered cigarettes. He and his ancient parents, Alf and Oma, were our nearest neighbors, a mountaineer family still living in the "temporary" log cabin Alf had built during the Great Depression—Oma was still waiting for the indoor plumbing he promised. Willis, a garrulous sixty-year-old failure to launch, whiled away his hours sitting under the pine tree in front of the cabin, waving loose-jointedly at passing cars and begging beers from anyone who stopped.

Unlike his lay-about son, Alf kept busy. Among other things, the old patriarch had been a bootlegger, only once arrested for it. "Twas my wife's cousin that lawed me. Soon as they turnt me loose, I burnt him out. Would of kilt him too, but for Oma." Alf's account of his wife's temper outsized her physical frame. He thought it hilarious that she'd addled him with a stick of stove wood for coming home drunk. "Why, I didn't blame her none for draggin me off in the creek after plantin a crop of pump-knots on my head. H'it renched off the blood, don't you know."

"Are you sure it was Willis?" I asked Connie.

"Absolutely. Nobody could mistake that dirty hair and moustache."

"So, after I see to Connie I go looking for him," Manny said. "Every chicken in Waldrup's goddammed yard scatters when I turn the Caddy in. Gravel flying everywhere. Naturally, Willis is nowhere to be seen."

"You could've been shot," Connie said.

"That old man isn't going to shoot me. He was hoeing corn. I march out there into the garden and light into him about Willis. He listens. When I finish he says, 'You'll want to tell that to Willis. I'll get him for ye.' We go to the house and he raps his hoe on the side of it. 'Feller to see ye, boy. Git on outcheer and say hey.'

"Alf is a trip," I said. "Never gets mad."

"Yeah? Maybe he should. Willis is a sicko. He comes to the door but won't step outside to take what he deserves. Snivels about asking Connie for a beer. I tell him to shut his lying trap, not to worry about the goddamned sheriff. 'If you set foot on my land again your dead ass is leaving in the garbage truck.' And I mean it too. I put the fear of god in him."

"How'd Alf take that?"

"Just nods and says, 'Well.' I shake his hand and come home."

"You called the sheriff?"

Connie said, "He wouldn't let me."

"And have the locals think I'm a candy-ass? No way. So I walk in the door and that fuggin snake nails me. I don't mind telling you, my stomach is still in a knot."

Liquor and nightfall brought a measure of relief. He asked to borrow the pistol. I reluctantly lent it to him.

The wail of an approaching siren roused me after midnight. Lights flashed through the trees at the Krugs'. No one answered their phone. I pulled on some clothes and went over. The back door was propped open. A female paramedic with a clipboard barked at me to leave. Connie invited me in. I gathered that she'd been putting a travel bag together for Manny rather than concentrating on the EMT's questions.

Mine could wait. "Connie, this lady needs information," I said. "Let's sit a minute."

I heard indistinct voices in the bedroom.

Connie told the woman that Manny hadn't been able to sleep. "He wouldn't quit flipping the light on, thinking he heard a snake. It got to where I thought I heard it too. Slithering."

The EMT scribbled. "He complained of nausea?"

"He's not a complainer. I wish he'd take better care of himself."

"The caller mentioned nausea."

"His stomach, yes. And he couldn't sleep. He was sweating and breathing hard. I had to call; I'm sorry. Will he be okay? Tell me he will."

Manny returned home six days later with a triple bypass and bag full of pills, appointment slips and rehab instructions. Pillow pressed against the crooked line of staples puckering his chest he cursed surgeons who couldn't sew straight. "In the furniture business, guys who sew like this sweep floors."

He was supposed to exercise on a treadmill. I set one up in their living room. They both used it. He took his medications faithfully and went on a low-fat diet. The insomnia persisted; he blamed post-op pain. Connie confided that it was really nightmares. Snakes choked him in his dreams. He only felt safe napping in the daytime, on the porch divan. At one month the surgeon was happy with Manny's postoperative progress but the sleep disorder persisted.

Sirens woke me again on the night of the fire. Flames at the party house were visible from my driveway. I parked up at the Krugs'. Though the lights were on inside, my call through the back door got no response. Around front I saw fire engines, private vehicles, an ambulance and the volunteer fire chief's SUV blocking the lake access road. People shouted and ran silhouetted by floodlights and fire glow. The blaze was confined to the far end of the building. I didn't suppose there was much I could do but went down anyway.

Connie met me on the lower steps. "This has gone too far," she said. Manny sat on the road beside the ambulance. An EMT had a blood pressure cuff on him.

"Is he okay? Are you?"

"He tried to put it out with a garden hose. He says he's fine but I want them to be sure."

"What happened?"

"There was this loud whoosh. We got out of bed and there was another one and a fireball. Manny told me to call 911. He ran out with that damn rifle before I could stop him."

"Rifle?"

"The sheriff took your pistol." She started toward Manny, who'd finished his medical checkup. He was talking to the fire chief.

With mounting concern I followed her.

"Hi, Doc," Manny said. "Take care of Connie for a minute, will you? I'm telling the chief what happened." He turned to the man. "I smelled gas. I didn't see the son of a bitch but it was Waldrup."

Connie and I walked to a spot with an unobstructed view of the dousing operation. They'd knocked down the flames but stinking clouds of steam and smoke still boiled from the charred wall. She asked, "Is it out?"

"Under control," I said. "What's this about the sheriff and my pistol?"

"You know those naps Manny takes? They make it hard for him to sleep at night. So I . . . You remember how it was the other time? Yesterday he was snoozing on the divan. I told him I was going to sunbathe and set out his binoculars." She paused, embarrassed.

"Makes sense," I said.

"So anyway, I went down. All of a sudden, there was shooting."

"Manny?"

"He didn't hear me yelling for him to stop until he ran out of bullets. When I got up to the house he said Willis had been behind the party house. It was me that called the sheriff. I'm sorry the deputy took your gun. He said, 'Rat shot or AK-47, doesn't matter. You can't open fire in this situation.'"

"And Willis?"

"Thank god, Manny missed."

No surprise there. Waldrup must have been two hundred yards away from Manny's position on the porch. The effective range of rat shot is approximately spitting distance.

"I meant was Willis arrested?"

She nodded. "He got out today. Manny bought a deer rifle. He can't handle that gun, not in his condition. He fired a test shot into the lake and hurt himself where they split his breastbone."

Manny and Connie had a rough go of it after the fire. Investigators recovered two plastic fuel cans, melted beyond any ability to yield fingerprints. Arson dogs were brought in but didn't turn up anything conclusive. The Waldrups claimed they'd been asleep until the fire trucks woke them. Pending a confession, the lead investigator said he couldn't file charges.

The strain of the impotent prognosis was showing when I had the Krugs over for supper a few days later. They hadn't mentioned the rifle to anyone involved with the investigation. Manny told me he'd propped the .30-06 on the deck rail when he decided to fight the fire. He was sure the Waldrups had the rifle now because it was gone after the firemen left and they didn't mention noticing it. In Manny's mind self-protection meant buying another gun. Connie refused to consider the idea. Tempers flared. During dessert, low-fat blackberry cobbler, I had an idea. "Why not put this on hold? Take a vacation. Call it a cooling off period."

"Concede defeat?" Manny fumed. "I can't let those sons of bitches get away with it. This is about respect."

Connie put down her spoon. "Manny, please. You're the one I care about. I don't want you dead or in jail. Listen to what Doc says. You haven't been the same since that snake bit you."

Which snake? I wondered to myself. The one in the pocket door? Or the one that wormed its way into the human psyche thousands of years ago to remind us that we've never got things all figured out? Whether in the guise of foe or risky ally, that serpent is a disrupter of worlds. It cares nothing for fairness, lucky charms, whistling in the dark or carefully crafted schedules that tick reassurance like a kid's stick on a picket fence. On some level aren't we wise to our own charade? But we cast the protective spells anyway, dance with serpents, drink the blood of cobras. My literalist client and his fellow pioneers of the digital age may be unequipped to register the serpent's existence but they're as vulnerable as anybody else. Let them call it bad luck or react instinctively as Connie did. She sensed the life being squeezed out of her husband and fought to save him.

That weekend the Krugs left for a month on the coast of Maine. I kept an eye on party house repairs for them. There were no further acts of vandalism. A good contractor and total lack of rain moved the job along. Connie's gardens suffered in the drought. I watered the plants within reach of a hose. While swimming in the lake one evening I found the .30-06 on the bottom, far out and partially covered with pond weed. In the confusion of the fire Connie must have given the rifle her best heave. I finished disposing of it for her.

I was sorry when she emailed to tell me they wouldn't be returning to North Carolina. Manny had put Lytle Camp up for sale. For a minute or two I envied the narrow tidiness of bulldozing a problem, and this card-carrying fixer of the unfixable wallowed in a Sisyphean funk. What was I getting, really, in return for the endless toil of pushing rocks uphill? An illusion of self-importance? Screw that. Why not just kick aside the rocks that can't be avoided and move on, no questions asked? Because, I decided, although self-assurance is essential, it's *always* an illusion. Regardless of the form it takes. We can plow straight ahead, ignore the inconvenient, ink confidence into our arms. I prefer mine in mythic context, widescreen, with a full soundtrack and option for color commentary.

A realty sign appeared across the road at Lytle Camp. So did a pungent odor at my mailbox. Draped over a branch of the nearby mulberry tree was a dead black snake. The bulge in its midsection couldn't still have been Rasta Ashley.

Music of the Spheres

"FUNERAL SPRAYS? You know how your intuition amazes me," Brad said, "but I'm struggling with this one." He was speaking to Kate Alango, his lover and creative partner in the cutting edge greeting card company, Kop a Platitude. The two sat at their breakfast table chasing morning cobwebs with second cups of coffee. Kate had awakened with an idea for a new line aimed at an untapped market, the soon-to-be-deceased.

"Terminally ill," she'd said, "is such a pastel euphemism. People are sick of the wink and nod."

Despite the caffeine, Brad wasn't focusing. He wanted to forget work for a while. Kate's half-buttoned shirt framed her cleavage beautifully.

She, noticing, finished buttoning the shirt. "Then how about Return to Earth?"

"Maybe, baby," he said, sounding less than convinced. "But okay. Here's a card. Two society types at an artist's funeral. One says, 'Frankly, I'd hoped for something more original.'"

"How very New York. Impersonal, stiff, formaldehyde finish. Would it hurt to add a little feeling? A couple of matrons stand at the casket of a departed girlfriend. One whispers to the other, 'Artie stopped buying the headache excuse.'"

Brad frowned.

"Dying wives will love it. What's more polite than informing an emotionally retarded male that Momma won't be fixing dinner tonight?"

Brad detected a chill in the ether. Kate had cranked up her cutlasses.

Bradford Stevenson has a special gift. He's able to "see" people's mental structures the way New Agers "see" auras. He says mentalities are more varied than most of us realize.

His own, for example, is a Rube Goldberg contraption of found objects networked with miles of pipe and wire. Lights blink. Cogwheels mesh. Pendulums, salvaged from grandfather clocks and a pocket edition of Poe, swing asynchronous tick tocks. Birds wing through his superstructure. A few never leave. Swooshed into the hereafter by a brass announcement at the business end of time, a glass-eyed owl now rides the bowsprit, searching eternity for mice.

Not all mentalities are mobile, Brad says, but his is, thanks to a sail and a rebuilt tricycle with monster truck tires. His customary seat on the trike is directly underneath a crooked finger of a broadcast tower raised to sky-tickling height. He shuns the common practice of decorating it with pennants—he's not selling used cars. Outgoing messages originate on an upright manual typewriter, each key linked to a remote striker. Think of a church organ sounded by hammers rather than air. "W" is the deep reverberation produced by a ball-peen tap on eight-inch diameter PVC. A similar pipe filled with water clunks "K." Fronting the rank of pipes, a motley selection of glass vessels dings out vowels. Incoming communications hum down to him on the tower's guy wires.

Music of the Spheres

Although he prefers audible conversation, Brad is equipped to send and receive via the emotional ethernet that conveyed Kate's displeasure. His detector is a popular design. Version 1.0 took shape in his baby crib as he thrashed, reaching for the fan paddling slow circles above him. Today his system resembles a helicopter rotor with ironing board blades and Hula Hoop control rings. It hangs inside the tower above his tricycle, rotating in the etheric breeze. Active control of blade pitch and speed converts it to a transmitter. Brad can kick up a variety of storms but seldom does. Some years ago he added a flywheel enabling preprogramed blade adjustments. During tedious discussions he's prone to make use of this autopilot capability.

How can men be so oblivious? Kate thought. The Funeral Sprays idea was one of two things she'd brought with her out of sleep. The other was a fog of dread. The babble about stupid greeting cards hadn't dispersed it. She buttoned her shirt and zinged Brad to attention but too late to prevent the fog from crystallizing into a decision.

Brad describes Kate's mentality as a viny castle, convoluted as the calligraphy of a medieval Celt. Organic-looking stethoscopes project along the ground, picking up vibrations he's unequipped to detect. She has two modest broadcast antennas, English and Spanish, but ethernet is her specialty. There's an antique Basque windmill, a carnival ride with wicker seats, and an intricately rendered solar system complete with major moons. She's also got the whirling ring of cutlasses, a daunting offensive weapon. Brad's ironing boards have been savaged by more than one encounter with it. The racket is dreadful, not to mention a threat to delicate control mechanisms.

⌘

It wasn't Brad's weird visual imagination that won Kate over to him. They shared a delight in perceptual nuance. The slither of an oyster slurped in the raw might set the mood for an entire evening. A blissful dissolution they'd shared while hearing "Manhã De Carnaval" in *Black Orpheus* inspired Kop a Platitude's bestselling card.

> happy anniversary baby
> i'd put a flower on our
> finger if we had one

Kate collected their breakfast dishes. "I know the cards were my idea but it sucks. Okay?"

"It's Dusky, isn't it?" Brad said. He watched her march the dishes to the sink. In they went, clattering.

She clutched the sink rim as if to keep herself from falling in. "How am I supposed get my head around this? He's dying? I should have divorced the asshole years ago." The countertop absorbed a cup-trembling thwack. "But I didn't. Then I couldn't because he was sick. Now this." She turned like a cornered animal. "The mistresses *du jour* aren't around; count on that. His mother's in a nursing home. Once again the wife is left holding the bag. Why couldn't he have a heart attack and be done with it?"

Brad went to her and gathered her in. Dusky's condition unnerved him as well. He and Jules "Dusky" Sandusky had been undergrad classmates in Charlottesville. They'd become friendly in the process of one-upping each others efforts to sabotage the heinously boring lectures of a general studies English instructor. Eventually the reMarx brothers, as they called themselves, shared an apartment, spent holidays at each other's homes. Kathryn Alango was the latecomer. An art major with too much forehead to be conventionally pretty, she nonetheless had a knack for causing men to forget whatever else was on their minds.

Her suitors generally fared no better than moths at a bug zapper but hopefuls didn't seem to care.

Brad had tried the gentleman's approach to courtship. Dusky, a happy-go-lucky rake who considered it unsporting to pass a doorknob without testing it, took Kate's as a special challenge. The outcome was never in doubt to anyone except Brad. The sounds filtering in through his bedroom wall often drove him to camp out on the living room couch, sonically blanketed with the smoky melancholy of Yvonne Lanauze fronting Duke Ellington's orchestra on "Sophisticated Lady" and "Mood Indigo." Brad dated other girls, fitfully, but was caught in a Martian orbit around Kate. The weather conditions there were monotonous: sunny and cold.

Dusky cheated on her through the remainder of fall term, Christmas break and after classes resumed. Brad kept his silence about it until the day she directly asked him where Dusky was. Brad told her, not mentioning the girl she'd find with him at the cross-town bar. Tensions in the apartment boiled over. Dusky accused Brad of disloyalty. Kate let herself be talked out of recognizing the plain truth and took Dusky back on condition that she always know his whereabouts. Not even *Asleep at the Wheel* could drown out the ecstasies of make-up sex.

Brad moved out, but the three of them had stayed in touch. Dusky was accepted into medical school. Kate went with him to Chapel Hill, held her artistic nose and took an ad agency job. Brad and his own new bride attended the couple's wedding before Dusky began his surgical residency. When he joined a practice in Norfolk, Kate opened a design studio there. Brad, by then an associate editor for the *Altamont Bugle*, launched Kop a Platitude as an outlet for pent-up sarcasm. His first series of birthday cards, designed by Kate, sold so quickly that he continued the long distance collaboration and quit the *Bugle*, to the chagrin of his wife. She saw it as proof of instability. The divorce was amicable.

All the while Dusky chased other women. The Sanduskys' marriage repeatedly strained, split and reconciled. In a letter to Brad, Dusky blamed his mother, Millie, for his sexual addiction; "I inherited her birth sign. It's neon and flashes OPEN ALL NIGHT."

That comment prompted a sharp retort from Brad and led him to surprise Millie with a visit when he was in Atlanta on business. She'd been flamboyant but not outrageous in the Charlottesville days. The last he'd seen her was at Dusky's wedding. Since then, they'd exchanged holiday cards. Her low-income efficiency apartment in a bad neighborhood shocked him but her physical deterioration was more appalling. She greeted him drunk, wearing a ratty housecoat and slippers. There was no possibility of taking her out to eat as he'd planned. Given the mess of fast food bags and boxes in the kitchenette he decided against trying to cook for her. He went to the nearest supermarket and returned with roast chicken, fixings and a gallon of sweet tea. Maybe the story she told as they ate was true; Brad hoped not.

She told him that Jules—she didn't call him Dusky—was already into sex as a kindergartner. The first time she caught him in the bathroom with one of his stepfather's magazines she'd forced the boy to waddle to the kitchen where, pants still around his ankles, she sat him at the table for a unique version of The Talk.

It began, "Jules, sugar, don't be embarrassed. It's your nature. I saw it the minute the doctor held you up and swatted your skinny little behind."

Brad tried to change the subject.

Millie didn't take the cue. "He kept grabbing at his pants. I wouldn't let him pull them up. 'No!' I said, 'they're fine where they are, sugar. It's what I'm talking to you about.'"

She said she'd intended to name him Chuck, after Chuck Yeager, the fighter pilot who broke the sound barrier. But, at birth, the baby's scrotum was all out of proportion to the rest of him, big and red as Rudolph's nose. "Those balls just sang out, 'We're here.' So I had no choice, don't you see, Brad? The nurse misspelled his name on the certificate. But, oh well. Isn't that a stitch?"

Millie cackled a throaty gale. "Jules didn't see the humor. Tried to run from the table. I sat his ass back down. 'They don't look so god almighty anymore,' I told him. 'But looks are deceiving, aren't they, sugar? If there's anything in the world I know, it's a horn dog. And you are one.'"

If nothing else, that atrocious account gave Brad a new perspective on the unusual makeup of his friend's mentality. Dusky was shielded by mirrors, a disco ball, impenetrable. Now, with scleroderma hardening Dr. Sandusky to leather inside and out, the defenses had cracked. He'd called Kate for help—three years after she left him for Brad. Her dilemma about how to respond had thickened the air at home for days. As Brad held her in the kitchen, she sagged in his embrace.

"I have to go to him, Brad," she said, lifting his arms away.

"Of course. Do what you need to."

"I'll call. Let *me* do that, okay? You know how he can be." Kate still called her husband on a regular basis but Dusky neither called nor wrote, perhaps not wanting to be reminded that he'd been dumped.

Jealousy never had to make sense. Brad said, "I'll be here."

Kate drove from Altamont to Norfolk, from Brad to Dusky, in a state verging on nausea. Had Brad fretted about the possibility of losing her again she might have unpacked her suitcase. But he hadn't. His concern was her welfare. So gallant. So bloodless. She'd fought an urge to administer heart massage to him with both fists.

Though well-schooled in the varied flavors of romance, she couldn't figure Brad out. He bared himself to her as no *man* ever had, fully and joyously. His devotion rang true at every chakra. She was sure their connection predated this life. How could she not love him? But he said his openness was only possible because his wellbeing didn't depend on her, that if one day she chose to leave she was free to go. Kate's inner feminist delighted in this, but the woman in her feared he might be telling the truth. Yoga, meditation and assorted pagan practices had not prepared her for a lover who claimed such equanimity. It sounded beatific but she suspected it was bullshit.

Ironically, Brad credited *her* with triggering his in-human peace of mind. Shortly before their affair began, he said, his long-frustrated love for her reached critical mass and imploded. He realized then that the communion he craved with life was already his; only a straitjacket of beliefs had kept him from knowing it. The more beliefs he suspended, the richer his experience. "You provoked me to freedom," he'd told her. "My fondest dream is to repay that favor. The day you join me on the green hills beyond the existential desert we'll let the raindrops turn our absinthe to milk, gaze back across the way we've come and be gentle with our ignorance." Kate felt as indeterminate as Schrödinger's cat when Brad talked this way. Perhaps his ex-wife had been right about him.

Kate was met at the door of her former home by an occupational therapist who introduced herself as Sara Gunn. Inside, they found Dusky seated in the formal dining room. He hauled himself to his feet. In a breathy monotone he said, "Wondered when you'd show."

The sight of him dispelled any temptation to jealousy. Her husband had shriveled to a husk. His jaundiced eyes were trapped deep in their sockets, incapable of roaming. Brown wisps on a blotchy scalp were all that remained of his vainglorious curls. Flesh-starved skin stretched taut across his cheeks and nose. Behind desiccated lips, Dusky's teeth were raised on their rootstalks as if repelled by his gums. Out of habit Kate gave him a peck on the mouth. It stank like a dead man's. She thanked goddess that the skeleton in Dusky's clothes kept its hands to itself.

Sara invited her to observe Dr. Sandusky drink a can of dietary supplement. After that, she added with therapeutic enthusiasm, she'd leave the two of them alone. She disappeared into the kitchen.

Dusky lowered himself into his chair but wasn't happy about it. "Hell with the damned supplement," he said. "Bring me an Oxycontin and vodka tonic. I don't need lessons in decrepitude now that you're home."

Sara reappeared with a small can, a soda straw and an odd utensil with a stirrup strap. She set the can and straw on the placemat in front of Dusky. "This is the chocolate flavor you enjoy." She handed the thingamabob to him. "Here's the adaptive opener. Slide it on your hand and push the hook under the tab. Show Mrs. Sandusky."

"This girl is driving me nuts, Kate. Get her out of here."

Kate, feeling as if she'd walked into the wrong house, stammered, "Let's see you do it."

Sara nodded, grinning. She was perhaps thirty, delicately featured. She'd pulled her russet hair up in a Japanese topknot. A sensible choice, Kate thought, as was the avoidance of jewelry. The patterned smock, jeans and jogging shoes were standard healthcare issue. During her years with Dusky, Kate had had occasion to study many such women. Those that attracted him resisted industrial anonymity in some personal detail. Sara, in addition to the topknot, expressed her individuality through fingernails. Necessarily short, they were filed in perfect almond curves. Fresh jade polish picked up the green of her eyes. Dusky's swinish misery dismissed her as a girl, but her manner projected an abundance of feminine confidence.

Dusky cursed, fumbling with the opener. His hands were curled, waxy white as though gloved in paraffin. Kate saw that he couldn't hold a scalpel, let alone tie the dexterous one-handed knots that were a surgeon's stock in trade. She was about to reach for the can but Sara said, "You can do it, Dr. Sandusky. No fair taking advantage of your wife."

"Kate," Kate said. "Call me Kate."

"What a strong name. It suits you. Dr. Sandusky is a lucky man."

He snarled, "Shit. Get out. I don't need you anymore. Kate, do this for me."

Kate glanced to Sara, then said, "I don't think so. Open the can and drink it. Then Sara can go."

"Well, damn," Dusky snapped. "You haven't changed a bit, have you?" He succeeded in prying up the tab without spilling much on the placemat. With the straw wedged between two fingers he stripped off the paper wrapper.

"Good," Sara said. "See what he can do, Kate? Illness is so demoralizing. It takes firmness and lots of encouragement to help some people maintain self-esteem."

Kate decided Sara would be sticking around.

"Life is a process for carrying ashes from one place to another," read the scrawl on Kop a Platitude's workroom whiteboard. Brad and the marketing director were brainstorming ideas for a Funeral Sprays card when Kate finally called from Norfolk. It was her third day away. He took the call in his office.

"Kate?"
"Hi," she said.
"Hi."

Brad and Kate exchange this greeting in a special tone of voice. "Hi" is their temple bell, a call to presence. Kate imagines the two of them as saffron-robed monks sitting opposite each other on Himalayan mountainsides, separated by an impassible rushing river. At the sound of "Hi," they leave the bodies behind and meet in midair, weightless.

Brad relaxed. "I miss you."
"Thank you."
"You're welcome."
Three simple phrases, a chord rich with overtones. After a time, she said, "It's so good to hear your voice."
"I've been worried. How are you? How's Dusky?"
"He's asleep. I wish I were."
"Tell me."
There was another silence. "It's bad. I think he's starving to death but he won't consider a nursing home. A therapist is doing what she can for him here and I'm trying to learn but it's hard. The pills affect his mind. He hates everything and everybody. When I looked in the mirror this morning I saw an old lady. Do you believe that I went out and bought hair color? Then I threw it away. It's . . . It's like . . ."
"Baby, I'm here."
"I can't stop remembering Charlottesville, the way he was then, your goofy engineer's hat on the end table. I was a bitch to come between you guys. Have I ever admitted that? Now, it's like I deserve this."
"Kate—"
"You know that port wine we used to drink? I bought a bottle. As soon as Sara left, I poured glasses for Dusky

and me. He won't drink anything but alcohol without an argument. Do you realize how sickly sweet that stuff is? How did we ever stomach it?"

"I'll catch a plane. I can be there in the morning."

"Don't. Things are confusing enough. I just need to hear your voice. We were so young."

"Some things don't change."

"Don't they?"

"No, they don't."

He heard an exasperated sigh. Her next breath was calmer. She ventured a playful dodge. "What you do to a girl ought to be illegal."

"What I ought to be, is there."

She was upset again. "*Dusky's* resentment is enough for right now."

"I don't resent you, Kate."

"You should. Don't make me resent *you* for not. On this planet, Brad, we need things. Love is measured in units of pain."

"You rescued me from that. I wish—"

"You're an alien."

"Best alien you ever met."

"He's waking up. Got to go."

Omar Khayyam's patriarchal Moving Finger flicked at Kate in her dreams. She set about erasing all It ever writ and woke exhausted. Dusky also had a hard night. In the morning she found him in a recliner, purple-lipped, complaining that a rodent was gnawing his esophagus. For once he didn't give her any guff about wearing the oxygen prongs. She took it as a sign of progress. Sara would be pleased.

Brad slept poorly as well, turning Kate's frazzled call over in his mind. He didn't like what the ethernet told him. Her moons were in full eclipse, her cutlasses too creaky to whirl. He feared she might be overmatched in Norfolk.

After an early Parks & Rec Advisory Council meeting, where he talked the Chief of Police into casting the deciding vote in favor of a downtown skatepark, he dialed Dusky's number.

The answering voice croaked, "Whozzis?"

Brad heard the familiar buzz of a drawn-out z. "It's Brad, Dusky. How are you? You sound like you just finished ten rounds in the gym."

"Dying'll do that."

"Kate told me you're having it rough. She called yesterday."

"Called you?"

"Yesterday. How can I help? If there's anything you need . . ."

"Uh huh."

"Dusky? Seriously, I feel for you. How's Kate?"

"Mine, Stevenson. Get it straight. Mine." He spat the phrases like bloody quids into a bucket. "Cut the crap. Not in the mood. After I'm gone. For now, you lose. Don't call again."

"Hold on, Dusky, you misunderstand. Listen—"

"Like hell."

"Hey, no arguments, okay? I'm *your* friend too. I care about both of you."

"Spin it on your stereo. That's all you get. Long as I'm around." The line went dead.

No wonder Kate's distress, Brad thought, if she were being subjected to the sort of wild haymakers her husband had just thrown at him. This wasn't Dusky's typical style of fighting. He lulled opponents to inattention, gutted them with a witty slash and then apologized as if the wound were accidental, "Oh, did I do that?" He had used his entire trick bag when Kate informed him that she was leaving him for Brad. She'd held her ground in the onslaught and Brad, to his own amazement, escaped without a scratch.

The invulnerability that surprised him then had since become second nature. It was another consequence of the psychological implosion that had permanently altered his mentality. Brad compared it to the film of the Bikini Atoll nuclear blast running backwards.

Kate had set it in motion by changing a ground rule of their relationship. They'd invariably held their card business meetings in Norfolk. Brad tested her boundaries if she and Dusky were on the outs, but nothing ever came of it. Then one Monday she phoned to say she'd be in Altamont that weekend. Could he recommend a restaurant? Brad kicked himself as he volunteered to show her the town. Dumb animals could learn; why couldn't he?

By the Thursday before her arrival he was so scattered that he spared the office staff and took a mental health day. At home he stared into the computer monitor, pondering his situation in doggerel verse. He revisited twenty years of hollowness, living as a broken chord without the sound of Kate's "Yes." Frustration poured through his fingertips in words breaking the confines of meter and rhyme. They spilled across the screen at increasing speed, aggravating the pressure he felt, not relieving it.

His broadcast tower began to vibrate. Pendulums swung erratically, losing track of time. The stuffed owl gripped the bowsprit for all it was worth as the ironing board fan swayed in widening excursions above the tricycle. He pedaled like hell but the monster truck tires squalled in place, enveloping him in smoke and fumes of burning rubber. The shaking in the tower worsened, threatening collapse.

His fingers typed on, trembling, uncaring as grammar and spelling were swept away by nonsense and nonsense degenerated to gibberish. Images of animal sacrifice burst in blinding flashes. Hooves trampled the keyboard. Even that became, at last, impossible.

At that instant the swarming energy winked out. Brad was a Pacific island, at peace and at home in the wide blue sea. Trade winds caressed his palm trees. The eternal tide lapped at sands bleached white in the tropic sun. Man and his works were expunged, nowhere to be seen.

This remarkable quietude extended to his mental contraption. The tower ceased to vibrate. Tires stopped spinning. Pendulums and ironing boards resumed normal function. But Brad had vanished. A single sheet of three-hole notebook paper salvaged from the quadratic thickets of Algebra II fluttered down and landed on the upholstered trike seat. On it was written a mathematical symbol:

$$i$$

Engineers and math freaks may intuit the significance of this development. For the benefit of those who skipped Algebra II or suffered through it like a year at the dentist, "i" is the $\sqrt{-1}$. The square root of -1 is the basic imaginary number, so-called because it doesn't exist in the real world. Any positive or negative real number, when multiplied by itself, yields a positive answer.

$$1x1=1$$
$$-1x-1=1$$

i is unattainable but no less valuable for that.

Brad had perked up in class the day his teacher revealed the mysteries of *i*. She described it as a gateway to quantum mechanics and Schrödinger's indeterminate cat, an unfortunate creature that sits in a closed box with an unstable atom and bottle of cyanide gas for company. If the atom decays, the poison is released and the cat dies. The odds are fifty-fifty. But until a measurement is taken the atom exists in both states simultaneously: decayed and undecayed. Schrödinger's cat is both alive and dead. It's the act of lifting the lid that eliminates one state of feline being. "Think of *i* as a bridge," the teacher had said. "It materializes to carry us across territory real numbers can't span. Then when we reach our destination it disappears again, leaving us on solid ground with a real result." Dead or alive.

What adolescent science fiction buff could resist such bait? Brad filed the factoid away, where it stayed until his implosion. Then I transformed to *i*. Brad ceased to be a real number.

He'd effortlessly welcomed Kate to Altamont. Over apple tamales at Café 12•22, she commented on his breezy manner.

"It's because I love you," he said, "and now it doesn't hurt."

The baldness of it drew an uneasy look.

"Don't worry. I used to think it had to be reflected off you to count. Now I realize it doesn't matter and I don't either. Hallelujah."

"What are you talking about?"

Exploring that question became an ongoing adventure for them both. They vanished in spaces unknown during his marriage. He wasn't sure whether it was because he loved her like there was no tomorrow or because the explanatory convenience of "Brad" had lost its receptor for personal anguish.

i was the revelation he wished for Kate. She was able to meet him in the air when they were together. But as long as a real Kate sat on a Himalayan mountainside or any other place, she remained exposed and at risk from landslides such as Dusky.

An email sent from Dusky's address arrived as Brad prepared for bed.

⌘

Damn it, Brad! Because of what you did, I
don't know whether to tell you this, but I

have to tell someone. DON'T DO ANYTHING. I appreciate your concern for me, in fact I love it, but this is my problem. Let me handle it. All I need is for you to listen.

Dusky's blood pressure was bad today. Sara called Dr. Prigogine and we went to the emergency room for tests. I don't understand everything, but Dusky is near the end. Hospice will be here in the morning.

I'll miss Sara. She has a better sense of humor than I do. Dusky bitches about her, but I saw how he primped when the doorbell rang. She promises to still drop by. I hope she does. They say the hospice people are good too.

Love,
Kate

He hoped she'd forgive his reply.

Dear Kate,

Baby, I'm sorry. Nothing else is coming. I'll try again in the morning. I wish there was more I could do. Please know I'm with you.

As always love,
b

He lay awake, conjuring inadequate fantasies of how best to support her. After midnight he bored himself into unconsciousness by chanting a mental sticky note to self: I need an answer before I wake up. As first light glowed on the bedroom wall, a rush of anxiety roused him. He stifled it, dozed again and got lucky.

Dear Kate;

Last night I went to bed feeling as helpless as you must feel. The veils are stripped away. It's down to you and Dusky and unanswerable questions.

Mr. Stevenson, your response please? What to say. How to say it. Whether, apart from the necessity of saying *something*, content actually matters.

There's a time for whistling in the dark with greeting cards. People like escapes and who's to blame them? But it's too late for that now.

This morning I dreamed that a friend visited me at the house where I grew up. Half his face was yellow from cancer. He wanted to talk, while he still could, about what mattered to him. We commiserated about friends we'd already lost. I told him about Dusky. We were just two guys who valued each other's company, glad of a chance to let each other know it. Then he was gone. I cried.

It sounds insignificant but, for as long as I can remember, my tears have been reserved for underdogs who beat the odds, never for sadness or pain. But grief set me off in this dream. I cried for you, for me, for Dusky, for all we've lost and all we will lose and not a thing we can do to stop it.

Somehow, though, I was still observing. The tears weren't all sad. The old underdog was mixed in there, crying for joy. It came to me after I woke up that human contact is an affirmation, a defiance. What we are to each other may be the only force strong enough to raise existence above the level of intolerable cruelty. Like Leonard Cohen says, holy or broken, it's still Hallelujah.

Much as I once hated it, you and Dusky touched each other. I hope you find a way to rediscover the comfort of that miracle.

As always love,
b

He received a disheartening reply.

Where did you pull this out of? You break my heart. Its tough on her, I know. I'm goinggto let her see this, like I didnt. Make you happy? Sje has nursy Gunn for company both of them are against me sick of this shit. cometo the funereal. I"ll be all ears.

Kate wrote later in the afternoon.

What am I going to do with you? I'm crying too. You drive me crazy, you crazy alien. You and your original Hallelujah. On Earth we listen to the version k.d. lang sings. It includes

a warning about people like you. Did I ever
tell you?

Love,
Kate

Ten days later, on the eve of the funeral, Brad flew
to Norfolk. The idea of staying at Dusky's house didn't
appeal to him any more than it did Kate. He booked a room
at a bed and breakfast and cabbed over to the funeral home,
arriving toward the end of visitation.

Except for Kate and Millie, demented beyond caring
in Georgia, Dusky had no family. But the funeral home
was busy. Pages of names in the guest book testified to
an extensive network of colleagues and friends. Floral
displays lined the walls. Several, propped on easels beside
the closed casket, were enormous. Brad spied Kate with an
elderly couple, standing off to the side. She wore a black
dress he hadn't seen before. It looked good on her. She
spotted him admiring it and excused herself to greet him.
The lines on her face were deeper, her embrace tired.

"Hi," Brad whispered in her ear.

"Hi."

He heard complication in the note she struck. "How
are you holding up?"

"I'm fine. It seems endless, but Sara and the hospice
people are walking me through it. Sara's over there." She
pointed to a sneaker-shod group across the room. "I'll
introduce you." She led him over and touched the back of
a redhead in a tweed jacket and jeans. "Sara," Kate said,
"Meet Brad."

Sara turned and drawled a friendly, "Hey."

"Glad to meet you," Brad said. "Kate says you've done
a wonderful job. Thanks."

Sara went subtly professional. "Don't thank me. Kate's a trouper. I enjoyed working with her and Dr. Sandusky."

"Did you get your schedule rearranged?" Kate asked her.

"I'll be there."

"Brad, Sara will be sitting with us at the funeral. She steadies me."

"Excellent," Brad said. "The more support the better."

The service was a lavish affair, held in the Basilica of St. Mary. Dusky had been a nominal Catholic, also, it seemed, a generous supporter of Church charities. The sanctuary was full of men in expensive suits and women with hankies. According to Kate, many of the latter were Dusky's old girlfriends. Despite the humiliating circumstances she carried herself with class. Dusky didn't deserve his widow.

Brad stayed over in Norfolk to assist Kate with the estate. They sifted through a chaos of papers before giving it up. Kate made an appointment with Dusky's attorney, intending to dump the job on him. Even so she'd be stuck in Virginia for weeks. "You've done everything you can here," she told Brad. "Go on back. Things will be piling up at work."

"There's no hurry. The B&B is livable and they've got a room for me until the middle of next week."

"No, really. I have to focus. With you in Altamont and Sara overseeing the medical bills, I can concentrate on the legal stuff."

"Sara's quite a woman. I like her," Brad said. He'd noticed the interlacing of their fingers at the funeral, how Kate relied on her. "I think you do too."

"She's easy to be with."

"Is that what you need right now?"

Kate rubbed her eyes. "I don't know, maybe." She blinked back tears. "Yes, Brad, it is. It's what I need."

He caught a flight the next morning. At home he rummaged through his CDs, slipped a reissue of *Masterpieces By Ellington* into the player and settled back on the couch. Liquid chords from the Duke's piano fell in perfect tinkling spheres, drenching Brad with the introduction to "Mood Indigo."

The Painter of Kitsch

"In the realm of kitsch, the dictatorship of the heart reigns supreme."
— MILAN KUNDERA, *The Unbearable Lightness of Being*

GENERATIONS OF NEGLECT had bleached the barn to the color of moonlight. Hunters who encountered this abandoned homestead in the Otter Creek Wilderness paid scant attention to the decrepit structure or the rock chimney standing guard in the woods nearby. Portable relics had long since disappeared and visitors who sheltered in the barn during downpours were usually more concerned with the tilting walls than the occasional flecks of pigment still lingering on the chestnut siding.

Joe Burchill was an exception. His memory, impervious to rot as the chestnut itself, had led him here. For Joe the barn was hulking and red and always would be. He saw and did not see the cattywampus peril.

His business was art, the marriage of antique rural scenes to weathered wood. On a golden October afternoon, the kind his work might celebrate, none observed the elderly painter studying the boards. Nevertheless he felt inhibited. Out of sight of the stiff-necked chimney his attention was drawn to a piece of siding with grain that eddied in attractive, unhurried figures. He took off his knapsack and squatted to clear the weeds from the bottom of it. There were no nails below the line of rusty scabs at knee height. Maybe he wouldn't need tools. The butt of the plank was damp in his hands. He jerked, rocking on his heels, but it didn't budge.

An adjoining board rewarded his first tug with pops of surrendering nails. Joe lifted, bowing the chestnut, struggling to maintain balance as he straightened his legs. Nails snapped higher up. He was pitched onto his back when the piece bucked loose. It vibrated in the air and fell, dealing him a blow to the cheek that shocked more than pained him. The skin there was shriveled like a dry apple, a numb ruin of scar tissue and badly knit bone.

He lay surprised at the absence of livestock smells in the musty breath issuing from the gap in the siding. From the loft, no velvet rush of owl wings. The entire forest had paused. He rolled over, drowning the silence with crackling leaves, and wheezed to his feet only to be engulfed by recollection.

Countless times his mind has flinched at the roar approaching fast behind. He watches himself pivot away from an ax stroke meant to take off his head. The toe of the bit carves flesh below his eye. It has the effect of a fingernail striking a match. Wonderment flares to blind rage. The hateful hours that follow are distilled into a moment of such bitterness that their taste has never left his mouth.

Joe recovered his bearings in the midst of a profane harangue wasted on an audience of dumb trees. He felt warmth trickling along his jaw and bent forward to spare his windbreaker. Blood spattered the ground and the plank that cut him. He'd have hammered his assailant to toothpicks but for a troupe of chickadees that flitted in to squabble about pecking order in the branches. The comedy reminded him of a few barroom fights he'd been in.

After the brawl moved on he stanched the blood with a handful of leaves and assessed the plank with a painterly eye. Better than a foot wide, sound, good surface condition. Six or seven pictures worth of blank canvas. Competitors in the truck stop art market might simply rinse off the blood and start painting. Joe had learned better. He scrubbed his wood with deck cleaner, then applied a stain-resistant primer. Otherwise, no matter how vibrant his colors, mildew and moonlight eventually seeped through.

He didn't look the type for such fussiness. A gaunt man, he went about in threadbare clothes and was often unshaven. The wispy fringe sticking out beneath the Red Sox cap had faded from black to dirty gray. On the side of his disfigurement several cheek teeth were missing; those in front were in poor repair. Joe's starveling build and cagey manner amply testified to hungers that began after an epidemic fever in Boston consumed his family and spat out a boy of nine to fend for himself on Gustin Street. The cousins who took him in care had no use for childish grief. Prohibition rewarded daring and toughness. Lightning fast tailboard thefts were succeeded by hijacking the beer shipments of rival mobs. He had cash in his pockets and excitement aplenty for any son of Erin until the North End woppoes ambushed his boss. Joe fled to Scranton and drifted southwest with the Alleghenies, a step ahead of the law and two behind his dream of a new start. Stability eluded him. Decades of manual labor, when he could get it, at last broke his strength. Only in the discard bin that the fortunate call retirement did he discover painting and, in art, consolation.

Visions of what should have been spilled out on his carefully prepared chunks of salvage lumber. Nighttime cabins floated in bubbles of windowlight. So warm were his snowbound cabins that viewers were tantalized by peeks through open doors. Other panels commemorated toil. A man might bend to a mule-drawn plow in an upland field or be shown at the sawbuck, working up stove wood. If Joe depicted the woman who embodied his happiness she'd be at her chores as well, shelling beans, feeding chickens, sweeping the porch. Her pride was honey-colored hair; he made a point of getting it right.

Although travelers paid top dollar for any Burchill rendering, the scenes didn't satisfy him. They missed the life. Also, he couldn't paint a decent barn to save his soul. All of them veered toward this one. Someway the undercurrents of the brushstrokes went out of control and trying to change things spoiled the picture. His frustration festered like a splinter buried too deep to see.

It had goaded him to return to this place. But sixty-year-old memories hadn't translated easily to roadmaps. The Turkey Run he remembered was dotted with small farms. No more. They'd let the trees take over. Second-growth timber cloaked the landmarks. Solving the puzzle had required a considerable investment of time, gas and tramping. The hike from his station wagon on the far side of the mountain had stretched to three or four miles.

He hefted the fool board at his feet. It and one other would suffice. It didn't pay to overload the mule, especially since he was it. He dragged the plank to the cabin site and leaned it against the chimney. Green with moss up to the narrowing above the firebox, the chimney reminded him of a monument at the head of a sunken grave. In a way it was. Inside the tumbled rim of the cabin's foundation stones a copse of dogwood had raised a corner of cast iron stovetop. All else had gone to ashes or just gone. Relatives of the tragic homesteaders had no doubt claimed the animals, hay and implements. Neighbors would have waited, gambling on the minimum length of a respectful interval, before racing to salvage silverware, flat irons, hinges and crockery. One had probably found an ax head in need of retempering.

Noise in the leaves sent Joe sprawling. His legs gathered under him as his fingers groped for a weapon. A gray streak disappeared behind the trunk of a walnut tree. Breathless with shame he coughed himself purple and raised his eyes to the high pulpit where a squirrel pronounced pipsqueak judgment on him.

Joe cursed his nattering critic. "Yeah, brother, tell it. Go on. Been waiting a while to get that off your chest, have you?"

Mindful of the hour he damned the squirrel to hell and marched toward the cockeyed wreck of a barn. The loft doorway, racked to diamond shape, yawned wide. Below it the main doors were slightly ajar and hemmed with black-berry brambles. The building leered, foisting vile images on him. Of Abner McConnell, hacked unrecognizable, lying in the yard. Of honey-haired Nancy as she cannot be, dangling black-faced and foul in despair. Of an oil lamp spilled, stretching forth its yellow tongue to lick the bed quilt and settle in to feast on wishes gone wrong. Of animal flight, unseen, wounded, listening, listening in his sleep.

Joe repelled these horrors with pictures of industry and potential. A farmer stands in his hay wagon lifting an aromatic forkful to a man who leans from the steamy loft. Summer is lemony in the air. Barn kittens toy with a pail while the cow looks on, lazily switching at flies.

But that was then.

Joe found the hammer and flat bar in his knapsack and knelt again before the plank with swirling grain. Beside it, the gap he'd created laid bare the barn's horizontal purlins. He drove his bar into the crack between the lowest of them and the board he prized. The nails gave up. Those at stomach level were rusted out. With that amount of freeboard leverage, the higher purlins were no problem. On the top plate a single nail resisted.

He allowed himself a moment of rest and glimpsed inside the barn. The floor was littered with empty sacks of the same umber color as the dirt. A barrel hoop, shaggy with spider webs, hung on a peg near the loft ladder. He wondered how many other hired men had climbed those awkward rungs. Had desire harried their dreams too, denied them peace? Had it paced and sniffed, made bold to leap into the world through the fleeting passway of an unguarded smile?

In the rafter shadows Joe saw the lines of a dress and high-topped shoes or so it seemed in the instant before he recoiled, realizing as he did that it was a trick of bad light. He dug his knuckles into the illusion. When it was rooted out he yelled in the direction of the squirrel's tree, "Come on. Where are you? Let's hear it!"

Disgusted by the lack of response, he spat and resumed work on the plank he wanted, twisting and levering. It tore free. He lowered it to the ground and crouched to trace the rough grain with his fingertips. Once again he strode new-tilled fields with a planting stick and pouch of seed corn, wishing for a harvest to call his own.

The squirrel resumed its chatter, observing that those mounded rows so present to Joe's touch were forever gone. The old man, aggrieved beyond endurance, forgot his board and palmed a walnut lying green in the hull. Folded at the waist as though seized by a bellyache he got to his feet and tottered away from the building, improving his angle of attack. Reflexes trained on an empty stomach cocked his arm. He reared and let fly.

A searing jolt behind the shoulder of his throwing arm kept him from watching exactly what happened. But whether from a ricochet hit or pure shock the heckler plummeted tail over teakettle to a whomping hard landing. Joe cursed the beast to the seventh generation as it recovered and ran off. He grabbed at his shoulder blade. Unable to reach the injury he rubbed the sore spot against a tree. The pain rippled but didn't slack.

Glowering at the barn didn't help either. It loomed in crooked confrontation, righteously indignant, punch-drunk and spoiling for a final round. The display infuriated him. He hadn't chosen his feral existence, had done everything he could to trade it for common domestic pleasure. It wasn't his fault that circumstance had time and again conspired to shut him out. Who could fault him for enjoying the scraps that came his way? Any man would have. Any man would have defended himself.

The barn mocked his excuses.

He imagined torching the hulk. Rafters groan, torn from their sockets on collapsing walls. The rotten roof twists and cries and crashes down on ill-fortune. There it will remain, sealed away until roots have sucked its bones to powder and generations of leaves bury it beyond recollection under a springtime drift of white bloodroot flowers.

But Joe hadn't the time for nature to take her course. His brush afforded a speedier transformation. It was within his power to erase, paint over, to redefine and make sweet, board by tortured board. The past stood defenseless before his skill. His the power to call forth the victorious, innocent flowers and, along with his customers, to glory in them. Now. The demand he served was endless.

A Relic of War

MY THIRD GRADE TEACHER informed our class that black is not a color. Nonsense, I thought; if black isn't a color, what's up with black crayons? It's clear now that Ms. Ketchum was correct, also that she didn't have a clue. Had she actually grasped the implication of her statement there'd have been a quaver in that lilting English voice. The shock of black will do that.

Half a mile from sunlight, resting against water-worn limestone in an obscure Ozark cavern, the reality of black is unavoidable. It's primordial and omnipresent, potentially suffocating. Black is the stuff the world is painted on and I'm down to one paintbrush: a Mini Maglite. It has to remain in my pocket until J.J. and Connor return.

Bad luck but really no big deal. We're old-school about lighting thanks to our paleontology prof, Dr. Fournier. Head-mounted electric lights aren't the best plan when caving for bones. Our gas lanterns illuminate a wide area—no bobbing beam—and they burn for twelve hours on a fill, big pluses on a dig site. So is the heat. Missouri cave temperatures hover in the mid-fifties year round, a bit chilly for lounging in subterranean humidity, especially when your clothes are damp with sweat and mud. The warm zone around the defunct lantern between my thighs has already faded from eyebrow to chest level. Soon it will disappear entirely.

We carry matches and extra mantles but who thinks about a lantern generator conking out in use? My spare and wrench are at camp. We've got a sweet spot there, close enough to the entrance to catch a little light but protected from the first arctic blast of the season. It was pecker-biting cold outside this morning and spitting snow.

Dr. Fournier had heard about this cave from the landowner, who told him nobody'd been in it but a few locals. If true it amounted to academically virgin territory. Nobody had to ask us twice. We laid on supplies for six days and drove down yesterday for a leisurely survey during semester break.

East of a dying town named Shepards Corner, J.J. turned his old Chevy Blazer off the pavement onto a woodland fire trail. We opened Mathilda's windows to bask in the smells of cedar and moldering decay. At one point a flock of wild turkeys blocked the road. Indignation at our talk of Christmas dinner sent them running through the dry leaves.

Eventually the woods opened to pastureland and our trail crossed a broad mountain creek. No bridge, just a knee deep low-water ford with a cobblestone bottom. The alternative to chancing it in the Blazer was a gear-laden trudge of uncertain duration in wet boots. J.J. tromped the gas. Mathilda plowed up a curtain of water, bogged down and died within crying distance of success. The water was below door level on her passenger side. I sloshed out and popped the hood. Our steed's innards were dripping wet but intact. J.J. cranked the starter. Mathilda refused to cooperate.

When J.J. got out to diagnose the problem I went looking for a farmer with a tractor. A footpath paralleled the creek upstream. Balls of mistletoe, heavy with berries, infested the arching sycamores. Nervous finches chowed down in the underbrush.

Today, I'm the one left behind. I could have stumbled along with a dead lantern but there wasn't much point. We're in a serpentine passage with multiple vertical levels separated by shelves of harder limestone. Where the shelves are incomplete it's possible to change floors by shimmying up or down with elbows and feet on opposite walls, something we've done repeatedly this morning. Clambering around a life-size maze is entertaining. However, barring another entrance, we're too far in to score any bones.

Connor promised he and J.J. wouldn't be gone long. We didn't imagine there was much more to see. Evidently a wrong assumption. If the passages continue on, my buds will explore them. Here I sit until their return, a way-marker to the exit. Such is life. After the rigors of the wormhole I can use a nap. Black is only a problem to the wakeful.

Paleontologically speaking, the trip has been a bust. We're often luckier. A dinky cave in the next county contained dire wolf, giant armadillo, rattlers the size of pythons, and a wealth of *Platygonus compressus*, an extinct peccary with fanglike tusks. *Platygonus*, Pleistocene ham on the hoof, surely needed them.

I'd rather have faced a herd of peccaries than the slavering pair of mega-sows that met me yesterday at a fenceline beside the creek trail. I was on their menu, perhaps with a tasty side of sweet potatoes. Fortunately the wire was in good repair. I followed it, hogs in tow, to a rustic farmhouse where a gentleman sporting his own swinish squint greeted me with a rabbit-ear shotgun. At his suggestion I got the hell out of here, trailed by the porkers. I was relieved to find Connor, J.J. and Mathilda waiting on dry land. Wet distributor cap, they said.

"Jingle Bells" is playing. Crowds and white tile. I share a hurtling capsule with New Yorkers drunk on eggnog and shopping. Jon Stewart whispers that my girlfriend wants a dreidel for Christmas. He surreptitiously opens his topcoat, so no one else can see. Hanging from the lining are rows of sleeping bats. I tell him Rayne is into recycled Dr. Seuss clothes. She'll look cute in the top I buy for her. But there's no box. I have to wrap it flat. The paper sticks to my fingers and tears wherever I touch it. I can't locate a needle and thread.

Enough. Pull it together, Dillon.

Awake again, back in black. I roll my eyes, turn my head, wave a hand in front of my face but nothing in the visual field changes. After a while this lack of feedback is disconcerting. Was the mistletoe the shade of spinach or canned peas? I close my eyes to see. Knuckle pressure on the lids reassures me that the images are internal. Closer to the peas.

Sensory deprivation is a bitch. If I sit too still, the tethers for my thought process dwindle to disconnected tactile islands. Paper-thin regions of bumpy cool and two blobs, like cups of hot and sour soup, which become feet when I project an intention to wiggle toes I remember having. With J.J. and Connor dawdling, maintaining physical integrity is job one.

Corrosive as black is to me, several species have adapted to it, wholly or in part. Twilight zone life-forms retain terrestrial colors near cave openings. There are green plants, brown bats. Salamanders and creepy crawlies may be paler versions of their above-ground cousins but are otherwise typical. They have eyes.

This particular cave is well supplied with twilight dwellers, perhaps because the mouth is large and south-facing. At winter solstice, ferns still prosper on the sunniest limestone blocks littering the floor of the entrance room. The boulders fell from the ceiling, a fact that gave us pause as we considered where to unroll the sleeping bags. Our safety concerns are apparently not unique. Evidence of previous human activity is limited to a single fire ring and a joke from J.J. about a moccasin heel sticking out from under a dumpster-sized rock.

The entrance or great room, as we dubbed it, is perhaps two hundred feet long and fifty feet in greatest width, with an irregular thirty-foot ceiling. On the floor, potential bone-bearing strata are few. Notable features consist of the death-from-above boulders, a colony of hibernating bats in the rear and, beneath them, guano Mt. Fuji.

Faint tinkling sounds from the vicinity of Bat Shit Mountain enticed us up and over the top of it. In a small grotto accessible from the back slope a hanging forest of soda straws dripped water into a terraced array of catch basins rimmed by delicate flowstone crusts. The layout could have served as a model for hillside rice paddies. Instead the pools grow translucent shrimp-like creatures the size of rice grains. They reacted to our lights with jackknife bursts of activity. The wreckage of a maladroit camel cricket lay mineralizing in the blue shallows. Stripes on its humped carapace remain visible after sixty-plus years, a relic of war forgotten by all but circling sharks. The Zero's young pilot, a rising sun prematurely set. Of his bones are coral made, and pearly sightless eyes.

Useless here in any case, beyond the wormhole. A procession of ghostly tumbleweeds rolls along the windless passage before me. Predatory fungi. They suck life but leave its color behind to decorate mud and stone. Invert world where ghosts alone may live. The balls gather, pulsating.

"No!" The sound hits like a pressure wave, shattering the gossamer menace. I jump up, crack my noggin painfully on an outcrop and am reconstituted. The lantern has crashed. A rhythmic, metallic click recedes to my right. "Damn it," I yell, grabbing for the crown of my head with one hand and my flashlight with the other. The pants pocket, stiff with drying mud, fights me for the Maglite. I pry it free and twist the bezel. Black recoils. On its wounded surface the browns of the passage congeal, lifeless perhaps, but comforting.

My lantern, glass globe miraculously intact, comes to rest at a narrow crevice between the floor and opposite wall. While bending for the Coleman I probe the crack with the flashlight. The bottom is quite a ways down. I shouldn't be surprised. It's a lower level. Ground floor, or second? I don't recall, only that we were on it before we climbed up here and there's at least one level above me.

"Connor! J.J.!" I shout. "Where the hell are you?"

The reverberation isn't saying.

I wonder if something happened to them. Don't go there.

My girlfriend Rayne isn't a cruel person. She doesn't wish anybody harm but she'd laugh her butt off at me down here losing it. She'd say it serves me right. I was supposed to be with her in Creve Coeur today, ramping up to Christmas at her folks'. I've met them and her kid sister Sue a couple of times. They're okay I guess, if a heavy dose of suburban propriety doesn't bother you and you don't have issues with people who name their firstborn for a cheesy barroom ballad. Rayne says Sue saved her life by not being able to pronounce the letter L as a toddler. Nobody except her terminally obtuse father calls her Raylene anymore.

Rayne Innes sounds more professional on stage anyhow. She's a theater major. Why not? John Goodman got his start in Missouri. Rayne has a playbill thumbtacked beside her dresser listing him as Oberon in an off-Broadway production of *A Midsummer Night's Dream*. It's from before he was famous.

She knows I love her, but leave the drama to Shakespeare. Holiday pilgrimages to my own blended parental units are as close to dine-and-dash events as can be arranged. I've been hearing who did what to whom since first grade. Naturally the identity of the aggrieved "whom" depends on the speaker. Counting ex-stepsiblings there are seven other pairs of ears for Sandra, Phil and their current hookups to pour crap into.

Rayne gets off on such stuff. She's all about family, endlessly engaged with the latest happenings and rumors of happenings. The necklace I made in Metalsmithing & Jewelry Design pleased her but this cave trip may be an even better Christmas gift: a juicy focus for conversation.

I'm lucky about the lantern. Spare globes we don't have. I stow the Coleman in a nook where it's unlikely to get kicked if I spaz out again. As an added precaution, I sit several feet away from it. These few minutes of light have done wonders for my mental state but I can't afford dead batteries. The flashlight goes into my pocket.

Black claims its own. I don't want to think how it rushed up my nose. Or about breathing it in. My lungs are blacker than any smoker's, invaded and occupied. Under the skin, black hollows me out like a cricket.

Enough again. Chill. Visualize the route to camp.

We arrived on this level by climbing up through a hole to my left. I scraped an arrow in the mud there with my boot. The arrow points this way. Wherever we changed levels I did that. To get out, travel against the arrows. I wish I'd thought to record our direction prior to each vertical shift. After the first drop we continue on to the left. Then things get hazy.

Turn it around; start in the great room.

We noticed the wormhole yesterday, a low horizontal passage opening at floor level, halfway back. The only decent mud fan in the joint originates there. Our test trench yielded nothing but a few twigs blown or carried in from outside. Nevertheless the wormhole represented a continuation of the cavern system. It had to be explored.

I crawled in, hoping but not hopeful. The passage looked as though it might peter out. It didn't. Neither did it get roomier. I could scarcely hold my lantern upright and was forced to retreat for consultations.

We might have skipped the wormhole in favor of a hike had the weather been better this morning. As it was we got an early start. Connor, who describes his physique as substantial, went in first. If he got stuck, J.J. and I could pull him out or at least not be trapped ourselves.

It was a near thing. I'm not claustrophobic but when your Coleman has to be cocked at a forty-five and the passage has you by both back and belly with no room to turn around, we're talking snug.

We soon broke a sweat from the heat of three lanterns and the sustained effort of wriggling with arms outstretched. Our situation grew increasingly grim the farther we crawled without locating a turnaround. I think Connor only kept going because he couldn't feature backing out. He diffused the tension by stopping occasionally to study the mud and announce he hadn't found anything. Really?

We struggled forward, head to toe like army worms in a too-tight tube, doing well to stay calm. Was it half an hour? It seemed longer before Connor whooped and kicked ahead. I didn't follow for fear he'd knock out my light. Ironic. When his flailing boots disappeared I whooped too.

It wasn't a chamber of course; it was this stack of serpentine hallways. But we weren't aware of that yet. What we *were* was totally relieved to find breathing room in a narrow flat-roofed passage about ten feet high. The wormhole teed into it under a ledge. I carved an X in the mud to mark the spot. J.J. added a granola bar.

A short distance to the left we noticed an irregular gap in the ceiling. The passage was too wide to shimmy up for an inspection. We walked on. The hall was devoid of formations and nearly barren of macroscopic life. No bat had ventured here, nothing with eyes. A millipede, blind and milky white, scuttled away at the approach of beings alien to its feeble imagination. What might once have been a spider was overgrown by a translucent fright wig. The disordered spider web we came upon next turned out to be tendrils of fungus feeding, we presumed, on thin air.

At a congenial break in the ceiling we climbed upstairs. The upper level resembled the first in size, lack of furnishings and snaky contour. I scratched an arrow rightward toward the wormhole but the earlier gap we'd seen from below proved unbridgeable. We backtracked. I scuffed out the arrow and dug another with my heel, pointing left. We dropped down to the first floor again at a crack where the hall narrowed impassably. Onward to the left. Up again, still left. Up to the third level, vacant as the other two. I think we went left. Yes, left, away from the wormhole. Up, briefly, in hopes of discovering another surface access, but a pancake collapse of multiple floors drove us down two levels and to the right. We passed a hole with an arrow pointing at us. Rather than retrace steps we took the earliest opportunity to gain a level. Then my lamp quit.

That's the route. I'm sure of it. What had me confused was the wall I'm sitting against. My left hand is rightward in the passage. For all I know the wormhole may be directly below, two levels down.

What's keeping Connor and J.J.? It's cold in here. I'm tempted to write the jerks a note and leave them to their own devices.

Rayne's been teaching me yoga. She says I'll be more flexible and centered. I do it mainly to watch her assume hot poses in a leotard. It pisses her off, though, to catch me with a locust-post boner instead of world peace. So I have to actually learn a few things. Sun salutations seem uniquely appropriate here where the sun don't shine.

The stretching feels as if I'm secreting a warm coat of armor. Muscles and tendons slide to their limits, grudging at first but soon well-oiled machinery. I drop to the deck for pushups, sit ups. Then deep knee bends, slow, imagining they're squats under a heavy bar. Pumping up until I'm solid and flawless. Also thirsty, but nothing I can do about it. We were unprepared for an extended excursion. The wormhole fooled us, not that we could have packed in water bottles anyway. Unless they were in a drag bag tied to a belt. The bag's a good idea; I'll have to make one.

Apart from my own noises the hall has been silent. But crickets, no, frogs are singing. How bizarre. Why haven't I heard them before? Has some black sun gone down somewhere? What are they like, these troglobite peepers, eyeless and transparent, unknown to science? Wide-mouthed clam heads with stick legs and suction-cup toes? They could belong to any of several genuses, geni, genera? Whatever. The species name will be *gollum*. Yes, my precious.

I'm getting ahead of myself. The taxonomic laurels are for later, when the frogs are pickled in a bottle. At present they're creeping me out. I cover my ears but the churring calls get louder. Tunes would drown them out. Where's my iPod? Not here. Too bad. Musically I'm lame as it gets. I'd kill to shut me up if I had to sing myself to sleep, but Elvis has left the building. I attempt the White Stripes, not getting past the second or third line of any song. Even Kings of Leon eludes me. So I vibrate through the first verse of "We Three Kings of Orient Are" over and over, with and without the rubber cigar. The frogs are not amused and embarrass me to silence.

Boredom is one thing. Being trapped in an inkwell with a chorus of angry frogs is another. They've already swarmed J.J. and Connor. A slimy gore-fest is underway. Revolting images.

Those are pearles that were his eies,
Nothing of him that doth fade,
But doth suffer a Sea-change
Into something rich & strange

The voice is female, English, Elizabethan. I should recognize it but my mind is turning to sludge, inescapable tar. The airy spirit chants on, "Ding-dong, bell. Ding-dong." Ms. Ketchum?

The frogs clap and giggle, tongues lolling, dripping acid mucus. They'll hear me breathe. Be still. The tar is stickier with movement but without it I sink. No saving vine to catch. A desert trap, this skim of water. Underneath, black placidly digests its victims.

As I walked out in the streets of La Brea.
As I walked out in La Brea one day

Mired and defeated, a mammoth trumpets in the distance. Grotesque hogs bristle on the shoreline, clicking tusks, squealing displeasure.

Sperm donor drunk splashes the point in vodka. "Disrespectful little prick. Sandra all over again." Rheumy daddy Phil. Sick-joke eyes and tombstone teeth. So white. "What did I do to deserve such an ingrate? Ought to cut you off right now."

Consider it done. Fungus drills the throbbing head. Thought-sipping spider webs breach the braincase, soon an empty shell. Those are pearles. Rolling away. Save them for Rayne.

Fall deeper as legions of black overrun lines of rhetorical defense. Negotiations are futile. Run for cover. Repeat.

Dr. Fournier will catch hell for this, but not his fault. We were fools sucked through a wormhole, lost in Gaia's gut, cryptic messages undeliverable until the cookie's cracked with fiery glow.

There is still a point. A still point unexpected at the bottom of the disappearing well. Safe in the heart of nowhere.

Slashes of light. Frogs on the hunt, "Dillon? Dillon?" I no longer fear them.

"There he is."

"Ah, shit, dude. Come on, man, not this."

"Why doesn't he move?"

Heat hisses on my cheeks. I'm shaken by a rude hand and a face full of J.J. I blink. He's still there. Connor stands behind him, lantern high.

Best not to mention the frogs. "What's going on?" I say, the light once again working its blessed magic on my thought process.

Connor remarks, "You look like shit."

"Do me a favor, dude," I ask J.J. "I banged the top of my head. Is there any fungus?"

"What are you talking about?"

I lean forward. "Just do it, okay?"

"Sure. Fine." He ruffles my hair. "You bled a bit, that's all. What happened?"

"Told you, banged my head." I stand, cautiously. "That spider we saw, the one with fuzz on it? You can't be too careful. Where have you been?"

"Shit, man," Connor says, "We were *so* fuckin lost. J.J. spotted one of your arrows."

"We should have kept making them."

"Why didn't you?"

J.J. shrugs. "I don't know, dude. It was your job."

"There is that," I say, feeling myself again.

Connor's antsy. "You didn't miss anything, okay, Dillon? Wherever you go it's like this. Up, down and sideways, the same thing. Let's get out of here."

J.J. shakes his lantern and frowns. "I'm running on fumes."

I fetch my Coleman. Though I didn't fill it this morning it's half full. J.J. kills his light. Pouring directly from one tank to another will be a wasteful mess.

"Got any paper on you?" I ask. "We need a funnel." Connor produces a single-serving bag of peanuts. I cut off the top of the bag and offer him nuts. He declines. We're too thirsty to eat. So I spill them, nip a bottom corner off the bag, blow out as much salt as possible and follow up with a rinse of unleaded gas. Between the three of us we're able to transfer the fuel with minimal spillage.

Moments later the Maglite is clamped between my teeth, illuminating the first homeward rabbit hole. Before my feet touch the lower level the flashlight has me drooling. So much for thirst. We don't make many wrong turns; it's a good thing. Connor, especially, is rattled. J.J.'s granola bar is a welcome sight. He picks it up saying he'll have it framed.

Once again Connor leads the wormhole procession. I'm second, although the light from J.J.'s trailing lantern does me little good. If I hold mine sideways with the flashlight projecting between the fingers of my tank hand I get a useful beam, like a one-eyed car on a country lane. We slither in laborious silence, six inches at a heave. The mud in my clothing has dried, chafing elbows and knees.

Connor bawls, "Oh, Jesus God, I can't see. I'm stuck." He's a yard ahead of me. The soles of his boots have ceased purposeful activity. They're twitching.

"What's wrong?" I ask.

"My lantern died. I think it's out of gas and I can't see. Oh, Jesus God."

"That sucks. We should have checked. But it's not so bad, dude. What are you going to do, take a wrong turn? Switch to your flashlight."

"I'm not kidding, Dillon. I'm fuckin blind."

J.J. shouts, "What's the matter up there?"

"His lantern's out of gas. Connor, chill. Use your flashlight."

"I don't have it. I can't see."

"What do you mean you don't have it?"

"I didn't bring it, okay? It's not pocketsize."

J.J. groans. "Dillon, what's he saying? You've got to do something."

The weight of circumstance bears down on my chest. I flash on J.J.'s gag about the Indian under the great room rock. Slow is worse, much worse. "Connor, it's not a problem. I'll loan you my Maglite."

"I can't reach. Can't get my arms there."

"Man, you know I'd bring it up to you but a lard-ass is blocking traffic."

J.J. growls a curse. Connor's freaking out.

"Dude," I command, fighting for his attention. "Connor, listen up. Here's what we're going to do. Put the lantern down for a minute and scoot over to your right as far as you can. Scoot. You'll see light on your left." His butt shifts, but his boot blocks the flashlight beam. "Good, Connor. Move your left foot."

He does. "I see it," he pants. "But I still can't reach." He bucks like a seizure with no room to move.

"No problem, dude. No problem. Just listen to me. I'm laying the Maglite down, right here, off to the side against the wall. Got that? I'm laying it down and J.J. and I are going to crawl backwards. Aren't we, J.J.? You too, dude. We're all crawling backwards on our bellies, skooching backwards until you have the flashlight."

Behind me I hear J.J. moving.

Connor blubbers, "I'll try."

"Make it happen. I don't want to have to drag your sorry ass. Okay, let's go." I do the worm in reverse. Connor thrashes, puffs desperately. Darkness in the shape of a boot swallows my light. "You're doing it, Connor. That's right. Another couple of feet. Keep coming."

"It's here," he gasps. "I've got it. Oh, Jesus God."

"Excellent." I'm as relieved as he is. "Now listen to me again. Chill it down. Chill it on down. We're cool. Everything is cool. When you're ready just head out. We're right behind you. Aren't we J.J.?"

J.J. mutters a response unfit for hysterical ears.

Connor is catching his breath. "How will *you* see?" he wonders.

"I got recalibrated waiting for you guys. We can chat about it later. For now you've got the flashlight and your boots are between me and supper. What say we book it out of here?"

Despite my response to Connor there are easier things than belly-crawling in the dark. With minimal visual cues it's hard to keep my head down. Connor develops a bad habit of stopping when I yelp, so I quit doing it. He can fret about my health after we're out of this hole.

I'm amazed at the absence of black. The darkness contains no particle of it, even in the densest shadows. Black is teasing me like I'm already supposed to forget it exists.

When I was a kid and had nightmares, Sandra used to march into my room demanding to know where the bogeyman was. Then she'd bitch me out because he'd disappeared. This was during her affair with the Chamber of Commerce guy. His idea of humoring the kid was slipping me an allergy pill in hopes I'd pass out. I treasure the night my bad dreams rid us of him. He stomped out half-dressed; "I can't sleep with that brat yowling, Sandra." For the record, I never yowled "Sandra."

Mommy dearest, if you want to meet black I can arrange an introduction up close and personal. But I know she doesn't want that. She's got her own bogeymen to deal with, always has.

A feeling comes, like the governor signed my pardon. I have no idea what I'm liberated from, certainly not this wormhole. Whatever it is I'm lighter than air and jacked to the max. Crawl, baby. I get on Connor's case, "Daddy, are we there yet?"

He stops. "What?"

"Are we there yet? J.J.'s picking on me."

J.J. pipes up, "Am not. Dillon's hogging all the room."

Connor laughs. "Don't you two idiots make me come back there."

"How much longer?" I whine.

"I'll tell you when," he says. "Count something. Count telephone poles. The one with the right answer wins."

We're skeptical. "Wins what?"

"A bigger piece of pie."

J.J.'s psyched, "Yum. Pie. Step on it, Daddy, I'm hungry."

Connor churns ahead. My lungs are pumping. The blind slither becomes a body thing. I keep my head, like the equally useless lantern, laid sideways. They're just along for the ride. I am the worm. My flannel shirt stinks of clay and old fear.

Suddenly Connor lets out a shriek with crazy echoes. I lift my face and open my eyes. Before me is a dim oval. Connor screams again in ecstasy.

"Keep it down, asshole," I yell, wriggling fast. "Remember the ceiling?" The constricting walls release me into a sea of cool air. I roll free. Behind me, J.J. is the lantern at the end of the tunnel. Then he's with us in the great room. We stare at each other.

"Holy shit," J.J. says, breaking the trance. "It's dark outside." Indeed it is.

Connor and I get busy fixing Colemans. J.J. sticks around until Connor's is lit, then puts on his coat and ventures out for kindling. We're thinking along the lines of a campfire visible from space.

J.J. is lighting it off in the fire pit when Connor and I join him at the entrance. We need wood. J.J. says he found a dead pine small enough to bow saw but he can't do the cutting. He twisted his ankle in the serpentine halls.

Connor's concerned. "I didn't know that. Why didn't you say?"

"What was I going to do, sit and cry about it?"

Connor erupts. "My lantern died, okay? I couldn't see anything."

I don't like where this is going. "Dudes, I'm just glad to be out of there. Where's your saw, J.J.?"

The night is starless, windy. Lantern light, aided by patches of snow blown into the lee of rocks and logs, casts trail hazards in high relief. J.J.'s tree tried to fall but was caught by neighboring branches. Connor volunteers for the role of sawyer to the widow-maker and does a masterful job. The pine snaps into pieces for us on the frozen ground.

Chef J.J. is at the campstove preparing a trio of freeze-dried favorites: chicken stew, mushroom stroganoff and shrimp ramen. He's boiling them together in a pot of creek water and will plate his deliciousness on slices of whole wheat. We pop tops on a round of PBRs. Fine cave dining demands no more than this.

Our fire leaps and sparks, reenacting magic older than names for the thing it dispels. A million years of fragrant smokes are engraved in hominin DNA. The tang of burning pine has us primed for good cheer. We manage to kill two six packs and dissect the college football rankings before wilting like octogenarians. J.J. is first to limp to the sack. Connor and I tend to the fire and aren't far behind.

Incoherent shouts disturb our slumber. It's Connor. We wake him up. Now he's afraid to sleep. He has to talk. We talk. He wonders if we'd mind him lighting his lantern. I don't. Neither does J.J., whose foot is throbbing. We talk about that. Connor quiets, then jerks awake again and curses us for letting him drift off. We agree that this cave contains nothing of paleontological interest. If the creek didn't rise we can leave in the morning and be home with a day to spare before Christmas Eve. Visions of twinkle lights flash in our heads.

Connor's restlessness persists. I try to talk him through it, revisiting my battle with black. It had me shook, I tell him, backed into a place I didn't know existed. I was safe there, regardless of what black did. J.J. snores, unimpressed. I encourage Connor to relax, let himself sink until he lands in his safe zone. I sound like a self-help group. Connor says he'll try but whimpers miserably every few minutes. It's a long night. The longest.

Morning breaks brilliant with sun. J.J. and I stagger out into it. Light pours down in painful dazzling sheets broken by tree trunks. It splashes up from snow-crusted leaves. We're drenched, painted again, seamlessly restored and embraced. Freezing to death seems a small price to pay for such luxury.

We start a fire. J.J. cranks up the stove for coffee, and I head for the campsite to pack gear. It's amazing how rapidly the sun has reclaimed me. The route through the great room rockfield that I earlier walked with confidence is now obscure. Connor's gas-powered night light reveals him among the boulders, scrunched down in his bag.

Rounding up our crusty laundry awakens him. "J.J.'s gimpy," I say. "You and I are in charge of baggage. Coffee will be ready in a minute."

He rolls over, farts and is asleep again.

Downslope in the same swale as the cave, Mathilda sparkles with frost. I swap her a load of dirty clothes and sleeping bags for a pound of bacon and a dozen eggs from the cooler in back. I also pocket a few specimen containers. We haven't identified the bats. Skulls from Bat Shit Mountain will settle that question.

J.J. has his extra-wide cast iron skillet warming when I return. The block of bacon slides into the pan with an aromatic sizzle. "I'll get some skulls for Fournier," I say, "but this trip has been epic. Let's take something else to remember it by."

"You mean besides Connor?" he sneers.

"He just cracked first. It could have been you or me."

"*We* did what we had to do. You didn't freak."

"Through no fault of my own. You slept through the story about the killer frogs."

"What killer frogs?"

"Never mind. I'll wake His Highness."

Connor stirs and grumps when I pick up his Coleman. I could use mine but his is handy. "Sorry, dude. There's work to be done. You can wait for me but no reason to. Go toward the big light. Special deal, today only, they're tempting lost souls with bacon and eggs."

"Dillon, bring it back," he fusses.

The ascent of Bat Shit Mountain is like climbing in damp dirt and smells about the same, with an added dash of ammonia. Leggy crickets interrupt their guano grazing to launch kamikaze attacks. They guard the cave's only fossil treasure. Under this pyramid lie the bones of pharaohs: the cave's first bats. I pose no threat to them. Combing the slopes for the remains of more recent inhabitants scores a half-dozen peanut-sized skulls. At least two different species. Dr. Fournier will be pleased.

I should call it a wrap, but music from the Zen grotto lures me again to the basin field and nurturing mineral sky, its soda straws bellied with droplets of natural time poised to ring out across the waters. The submerged cricket shell wavers and is still, resting on its side, a suit of armor, breached. I reach for a specimen bottle then stop myself. Some wreckage is best left in peace. All I really want is to be in Creve Coeur surprising Rayne with a pair of pearl ear studs. She's a nut for jewelry.

I'll run you to the sea, she said

S OME PERSONALITIES CAPTIVATE US with their flow. They need only walk into a room to touch and be touched by everyone in it. My late wife, the artist Carla Rosselli, was one of these special people. She felt no need to jazz up her brand with eccentricity or fits of pique. Although a few critics might disagree, she didn't trade on mystery either. Carla was hardly unique in refusing to invent explanations for her work. She had an honest fear of jinxing her creativity. In at least one instance she was also protecting a source. I'm thinking of her breakout series of landscape oils, the Portraits of Gladys. Who, some asked, is Gladys and how do barren rockscapes reveal her? Carla chose never to answer. Now, with her gone and "Gladys" no doubt dead as well, I'm free to address these questions. To be honest, I feel compelled to. Explanation has a place in the order of things. Perhaps it's just the ghost dance of a bereaved husband but, regardless of our poses, who among us doesn't dream of being understood?

Those familiar with the Gladys canvases may be interested to learn that a pen and ink study of a hermit lady who lived high on a Colorado mountain was the first of the series. A bust portrait occupies the center of the page. There's a mineral aspect to the weathered slabs and cracks of Gladys's cheeks, a metamorphic veining to the waves of hair. In that context, the animation of the eyes is startling. I vividly recall the desire in them, childlike and predatory. To engage with Gladys was to be simultaneously affirmed, violated and rebuffed.

The lower left corner of the sheet contains a full-body cartoon. Gladys holds a Winchester carbine as she stands near the isolated timberline cabin where we happened upon her. She's dressed in her wool shirt, trousers and, in a flight of Carla's imagination, a boonie hat. Opposite the cartoon Dylan Thomas is quoted in loopy cursive: "I'll run you to the sea, she said." Thomas's youthful tales of Welsh magic and horror fascinated us that summer. Outside the orbit of our budding romance cities burned and dreams died screaming. It was 1968.

Carla's earlier drawings from the trip we'd taken to the Rockies had been different. Her travel sketchbook is filled with bobble-headed jays, ruined cabins, lichen-clad boulders. People, including me, are represented, not always in flattering poses. But Gladys is conspicuously absent. Her portrait didn't appear until weeks after Carla and I returned to Manhattan.

She told me it came out of Gladys's refusal to let me photograph her. "If you want a picture," she'd said, "take one of your girl. Somewhere else." I've mentioned the rifle. Carla and I retreated across the rockpile guarding the old lady's privacy and surveyed our alternatives for getting down the mountain. Shadows were creeping up the Gideon Creek valley toward peaks mantled with July snow. They, and we, were separated from the valley floor by a couple of thousand vertical feet of conifers and aspen groves. We'd been hiking in and above such timber for hours, a slow process, and evening chill sets in early at altitude.

It was no big deal to us. We were young, stoked on counterculture freedom, and freedom equaled mobility. A whim to visit the West had sufficed to lure us out of Greenwich Village. Thumbing rides was still an accepted mode of transportation, easily accomplished if one of the hitchers happened to be a cute hippie chick.

Our introduction to the Gideon Creek mining district was serendipitous. A fisherman at a gas station in Buena Vista offered to drive us to Rhyolite, an abandoned town nestled near the continental divide on the upper Gideon. After a jolting climb up an unimproved road he dropped us off on Rhyolite's dusty main street. If the bears didn't get us, he joked, we'd probably freeze. We shouldn't worry though. He'd be back for the bodies next weekend. On behalf of the county he hoped we carried contact information for next of kin. I grabbed our gear out of his Travelall. Carla sweetly wished him good fishing.

Rhyolite dazzled us. The air was infused with a resinous scent of pine. Rotten boardwalks fronted the general store, church and courthouse. There were no hitching posts; the livery stable wasn't more than a hundred yards from anywhere. Sandwiched between a narrow gauge rail line and Main Street, at the lower end of the commercial district, lay a fallen-down ore mill. Chipmunks scampered to lookout posts on the sunblasted timbers, giving us the eye.

Gideon Creek rushed noisily behind the single row of buildings on the other side of the street. We turned the water music into a tinkling piano at the hotel. Its first floor windows were covered with plywood. I jimmied the lock on a side door and we went in. No barroom, only a kitchen, small retail area and public parlor. The furnishings remained in place, including a 1922 wall calendar advertising Sun Maid raisins. Upstairs, the guest rooms featured intact window glass and rough-sawn plank walls. Beadboard ceilings bellied down, their tongue and groove joints threatening to separate. Dry, coffee-colored leakage stained the white paint. A room with a view of the valley tempted us, but fooling around on the bedsprings scared a family of packrats in the chest of drawers. The rats convinced us to forego sleeping under a roof.

We pitched our borrowed tent in the soft pine duff above Rhyolite. Next morning Carla spotted bighorn sheep on the peak west of town. As our acclimation to the altitude improved in the days that followed we graduated from casual sightseeing and panning for gold to scaling the dizzy inclines where miners had wrested livings from glorified gopher holes. Jenkins Pass over the continental divide lay six miles up valley according to a Forest Service sign. That hike would be a perfect climax to our stay.

At first light we broke the ice on a pot of drinking water, filled canteens, bundled up and set out. The day warmed under an intensely blue sky. Our coats were stowed before we reached the last of the trees. Ahead lay an expanse of willow brush dotted with beaver ponds. In the far distance the road snaked up an impressive slide-rock pitch to a notch between peaks. It looked to Carla more like work than play. Sheep Mountain was now behind us. Its summit was high enough to afford a view over the divide and seemed approachable by way of a saddle ridge. We could save a couple of miles and drop down the back of the mountain to Rhyolite.

We cut across the soggy, chest-high willow brush, jumping small beaver channels and splashing through streams to a game trail that led us up the saddle. From the ridge the futility of attempting the final thousand feet to the summit was obvious. Too steep. But a dry meadow gradually fell away to the south between Sheep Mountain and the divide until a kink in the jagged spine boxed it in. Perhaps the lake we saw down there fed Gideon Creek, perhaps not. At that moment we didn't care. Entranced by the view we stretched out on Eden's own grass, shucked the damp trappings of fallen man and made love in the warmth of the alpine sun. We woke invincible.

In sun-dried clothes we hiked south, then east around Sheep Mountain, descending only as far as timberline. Lower down, rockslides and tangles of deadfall hampered progress. The meadow on our right kept dropping away, a good sign. Eventually the mountainside took an abrupt turn to the north. It was as if a corner of the slope had cracked off and gouged a vertical swath through the trees down to the creek. Across the valley I recognized the tailings pile of a mine we'd explored upstream from Rhyolite. Thirsty and freshly oriented we scouted for a spot to refuel and absorb the scene. We stepped carefully crossing the avalanche chute but loose stones skittered into others. Stampedes of them leapt and clattered out of sight. We eased upward toward a parapet of boulders.

Behind it lay a dry cirque with a rocky meadow where the lake should be. In the middle of that was a log cabin, silver with age. We saw no evidence of diggings. The cabin's location was crazy even by mining standards but it appeared to be intact. Something like rawhide was stretched over the window beside the half-open plank door. A woman with a head of iron gray curls stepped out toward us, preceded by a rifle barrel. "What do you want?"

As natural as could be, Carla replied, "To meet the queen of the mountain."

"How'd you find me?"

"The day led us here."

My hands were in the air. "We were just going to rest a minute."

"Think it's purty, do you?"

"Not pretty," Carla said. "Pretty is safe. Beauty isn't."

"How'd you figure that?"

The question caught Carla by surprise. "I didn't, before."

"You'd best sit." The old lady indicated a flat boulder for us and sat on a rock nearby. Carla took off her pack and did as she was told. The queen sized me up. "What about you, Pancho?" she said. "Gonna stand there like you're caught thieving cookies or you gonna sit?" She lowered the hammer on her Winchester and laid the gun carefully in the grass.

I shrugged off my packframe and joined Carla. "Would you like some dried fruit?" I asked.

"Crashing around wore you out, did it? How's your water?"

"We have enough."

She retrieved the rifle and stood. "Gimme your canteens. I'll fill 'em and bring a bite of food."

"We're fine," I said.

A stern look convinced me to produce the canteens. She looped the straps around her knotted root of a hand and headed for the cabin. We were instructed to stay put.

Carla and I stared at each other.

"Far out," she whispered.

I was less enchanted. "Soon as we get the canteens, let's split. Who does she think she is, Daniel Boone?"

"I don't care who she is. This is real. Do what she says."

"The hammer on that .30-30 was cocked."

"It's not a picture postcard, baby. Things happen here. Give yourself to it." She nipped my earlobe.

"Here she comes."

Our benefactor had left the weapon indoors. She returned our canteens and gave us each a strip of dried meat. "It'll get your strength up."

"Sorry we scared you," I ventured. "Didn't think anybody lived around here. You're the first person we've seen."

"Ain't I the lucky one."

"I mean you must not get many visitors."

"That's the way I like it."

Feeling surer of myself, I blathered on. "This is a far-out place you've got but what about food and water? It's a hell of a hike."

"He always like this?" the woman complained.

Carla paused from her jerky. "I'm working on him."

"Why bother?"

I stopped chewing and laid the remainder of the strip on top of my pack.

"This is good," Carla said, meaning the jerky.

"Don't worry, Pancho. That meat ain't my last caller. Leave your girl with me a while and I'll teach her."

"I think not," I snapped, careful not to raise my voice.

Carla flashed a streetwise smile I'd never seen her use before.

"You sure about him, girlie?"

Carla put her arm around me. "Mountains come in all sizes."

"Dumb as a rock, is he?"

"More like inscrutable. *He's* not pretty either." Her voice took an aggressive edge. She shed her Army surplus boonie hat and shook her hair free. Straight backed, perfect breasts and jaw jutting out, she said, "And neither am I."

The woman's face went soft. For a second she almost appeared confused. I clapped a restraining hand on Carla's thigh.

"That's a sparker of a girlfriend you've got, Pancho."

"Her name is Carla, and mine—"

"Is Pancho. Don't matter what they call you where you came from."

Carla tensed. I patted her leg. "It's cool, baby. Pancho, as in Pancho Villa? I like it." Actually, I did.

She kissed my neck. "Okay, *mi General*." Leaning her head on my shoulder she asked the woman, "And what should we call you?"

"Suit yourself," the queen sulked. "I generally know who I'm talkin' to."

Carla thought a minute. "Gladys. Gladys suits you. Don't you think so, Pancho?"

Gladys's lips pursed. "If you ain't just a one," she said to Carla. "Finish eatin' and skedaddle. You got a ways to go. Don't think of bringing him back here."

That's when I asked to take her picture. Her gruff refusal was posturing but I let it ride. Carla and I repacked our stuff. She held out her hat. "Gladys, this is for you."

"What do I want with your hat?"

"You always like this?" I scolded.

"Ha, Pancho, ain't she just a one." With the hungry expression Carla later captured in her portrait, Gladys took the hat and turned away. "Git, before I fetch my rifle."

The descent of the avalanche track required total focus. A misstep could break a leg or worse. But the steepness was exhilarating. We whooped, hurtling from bush to stump to grassy hump, clutching at saplings for balance. Down, down past files of evergreen spectators on the sidelines. Down five hundred feet and five hundred more and still skipping down dodging heaps of snarled limbs until we ran out on a lush pasture above Gideon Creek and collapsed, gasping for breath.

With the last rays of sun abandoning the peaks our rest was short. We followed an overgrown wagon trail downstream and arrived at camp with the evening star. At moonrise we bathed in the mightily cold creek. Soon after, Carla bent near our campfire, drying her hair.

"Why did you give her your hat?" I asked.

"An offering maybe."

"For the meat?"

"No. She's like you, another mountain. Mountains stake out territory. They always know where they are and where they'll be." Carla picked creek debris out of her comb and flicked it into the fire. "Not me. I'm water. I flow, never too sure about anything else. What scares and attracts me about you mountains is your certainty. It's what makes you beautiful. Maybe my hat was a gift to something water doesn't understand."

She resumed combing. Firelight lit the curtain of her hair with copper. I watched, mystified. "You were on the verge of picking a fight with her."

"She had to respect me. Otherwise, she might not remember mountain's thirst for water."

"Your hat?"

"Was leaving it too cruel?"

That day inspired Carla. Her painting became obsessed with exploring the push and pull she'd discerned in beauty. Each new canvas was, in a sense, another hat for Gladys. Critics who classified those early landscapes as neo-romantic upset her. She'd come to see romanticism as a peepshow thrill. For her, an honest rendering of any great sentiment entailed its opposite. Where there was ecstasy, anguish lurked in equal portion. Alienation was the other face of ravenous want. The question of voluntary engagement with such monsters gradually took form in her work. Knowing the thing whole, it seemed to ask, how strongly dare we feel?

As for herself, my wife continued to embrace what frightened her. Numbness, not pain, was the great enemy. Much better than I, she lived the vitality she painted. Yes to curiosity. Yes to new experience. Yes to what Zorba called the full catastrophe. We traveled; we danced; we sang.

No one, flowing or rooted, is prepared for pancreatic cancer. Carla soldiered through the diagnosis and our search for effective treatments. She endured the industrial efficiency of hospitals, the flaccidity of weight loss, the sores, nausea, jaundice and stenches. I did my best to support a proud woman as she suffered the countless humiliations of rotting away. She cried in agony. I cried with impotence. Before coma relieved her suffering she was reduced to a dull-eyed skeleton with a gaping, crusted mouth. Four obscene days later, her breathing stopped. It was a horrid relief.

I couldn't bear to take her smudged water glass from the bedside table. On the last morning she painted she had me improve the light in her studio by pulling a window curtain aside and draping it over the hat rack. I left it that way; to disturb the arrangement would have been to lose her more. At every turn her long-ago voice asked me, "Was leaving it too cruel?"

Yes, it was, though grief prevented my doing anything about it. Friends disposed of the clothes—not "her" clothes but "the" clothes—and stored "the" art. I threw myself into my law practice and avoided things with too much of Carla about them. A part-time secretary answered her mail.

Then, last month, an advertisement featuring one of her paintings surprised me in a magazine. After I threw it across the room, my cowardice shamed me. I went to the storage facility and retrieved a crate of her work, including the Colorado material. In it I rediscovered Gladys. Now, for an instant or an hour, as I'm able, I scratch out these notes and recall Gideon Creek by moonlight, the bracing sheen of snowmelt on young skin, Carla's squeals and the chorus of water and stone. Did Gladys really dare to wear the boonie hat? In the moments when I think she did, Pancho's heart aches for the mountain queen.

Afterword:
Literature as Magic Theater

L ITERARY FICTION roughly divides into camps of authors who, in the tradition of Dante, Dickens and Tolstoy, intend their work to say something of social importance, and those content to produce art as art, echoing Chekhov; "My concern is to write, not to teach!" Chekhov's rejection of the moralizing orthodoxy of his day freed literature to pursue visions that may relate to readers only aesthetically. His approach has now congealed into an orthodoxy frequently timid or AWOL in the face of big questions. Paraphrasing Prufrock, how should the artist presume?

There's nothing wrong with art for art's sake, as far as it goes. But if that's no further than its frame, a Fabergé egg has the same social relevance. The pursuit of autistic excellence has, predictably, resulted in the cultural marginalization of its product. Writers with a more community-minded vision of art's potential need not return to the old teaching model to contribute to the debates of the day. It may be enough—and is certainly less prescriptive—to catalyze new ideas, a point driven home to me a few years ago by a visit to virtual Ireland.

The Celts believed that the veil between everyday reality and the Otherworld thins at special places and times.

It's a borderland I'm not familiar with, but I can say that *some* veil was in tatters at my house when the alarm clock buzzed at oh-god-thirty on the morning of winter solstice, 2007. The occasion was a live webcast of the dawn at Newgrange, a 5,000-year-old passage tomb in County Meath. Ages before the Celts, a millennium before the great circle was raised at Stonehenge and five hundred years before Egypt built its iconic pyramids, Irishmen hauled hundreds of thousands of tons of rock slabs and soil to create Newgrange and other monumental cairns on the hills overlooking a bend of the River Boyne.

The structures are artifacts of a megalithic Stone Age culture dispersed along the Atlantic and Mediterranean coasts of Europe. What possessed the builders to undertake their architectural feats has been scrambled by a 250-generation game of telephone, complicated by war and migration. Today Newgrange is a hieroglyph, a gently sloping grass-topped dome nearly two and a half times the diameter of the Stonehenge circle and forty feet high. Around the perimeter a line of blocky gray kerbstones, each weighing a ton or more, supports the base of a white quartzite retaining wall. In the southeastern quadrant a door slab leans beside a man-sized entrance framed by rock pillars and a platter-like lintel. Above the lintel the quartzite is neatly backset and features a rectangular transom or "roof box" opening. Both the roof box and doorway access an up-sloping interior hall. Sixty feet of massive standing stone walls and flat ceiling slabs end in a three-lobed chamber. There the ceiling sweeps upward twenty feet in a conical dome. To the right at ground level, in the largest of the closet-sized recesses, a granite basin once held ashes of the dead and items sent with them to the afterlife.

Scholars describe the interior layout as cruciform, a concept no doubt foreign to mentalities innocent of alphabets and predating Christ by 3,000 years. The connotations of the term tinge them anyway—another set of ideas not likely available to the builders But this is speculation; the belief system they clothed themselves in is anybody's guess. Ancient Irish ghosts will wear almost anything these days, no matter how ill-fitting.

The intended meaning of designs pecked into the stones at Newgrange has been lost as well. Some of the pictographs are doubled spirals, winding inward then reversing course at the center and winding out again. The site's signature design is the triskele or triple spiral, a set of three doubled spirals interconnected in a cloverleaf pattern. It echoes, in outline, the chamber floor plan. Triskeles appear on the entrance kerbstone and rear recess wall. Perhaps the builders used triple spirals to represent the new moon's three-day sojourn in the land of the dead or the related trinity of birth, death and rebirth. Did triple spirals signify a triple reality consisting of the natural world and spirit worlds above and below? Who knows.

Across the millennia the chamber remained dry and far more intact than its meaning thanks to slumping soil that sealed the entryway, a common occurrence at megalithic Irish tombs. Celts understood the old mounds as portals to the home of the legendary Tuatha Dé Danann, people under the hill. The Celts may not have realized that the sites served astronomical purposes. From December 19th-23rd, when solar fire is weakest in northern latitudes, sunlight streams through the Newgrange roof box at dawn, briefly lighting the triskele at the rear of the chamber. If the door is open a second golden beam illuminates the passage floor.

The show occurs around the time of a winter salmon run on the Boyne. But although opportunities for a full belly are worth noting, it strains credulity to imagine that Newgrange functioned primarily as a gigantic kitchen timer. Possibly the beam signed the sun's commitment to push back the advancing night and dreary Irish winter.

Or the sun's penetration of the earthen mound could have been an act of fertilization. Gods frequently chose this method of injecting themselves into earthly affairs. The Babylonians said a ray of light impregnated the mother of Tammuz, a male deity who cycled annually between birth and death. Mitra, an Indo-Iranian sun god, was born in a cave at winter solstice. In Greece, King Acrisius kept his daughter Danaë in an underground chamber to prevent her foretold pregnancy. Zeus got to her as a shower of golden light. Christian painters depicted the conception of Jesus with a heavenly beam. Cartoonists still convey the birth of bright ideas with illuminated lightbulbs. Whatever the Irish details, the importance of the solar shaft at Newgrange is certified by the hard labor expended to reveal it to those intended to bear witness.

Nowadays the Office of Public Works (OPW) in County Meath conducts an open lottery for the opportunity to observe from inside the chamber. More than 28,000 requests were received for the fifty solstice dawn tickets issued in 2007. OPW addressed excess demand by staging a webcast of the event. That's what got me out of bed in the wee hours.

A trio of commentators, sniffling in the chill, stood outside the monument with a throng of visitors and handled the play-by-play. Cameras panned the refurbished quartzite wall and a lightening horizon across the misty river. Other video eyes watched the dark entrance passage from the perspective of a lottery winner. The sun soon peeked above the distant trees. As promised, sunbeams appeared and strengthened impressively along the passage wall and floor.

In my half-awake state the amber ribbons seemed almost tangible, yellow brick roads linking the heavens with the underworld. Did the honored dead once travel them, or shamans in charge of the annual ceremony? Irish lore about rainbows and leprechaun gold had to start somewhere.

Time may be the least of our separations from the Stone Age *zeitgeist* of 3000 BCE. Consider developments in the realm of symbols. They've come a long way since triple spirals were state of the art. Via electron streams directed by a symbol mechanism known as Windows Media Player, 300,000 people joined me at the solstice dawn. We observed it in a land populated by images full of significance but lifeless and devoid of substance. The filmmaker Godfrey Reggio has described such environments as synthetic nature. We often prefer it to the genuine article.

Online archival data tells me it was raining lightly and 39.9° F in my town when the dawning sun worked its magic in County Meath. I'll take the website's word for it; I was in digital Ireland. My trip there was unblemished by airport delays or lost bags. Unlike the OPW commentators, my nose didn't burn or drip in the frosty morn. I had the advantage of multiple viewing positions. No actual visitor could manage that. Of course there were limitations. I couldn't hear the whooper swans begin their day on the Boyne or smell the riverine funk. Having avoided the cold I also missed the warm, musty shock of underground air, the texture of passage stones, claustrophobia and the camaraderie of lottery winners stuffed in the burial chamber.

The builders' solstice experience probably differed from my encounter with its facsimile in a second regard. Martin Buber distinguished between the communion of I-You (Thou) relations and objectified I-It interactions. Antique pictographs, words or files rendered on a display monitor are examples of It; they are objects. The same is true of the things around me. I observe or use my coffee cup but sense no presence between us.

Five thousand years ago the Irish sun, trees, rocks, barley, the Boyne and the salmon in it might have been perceived in the I-You mode of awareness, as fellow spirits with whom men shared living relationships. Surviving animist cultures are at pains to maintain harmony with spirit beings. Animals and plants offering themselves for human use are formally appreciated. Demonstrations of respect ensure proper behavior of the sun, moon and rain. If malicious spooks are about, they are dealt with.

But belief systems morphed along with cultures. Stronger gods absorbed or banished lesser spirits. Yahweh vanquished his Middle Eastern competitors and emerged as the monotheistic victor in the West. Old understandings were bent to fit new realities. Man alone among earthly creatures retained a spiritual dimension. Souls in need of communion had to seek God in his otherworld. There, not here, worshipers were assured of paradise.

This transformation was succeeded by another. Martin Luther declared the common man's competence to read scripture, undermining the authority of God's priestly representatives. Within two centuries the Enlightenment laid successful siege to the tyranny of holy writ in matters of science, arguing that empirical evidence processed according to the rules of reason—based in the symbolism of language—trumped unverified wisdom received from any source. Earth's place at the center of the universe was an early casualty. By the nineteenth century God himself was on trial. Ivan Karamazov accused him of permitting cruelty to children and other innocents. Friedrich Nietzsche declared him dead, killed by man. "Is not the greatness of this deed too great for us?" he asked in *The Gay Science*. "Must we ourselves not become gods simply to appear worthy of it?"

Artists continue to tear at the heavenly corpse and are not struck by lightning. An impatient Ayatollah Khomeini called for volunteers when Allah failed to make a divine spectacle of Salman Rushdie's blasphemy in *The Satanic Verses*. Khomeini's fatwa inadvertently acknowledged man's revised place in the cosmic order. Cormac McCarthy's novel, *Blood Meridian*, cast the new boss as a white giant of a man, Judge Holden, who certifies his lordship with orgies of violence. Paraphrasing Karamazov, Holden tells fellow members of the Glanton gang, "The truth about the world . . . is that anything is possible."

But God did not go quietly. Holy wars are back in style. Christian conservatives complain of religious persecution in the United States. Some advocate the replacement of secular jurisprudence with Mosaic Law and punishments. Brutal applications of Sharia Law persist and spread in certain Islamic societies. The vehemence of fundamentalist objections to modernity may, in part, be rooted in the Enlightenment's psychological fallout. Personal convictions of truth, including awareness of transpersonal presence/connection, are discounted when the empirical method can be brought to bear on public questions. Subjective I-You evidence must bend the knee to reasonable I-It facts. Technological society depends on the willingness of skilled people to privilege the cognitive mode of reason. Public schools teach It. Some carryover into private worldviews is to be expected. Reason reinforces the identification of God as a conjectural object. There can be no living relationship between It and me—whoever *I* am. *How* I am is existentially alone. Yikes. Nevertheless, the tangible benefits of Enlightenment thinking suggest that its overthrow will be an uphill struggle for religious conservatives.

Annie Dillard described the Western spiritual arc as a transition from pantheism to pan-atheism. Cognitively inevitable or not, challenges posed by the ascendance of reason extend far beyond congregations of the devout. Rational processes are morally ignorant, serving any master.

The domain of binary code is nonjudgmental. It buffers the consciences of those who push buttons with nasty effects, regardless of politics. And there's more. If animists were deluded about spirits living in trees and Yahweh turns out to have been a metaphor, what of my own spirit? It is a small step from Judge Holden to the demented Tin Head and his hapless brethren in Annie Proulx's *Close Range*. But it's a hellish leap for me. If things happen just because they do, my perception of myself may be another mirage, an illusion thrown up by a dusty symphony of molecular collisions. The end of all our exploring could be nihilism. Welcome to the big disconnect, the ranks of It. Does it come down to Townes Van Zandt's twangy despair and a lifetime of "Waitin' 'Round to Die"?

So there I was, staring out from the virtual depths of Newgrange. Pixelated ribbons of amber light appeared and inched toward me. I don't know what I expected. The experience was less a neo-pagan awakening than a comfortable rush of generic magic. At one with those who dreamed up this place, the generations that cursed the weight of the rocks and limped on crushed feet, those who died positioning the slabs just so. Shamanic sing-song. Knots of farmers nervous in the frosted grass. Little kids, thumbs in mouths, peeking wide-eyed from behind a parent's leg, wondering, shushed. Most of all the company of those who, through the ages and believing any number of things, realize the irrelevance of baggage on a golden road. Has the joy of existential connection ever been more universally evoked than by a well-framed sunbeam?

Whether or not the triskele symbolized a triple reality for the Newgrange builders, their monumental display of the solstice dawn showed me that I am embedded in one. The evolution of angst seems less a product of change in the physical universe than of developments in two others.

I doubt that trees literally quit talking to us because their spirits died or were imprisoned by gods. Is this objectively correct? In the privacy of my subjective universe it doesn't matter. There, my word is law. As absolute monarch of your own subjectivity you are free to your own opinion. The limits of the subjective cosmos aren't entirely clear but I'm pretty sure that my body is outside it. I *have* a body; I *am* aware. Subjectivity is the home of Buber's I-You feeling.

Does awareness have substance, or is my substance a carrier for self-modifying patterns of information networked such that the network is able to detect itself? Either way, my beliefs on the matter reside in a third realm. Though definitely insubstantial, the conceptual universe is a joint human venture. Words, signs and symbolic images interact to construct detailed and powerful models. Tables are distinguished from wood, disgust from disdain. Through models I understand myself and my surroundings. What I mainly perceive when I look at a table is a nested set of conceptual models. Without it, all I'd register is non-uniformity in the distribution of stuff and that doesn't tell me much. But models are not the actual physical or subjective entities they masquerade as, sometimes with deadly consequences. Is God Protestant or Catholic? Shi'a, Sunni or Hindu? On a lighter note, I once wore a beard. After I shaved it off, casual acquaintances noticed the bare face. Close friends asked if I'd lost weight. The map is not the territory, cautioned Alfred Korzybski, father of general semantics. Models evolve. They can break down or be superseded. Copernicus, Van Gogh, Einstein and Kafka created new models that more closely approximated physical reality and/or enlarged the conceptual universe. They made it possible to imagine in ways not previously considered.

Atoms, awareness and models are my triple reality. I have a body. I am aware. I interpret experience. If that re-visioning fuddles the ghosts of Newgrange they must at least feel kinship with their descendents' ongoing urge to build. Mighty phallic pride is on display in Dubai's 2,717-foot tall Burj Khalifa skyscraper. Recent projects in the conceptual sphere are as impressive. Western-style psychological individuation turned believing peoples into thinking persons, at grievous existential cost to some. Mathematics progressed from counting to calculus to contemplating its intellectual limits. From equally humble beginnings, art built upon art, text upon text. Towers of metaphysics dwarf the steeples of religions they proclaim. Manhattans of the mind enable, shelter and limit us. They hide some things and frame or create others. Within their realm, models *are* the territory. Outside it, they reverberate through the physical and subjective worlds.

Like seers of old, artists prowl the conceptual universe as framers and tinters of views. In an objectified age when man doubts his significance in the Big Bang cosmos and, by default, sees himself at the center of a marooned subjectivity, the arts were bound to notice. There's nothing particularly surprising about literature's postmodern fascination with its own textual edifice. Maybe there's nothing else to write about. Maybe we shouldn't think in terms of "about." Susan Sontag justified her focus on form by dismissing the idea of artistic content as a hindrance. Content has no meaning independent of interpretation and contemporary interpretation amounts to the revenge of intellect on art. Interpretation stifles art's immediacy. "In place of a hermeneutics," she wrote, "we need an erotics of art."

"Immediacy" isn't "in" the art, of course. It's a subjective state, a temporary suspension of intellectual concepts, an openness on the part of the artist or the beholder of art. Immediacy was the state I found myself in when touched by the Newgrange beam. Sleepy ignorance had rendered me unusually vulnerable to it.

Grant Sontag that the thickness of models stacked between awareness and what it perceives affects the sensuality—subjective quality—of the encounter. As with food, minimal processing allows the flavor of ingredients to shine.

Perhaps Sontag would grant the value of striving to understand. Multiple levels of operational models, however imperfectly shared, are required to translate squiggles on paper into her admonition against blanketing art in concepts. More broadly, a deer in the headlights that doesn't flee by instinct or education courts disaster. The difference between my triple reality and the "blooming, buzzing confusion" of immediacy William James attributed to newborns is a painstakingly constructed conceptual universe, i.e., interpretation.

Our instincts deeply distrust mysteries and reward solutions—explanatory models—with the visceral jolts of satisfaction we call epiphany. But mysteries are legion and bewilderment unpleasant. Avoiding unknowns is often an option too. There is comfort in a status quo, especially for the comfortable, and no assurance that leaving it will reward us with a better or even livable alternative. Celebration of certainty was probably at the heart of why ancient Irish divines crouched in the darkness awaiting sunlight and omens. Any Catholic in the Middle Ages could raise her eyes in the cavernous space of a Gothic cathedral and read God's contract in the light streaming through the rose window above the entrance.

But ours is an era of *un*certainty. Art can soothe that discomfort with a distracting retreat into technical self-absorption or by shoring up suspect models. Alternatively, it can challenge us to give those models a good shake and see what falls out. When it does the latter—especially when encountered in a state of mind where the boundaries of self and other and this and that are permeable—wild light flashes through gaps in the conceptual universe and may spark the fluid magic of recombination. Out of immediacy's hat might pop the epiphany of a new model, even a triple universe. Surely Sontag's erotics of art would have included a chapter on baby-making. She could have entitled it "Conceiving Hermeneutics."

Like the shopworn literary case of Chekhov v Tolstoy, Dostoevsky, et al, the form and content model of art directs attention to secondary issues. Except for some automotive experts, the essence of cars isn't their physicality or the curve of a line. Cars move. Art arranges things, literally or figuratively, but its power depends on the significance of the immediacy that gave it birth and a work's ability to involve an audience in that.

Dostoevsky's Grand Inquisitor grabs readers by the throat. Picasso was always a master of form, yet "Guernica" has a unique ability to stop people in their tracks. Flannery O'Connor's grotesque characters, beset by what she believed to be flawed models and the dire epiphanies she labeled moments of grace, are preachy but still hard to look away from. Bob Dylan inspired a generation of Americans with songs that he, Chekhov-like, disclaimed meaning anything by. Perhaps understanding that the most important epiphanies are personal, some authors seem less concerned about how their characters solve problems of living than immersing readers in them. McCarthy introduces us to the tender mercies of Judge Holden or drops us onto *The Road* and, with a sneaky skyward glance, is gone. Proulx, dispensing with that *Cool Hand Luke* flourish, rides off "Brokeback Mountain" spitting in the dust, hopes we brought our canteens.

I'm with McCarthy and Proulx. Might we agree to wink a little at each other's revelations? And might we sometimes aim for more than aesthetic and/or pedagogic values in our fiction? Literature, accidentally or on purpose, is capable of functioning as Newgrange does. It can use the technical wizardry at its disposal to invite us into otherworlds where the unsettledness triggers our own and supports a state of reader immediacy. There lies magic and the opportunity to remake worlds.